Warriors of
ALAVNA

Warriors of Alavna

N. M. Browne

BLOOMSBURY

First published in Great Britain in 2000
Bloomsbury Publishing Plc, 38 Soho Square, London, W1V 5DF

The moral right of the author has been asserted
A CIP catalogue record of this book is available
from the British Library

ISBN 0 7475 4694 0

Printed in Great Britain by Clays Ltd, St Ives plc

10 9 8 7 6 5 4

For Paul

Chapter One

The Call of the Warrior's Veil

Dan watched with horror as Ursula was swallowed by the yellow mist. He tried to call her name, but she didn't stop. He had no choice but to follow her.

It was obvious close to that it wasn't a mist at all in the ordinary sense. He could see moving shapes through it, but they were distorted as if through rippled glass or water. He could not see Ursula. He didn't like it. He took a step forward. The mist enveloped him, colder than ice and oily. It had a surprising solidity. He entered it and it surrounded him; a mass of oily droplets that held him like a fly in a web. No ordinary mist. He shut his eyes instinctively to protect them and took another difficult step. The mist clung to him, resisted his movement. He struggled forward and the mist released him with an almost inaudible pop into some other place. There was no sign of Ursula. He was standing in deserted marshland. It was warm and bright sunlight forced him to squint. There was no sound apart from the twittering of birds. No movement except for the ruffling of the tussocky clumps of wild grass in the breeze. He looked back; the yellow mist impeded his view of the frozen field he'd just left. Where was Ursula? She had left him at an angry run but even so she only left an instant before him. Why couldn't he see her?

He replayed their conversation in his mind. He hadn't meant to upset her. They had been paired up for the history field trip round Hastings. Miss Smith thought girls kept boys out of trouble – she was an older teacher and must have been due for retirement soon. Dan had never had much to do with Ursula; she hung around with the other misfits in the year group. They were all lumped together in his mind, plain girls, fat boys, the non-starters. Ursula was one of those different ones – she was enormous, over six foot tall, fifteen years old and not just tall but heavy with it. She was solidly built, verging on the very fat. Broad shouldered and long limbed, she disguised her bulk in baggy tops and loose trousers. The effect was unflattering. She towered above her classmates, a massive cylinder of black sweatshirt and pale flesh. She wore her fine blonde hair very short at the sides and back but hid her cool, blue-grey eyes under a long fringe. Her impassive face was almost sullen. She rarely spoke. He'd been telling her about his training regime. She hadn't volunteered anything, and scarcely answered his questions so he'd set up a steady stream of near meaningless chatter to pass the time. He'd got a trial for the local football club and was a county runner. He'd been showing off, in a half-hearted way and suggested that Ursula tried weight training. He hadn't meant anything by it, but she'd run away from him. The mist had come down while he was talking. He was just about to comment on it because it had merely appeared. To the south everything was unchanged; to the north he could see nothing but the odd yellowness. She had run north. And this was what she had run into ... except that it wasn't. She wasn't here. The marshland offered little cover and Ursula had been wearing a bright red anorak.

It never occurred to Dan to go back without her, any more than it had occurred to him not to follow her. There was a small hill, more of a ridge really, to his right. Perhaps if she had really moved fast she could be behind that hill. She would have had to be a surprisingly good runner, though. Dan began to run too, but carefully, because the ground was uneven and soggy – ankle-breaking conditions. It was strange. The sky was blue here and it was warm. He took off his jacket and tied it round his waist. It was suddenly a beautiful day.

It was not a beautiful day for Ursula. She had run from Dan because she was in no mood for any more jokes about her weight and height. She coped well, mostly, but it had been a bad day. There had been a letter from her father that morning telling her that it wouldn't be convenient for her to visit as planned this weekend because his new baby was sick. This had produced the usual hysterical outburst from Ursula's mother and the usual stoic response from Ursula. She sometimes wished he would give up the pretence of loving her altogether. Dan wasn't really the problem, though she had enjoyed listening to him talk and show off a bit like he did for more normal sized girls. It was everything really. The Richard twins giggling at the bus stop and some stupid stranger asking her what the weather was like up there. Everything. The mist was a surprise. She hadn't been paying much attention to her surroundings but the mist she couldn't ignore. The colour was sickly, like smog, or like smoke from a witch's cauldron. It clung to her like a fine net, like a cold shroud, freezing the marrow in her bones with its oily touch. She shut her eyes as if she was underwater. Determinedly she strode through it. She wanted to wipe it away, her face felt slick with it and sick with the feel of it. It was not natural, not natural at all. She began to panic. As a toddler she had once got stuck in the small gap under her father's shed. She felt the same fear bubbling now. Then, abruptly she was through it and somewhere else. She heard a pop, like the sound you hear in your ear when the altitude changes on a plane. She was trembling all over and dizzy.

Everything felt wrong. She opened her eyes. Everything *was* wrong.

She was in the middle of a stone circle, surrounded by people. There must have been six men, and a woman, dressed in some historical costume: cloaks, breastplates, strange hairstyles. She didn't really take that in. All but the woman were armed with swords. All of the swords were pointing at her. It could not be real. Her mind rebelled at the evidence of her own eyes. She didn't want to be there. This was not what happened when you were on a history field trip! Ursula was not a coward. Her brain didn't really accept what her eyes told her but her heart did. It began to pump adrenalin at a fearsome rate. She stood up a bit straighter and squared her considerable shoulders. Trying to control her shakiness, she adopted her 'If-you-mess-with-me-you'll-be-sorry' look, perfected at bus stops and in dinner queues over many years. They were all staring at her so she stared back. She looked at them one by one. Boys often backed down when she did that. These men did not. There was not one of them that did not have the cold hard eyes of a psychopath.

'Oh God!' she whispered in her mind and it was a true prayer.

The woman threw back her head and howled. The sound lifted every hair on the back of Ursula's neck and she shuddered. It was not a sound she would have thought a human throat could make. The men looked discomforted and she noticed one or two grasp their swords a little tighter. The woman began to chant. It was like the sound monks made. In contrast to the unearthly howling, her voice was deep and melodious. It reverberated around the standing stones until the air seemed to thrum with it. It was very beautiful but utterly alien. Ursula felt her body tingling and even her heart seemed to slow to beat time to the woman's chant. It was something more than music, the notes had a force to them that did something to the air. It was as still as the moment before a storm breaks but the very atmosphere felt charged with power. The air crackled as the woman raised her arms and Ursula felt a jolt like an electric shock on the skin of her own arms. What was going on? She strained to hear the woman's words. They were in no language that she recognised.

The woman's voice was becoming more insistent, the rhythm faster, the pitch higher. Then the woman looked at Ursula. It was a very direct look. The woman's eyes were an extraordinary emerald green, intense and searching. They were more frightening than the swords in the hands of the men. But Ursula was used to being afraid and of pretending not to be. She would not give this woman power over her by showing her fear. Ursula stared back implacably, her own eyes as hard as she could make them. The woman gave a little cry of surprise and crumpled to the ground in a graceful and dramatic swoon that Ursula would have been proud of.

The rite, if that is what it was, was clearly over. With the woman's fall into unconsciousness the charged quality of the air ceased at once, almost as if someone had thrown a switch and shut off the current. There was a strange noise, a kind of implosion almost out of her hearing range, that Ursula sensed rather than heard. A couple of the men muttered to each other and pointed. Ursula, swinging round to follow their gaze, half expected what she saw. The mist was gone. Not a wisp of it remained. There was nothing unusual in the view. Beyond the stones there was only flat and marshy land stretching as far as the eye could see. There was nothing unusual about it, except that it bore no relationship at all to where Ursula should have been. There was no sign of Dan or any of her classmates. There was no sign of the car park where their coach should have been parked. There was nothing but the marsh and the standing stones and no one but the men with their swords still drawn.

~ Chapter Two ~

The Red-haired Girl

Dan could run all day. It was what he did, but he could still find no sign of Ursula and he was beginning to get anxious. He was quite sure that if she'd been ahead of him he would have found her by now. He was the fastest runner in the school, even cross-country. He just knew that Ursula could not be that fast on her feet. He was thirsty. He stopped for a moment and bent to catch his breath. His watch said it was 2.00 p.m. It had stopped. The golden quality of the afternoon light suggested it was much later than that. They were supposed to meet back at the coach by 4.30 at the latest. Perhaps Ursula had turned back immediately. Maybe he'd missed her in the mist. It was frustrating but he'd have to tell Miss Smith he'd lost her. He didn't like the thought. If Ursula wasn't at the coach already, laughing at him, they would have to make a proper search party. He hated giving up on anything but what he was doing was mindless.

He'd left a can of coke in his rucksack. He'd go back, drink it, find Miss Smith and then do whatever had to be done. He hadn't finished the assignment, of course, so he'd be in trouble for that too. He had to admit he'd enjoyed the run in the clean air, silent but for the sounds of birds. He must have run quite a long way from his starting point because there was not even the distant hum of traffic.

He turned around and began to jog back. The mist must have dissipated because he couldn't see even a hint of a yellow tint in the clear air. He was pretty sure he'd run back to where he'd started, but he could not find the tree where he'd left his rucksack. He couldn't see the car park or hear the road. The land was completely desolate. He was lost.

Dan had read somewhere that you could not walk for more than five miles in any direction in Britain and not come upon some kind of habitation. That then would be his plan. He'd carry on running until he found somewhere with a phone, then he'd ring the school to let them know what had happened. He'd be in trouble but that couldn't be helped. He was more worried that if he got home too late there would be no one to put his sister, Lizzie, to bed. His father's shift would start at six and he didn't always remember to ask their neighbour, Mrs Ainley, to keep an eye on her. 'I'm sorry I forgot. All right?' was his father's favourite phrase.

If Dan kept running he would be OK. He quickened his pace, dogged by unease. It didn't make sense for him to be lost any more than it made any sense for Ursula to have disappeared. He couldn't come up with a satisfactory explanation for either event and that bothered him. The land changed as he ran. Marsh became wood. He hadn't noticed any woods round the history study area. It was difficult to run. There was no obvious path. Somehow he had got himself very lost.

Eventually he came to a clearing with a roughly made cabin. It was small and windowless, more of a hut really. The door had no handle and was slightly ajar. He pushed against it, gently. 'Hello! Is there anyone there?'

His voice was husky and the creak of the door made him jump. A couple of birds launched themselves, in panic, at the open sky. It was hard to see in the gloom but the cabin was not a wood store as Dan had expected. There was a blackened hearth in the middle of the small, single room. There was no chimney and a strong smell of woodsmoke pervaded the air. There were some shelves on the wall with pots and woven baskets on them. That was about it. Perhaps it was a den for some local kids. Whatever it was used for it was of no use to Dan, there was no phone there. He had a quick look outside just to check there was no one around. It was then that he found her.

She was lying face down on the earth. She had some sack-like dress on and a shawl of a bright, coloured plaid. Long auburn hair spilled over her shoulders and made a kind of fan of reddish gold against the earth. Her feet were dirty and bare and she lay in a puddle of mud that he somehow knew was not mud, but blood. He knew she was dead.

Conscience compelled him closer. There was a chance she was still breathing. He could not bear to draw back the hair to see her face, but he made himself touch her neck for a pulse. The flesh was quite cold. The woman was dead, murdered by the look of it. Flies were beginning to settle on her. He batted them away.

He'd read a lot of crime books and watched a lot of murders on TV. It did not prepare him for this. Dan was trembling now quite uncontrollably. What if the murderer was still about? What if he'd got Ursula? A part of him wanted to run away. Another part, the larger part was morbidly curious. His conscience told him it was his duty to attempt to identify her, so he could tell the police. He would need to tell them enough details for them to know that he had not made the whole thing up. As if anyone would.

It was not the first corpse he had seen. He had seen his mother, after the nurses had tidied her up a bit. His grandmother had been furious about it, but Dad had insisted. He said Dan had to know it was true. Dan had to see that all that made her his mother had gone, so that he would understand. He had seen, but he hadn't understood, then or now. He wasn't at all sure that his father had either. Still, it meant he had seen a dead woman before. He could do it again. It had to be easier than before, this one was a stranger. He made himself pull back the beautiful hair. The girl was about his age, year ten or eleven. Her brown eyes were wide open. Their terrible blindness shocked him. She had been very afraid. Her mouth was open too. He let her hair drop and ran for the bushes. He was violently sick, just as he'd always read people were in such circumstances. The books had not prepared him for his own body's shock and shivering outrage. Someone very twisted had killed that girl. Dan had a hanky in his pocket. He wiped his mouth, though he could do nothing about the sour taste in it. He had seen a young girl slaughtered and it seemed that nothing would ever be the same again. The world seemed a bleaker, darker place. He felt cold. He untied his jacket from his waist and, shivering, laid it gently over the girl. It seemed the least he could do.

He didn't think the killer was still about, but he looked around for a weapon just in case. Knives were bad, in a fight they could be used against you. You could be excluded from school just for carrying one, but something was better than nothing. He went back to the hut. He wanted to wash his hands, cleanse himself of the horror outside, but there was no tap anywhere that he could see. Keeping the door open for light, he looked around. He needed a weapon. He also needed some clue as to why the girl had been killed. What could have been going on for the girl to be dead in the middle of this wood, miles from anywhere? Could the girl have been living here as a runaway? Behind the door was a carved wooden chest, the only bit of furniture in the room, apart from the shelves. Even to Dan's ignorant eyes the chest looked too valuable to be in a wooden hut. Nicked, no doubt, he thought. Pulling the sleeve of his school sweatshirt over his hand, so as not to disturb any finger-prints, he cautiously lifted the lid of the chest. Inside, the chest smelled of Christmas, of some pungent herb, was it cloves? He strained his eyes to see what was in it. He was disappointed. It was full of old clothes. He'd expected something that might be a motive for murder. He groped around, checking for something more. At the very bottom of the chest he could feel some hard object, wrapped in cloth. It was longer than a rifle and very heavy. Lifting it into the sunlight, he carefully unwrapped it from its layers of cloth. The last layer was thick with some foul-smelling greasy stuff. He peeled it back, gingerly, uncertain what it was and what it was covering. It was covering a sword. That he hadn't expected.

The hilt was breath-taking. It looked like it was made

of gold and silver interworked on an elaborate pattern of knots and loops. The patterns were so complex; his startled mind could make no sense of them. The blade was very long and double-edged. It looked sharp as a kitchen knife. Even if it had been blunt the sword's weight alone would make it a fearful club. Dan didn't know what to do. He was sure it was stolen from a museum. He had a vague recollection that to take stolen property was also a crime, but it was a weapon, and he needed a weapon. He was a bit worried about finger-prints too. He didn't want to spoil any that might be on the hilt, but if it was to be any good to him, he had to hold it. The unwanted image of the murdered girl haunted him. He was afraid it always would. He was in trouble already, but he was alive and he wanted to stay that way. He would take the sword as a weapon and turn it in to the police as soon as he could.

Carefully he wiped the grease from the sword with the cloth from the chest. He held the sword high to inspect it and the blade flashed, brilliant with silver light. It was very heavy, designed for a tall man and a strong one. It wasn't a sword for fancy fencing, that was clear. Its beauty could not distract Dan from its brutal power. It was a blade made for hacking flesh from bone. It reminded him of nothing more than a butcher's cleaver. It was a chilling thought. "Bright Killer". The name came unbid-den to his mind. Heroes always named their swords. He was no hero he knew. It was not at all appropriate in the grim circumstances to name a sword as if he was a child playing, but the name existed now. He had thought it. He could not un-name it. The sword was for him "Bright Killer".

It was also far too long to wear at his hip, even if he could find a way to walk without tripping over it. He had seen a film once where the hero carried a great longsword on his back. He might manage that if he could find some rope to lash it to his back. It would also be a better way of dealing with the sword's weight, which was considerable. Dan was an experienced runner. He knew how even a light weight dragged you down over any distance. Unexpectedly, he found what he was look-ing for straightaway. The remnants of a leather harness were stowed neatly on one of the shelves. It looked as if it had something to do with horses so it was strongly made. It is extremely difficult to tie something to your own back, but with a lot of fumbling and some judicious knotting, Dan managed to strap the sword diagonally between his shoulders. The hilt was just level with the tip of his left shoulder blade. With a bit of contortion, he could reach for it over his head and pull it free. He earnestly hoped he wouldn't need to. It was extremely uncomfortable and he couldn't secure it tightly enough. Even before he started to move off, he knew it was going to bruise his back black and blue. Still, in spite of the discomfort, its stolen status and his complete ignorance of how to use it, the sword made him feel safer. It was another thing that didn't make any sense.

He set off more cautiously this time and more anxiously. He didn't run, though he wanted too. He knew he would make too much noise. He had no experience of moving quietly and that worried him. He was an easy target if the murderer was still around.

He had gone less than ten metres when he became convinced that someone was following him. Someone who wasn't making too much effort not to be heard. Dan didn't pause to think, he just ran. The sword clattered against his bones. His feet snapped fallen twigs indiscriminately. He dodged branches and leaped over stones to the rhythm of his frantic heartbeat. His blood roared in his ears. Inevitably his make-do sword harness let him down. The knots broke and the sword fell. As it fell, it caught him a hefty blow to his back, knocking him forward and upsetting his balance. He landed face down in a sprawled heap – just like the dead girl. He tasted earth and blood and salt, from his too dry mouth. His nose was bleeding. He struggled to his feet, grabbed the sword and turned to face his nemesis. It was the biggest dog he had ever seen.

It was like no dog he had ever even heard of, something between a wolf and a red setter. Its massive head was level with Dan's shoulder and its teeth were bared in a terrifying display of natural weaponry. A deep growl issued from its throat.

Dan was not confident he could deal with the dog before the dog dealt with his neck. It must have weighed more than Dan and had all the swords it needed in its mouth. Dan felt the rivulets of sweat trickling down his face. He tried to control his trembling and hoped he didn't reek of fear. The dog never took its eyes off the huge sword.

Dan had to make a decision. He could run for it, but four legs would outpace him and he couldn't run and fight. He could charge and hope he could find it in him to drive the sword home, into the dog's massive chest. He wasn't at all sure he could do that. He could wait for the dog to leap at him and gamble on having the speed to ward off the attack. In the end he did none of these. The dog was injured. He could see it now. Dried blood caked one of its hind legs and there was a gash around its neck. Maybe it belonged to the girl. Maybe it thought Dan was stealing the sword. After all he *was* stealing the sword, if only to hand it in to the police.

Like a sudden gift from God, Dan found his place of calm, somewhere, the other side of fear. It was a place he only usually found when he was playing football or running. It was a place where the world slowed down and he had time to dodge a tackle or control a pass or shoot for goal. It was a place of calm, unhurried certainty. In it

23

he made his judgement. He laid down the sword and waited, one, two, three heartbeats. The dog stopped growling and advanced, it sniffed the sword and whimpered, rather piteously for a dog of its size. From his calm place, Dan could see that in spite of its impressive size it was still a young dog, with too-big feet and a disproportionately large head. Very deliberately, Dan moved forward. He was perfectly balanced to run at any second. He was no longer shaking and his voice was calm and level when he whispered softly, 'It's OK, boy. I won't hurt you.'

The dog was like a coiled spring, or a cocked gun, wary and ready. Dan patted its head, still making reassuring noises. The dog did not relax, but made no move to attack. It was clear that the dog had been badly wounded, the gash in its neck was particularly deep. It was breathing hard from its abdomen and panting. It must have been nearly mad with pain. He wished he had some water to share with it, to show it that he meant no harm. Dan had nothing but his kindest voice and calmest manner. He did what he could with those.

'Was it your mistress who was killed? Poor dog! I have nothing to give you and you are such a beautiful dog, aren't you? The handsomest dog I've ever seen.'

It was true. Dan had always wanted a dog. It had always been out of the question. He had never seen such an animal as this, lean and muscled with extraordinarily intelligent eyes. He could not but admire it. It still might kill him but it really was a wonderful dog. He could not have cold-bloodedly charged at it with the brutal sword. The sword, that was his problem. He needed to pick it up without threatening the dog. The dog was still alert and ready. He'd been lucky so far. The dog tolerated his touch and voice but that was all.

Suddenly the dog growled, as if in warning, and flattened himself to the ground. Its ears were down. It held its body even tauter than before, muscles bunched ready for fight or flight. It was clear that it had heard something. Dan stopped his whispered crooning and dropped to the ground, ducking his head down to make the lowest profile he could.

Distantly he heard voices. There were two voices, male. He could not hear what they were saying. The dog's teeth were bared but it didn't growl. Dan had good instincts and he trusted the dog's. Danger. Dan held himself very still.

He had fallen in a particularly dense part of the wood. It only now struck Dan how green it was for late autumn. He would be hard to spot if he could keep quiet. The hilt of the sword jabbed into his side. He closed his hand around it, carefully, hoping the dog would not object. The feel of the cool metal of the hilt under his sweating palm made him feel stronger. The voices were louder now. There were definitely two men speaking in undertones and moving quietly. Dan strained to make out the words. They did not sound English, the intonation was wrong. Was it Italian maybe? He could hear them clearly now, though he dared not lift his head to watch them. The dog remained completely still but Dan felt that he could sense its hostility towards the approaching figures. It was quivering with fear. That did not offer Dan much comfort. Dan was again exiled from his place of quiet certainty and was very afraid. He could hear the voices of the men even more distinctly now. They were coming right towards him. He recognised the language – just. He had never heard it spoken before except in class. They were speaking Latin.

~ Chapter Three ~

In the Camp of the Standing Stones

One of the men approached Ursula with long, easy strides. He sheathed his sword, as he walked. That didn't make her feel any safer. He was a big, muscular man and quiet menace was in every step. Ursula specialised in looking impassive. It worried people and ncouraged them to leave her alone. She kept herself very still and fought to keep fear out of her eyes. It would not help.

The man spoke. She listened. It meant nothing. He tried again. He wasn't speaking English and she was sure it wasn't German or French.

'Don't you speak English?' She was pleased that her voice sounded even and surly.

'I ... know some ...' he sounded amused, though his face too, was hard to read.

'Why are you threatening me?' She was annoyed that she sounded slightly petulant.

27

'Rhonwen called you through the Veil. You are a warrior? Warriors are danger.' He shrugged matter-of-factly. His English was perfectly comprehensible, she just had no idea what he was talking about. 'Where are your weapons?' He asked the question quietly enough, but his voice was as sharp as his sword. It was Ursula's turn to shrug. 'My men can … search … You want?'

Two of the men were tending to the woman who had fainted. The remaining three were watching the interchange with wary interest. Their grip on their swords had not faltered. No, she did not want to be searched, least of all by thugs in antique dress.

She took off her anorak with deliberate movements, keeping her eyes on the man's face. The anorak had loads of pockets. If he regarded her bus pass and her biro as weapons, he could have them. She emptied the pockets of her school trousers. Two boiled sweets, thirty pence and a crumpled paper tissue. She threw them on the floor disdainfully.

'I have no weapons.'

Searching through the pockets of her anorak, it seemed that he agreed with her. He shrugged again.

'Rhonwen no good at warrior hunt. How old are you, boy?'

Ursula was not surprised at the question. She was used to people mistaking her for a boy. These days she cultivated it. She always wore cropped hair, trousers and loose tops. She kept her face impassive.

'Nearly sixteen.'

'You have too much flesh and are too old to train. Can you ride?'

She didn't think he meant a donkey at Whitby Bay, she shook her head.

'Well, Gift of the Goddess, you must drink the Cup of Belonging and hope the Goddess knows more than I do. You are with us now.'

He signalled for the men to sheath their swords, turned his back and walked away. She was dismissed. She felt her anger boil. She wasn't *with* anybody. She wanted to know where she was and what was going on. She could see that she was far from where she should be. She demanded an explanation.

'Oy you!' she shouted, deliberately uncouth. It was not the most sensible way to address an armed man and even as she did it she wondered at her foolhardiness. The atmosphere changed in an instant. Swords were back in hands; eyes flickered their interest. The leader turned very slowly, like a gun-fighter in a Western.

'If you want to live, never speak that way to me.'

All humour had left his eyes, which were cold as a winter sea. Ursula wanted to crawl under a stone and hide there, but some instinct forced her to answer. Of course, it might have been an instinct for self-destruction.

'I want to know what is going on. Who are you? What is all this about? I need to go back to catch my coach.'

The man stared at her expressionlessly but she thought he looked slightly less likely to kill her than he had before.

'I have no time for this. We cannot stay here much longer.' His face remained expressionless but his tone was irritated. Nonetheless he answered her. 'I am Prince Macsen of a lineage that takes days to say. You are here. You cannot catch your … coach. I regret, you cannot go back to wherever you came from. After the rite someone will explain. Come.' He signalled for her to follow. He sounded weary, but he did not sound like he was lying. She did not know what he meant by not going back. Did he mean that he would not let her?

The man looked like no one she had seen before. He would not have looked out of place at a fancy dress party – his size and physique would mark him out anywhere but a Hollywood film or maybe an American football stadium. He was bigger than Ursula by several inches, which must have made him at least six feet six inches tall. He moved with the same innate balance as Dan, but somehow she didn't think he was a footballer. His hair was long and plaited down his back and the lower half of his face was almost hidden by the most extraordinary moustache she had ever seen. It was a pale gingery gold and was so long it hung to below the level of his chin.

Draped over his broad shoulders was a heavy plaid cloak in rich greens and rusts. Under that he wore a long tunic, yellow and green striped trews and soft moccasin type boots. A thick gold-coloured necklace circled his neck like a serpent and another massive ring coiled around his right bicep. Both bare arms were elaborately tattooed with swirling patterns all around the wrists and forearms. His sword hung from a scabbard of finely tooled leather, embossed with silver and gold. It seemed to belong there. He wore the sword as naturally as Ursula would wear her school rucksack.

Her mind refused to supply her with a credible explanation of what was going on. Her imagination ran wild. She kept herself outwardly calm and retrieved her anorak from the ground where he'd abandoned it. Tying it round her waist, she followed "Prince Macsen" mainly because she couldn't think of anything else to do.

The men had carried the woman to a tent a little way from the standing stones. "Prince Macsen" followed and his remaining men walked a few paces behind Ursula. She found that less than reassuring. None of them was quite so enormous as their leader but for the first time she felt physically diminished. She could hear them chatting in some foreign language. Adrenalin made her stomach queasy but she was determined not to let her uncertainty show.

They laid the woman inside the tent and emerged a

31

few moments later with an amphora and a goblet. To Ursula's eyes the goblet resembled some priceless artefact of gold, studded with gemstones. It had to be a fake; such things did not exist outside a museum. The men, including Macsen, squatted on the ground. Macsen indicated that she was to do the same. She could not squat for any length of time; she didn't have the strength so sat cross-legged, like a little child. She felt foolish. There was a small campfire, though its heat was rather unnecessary for such a warm day. The man handed the goblet and amphora to "The Prince" who sighed.

'Rhonwen should do this. It is a priestess' rite. Kai has some of the old druid blood, and a little of the talent that goes with it. He will try and take her place. It will be fine. We haven't time to waste and Rhonwen may not wake for several watches.'

Macsen nodded his head and the man called Kai started to chant and throw rust-coloured powder from a small pouch into the fire. Although Ursula listened hard, the words were incomprehensible. This chant was not in English; it might have been nonsense syllables for all the sense it made. At first nothing much seemed to happen. But as Kai gained confidence his voice grew stronger. As his sonorous baritone rhythmically intoned the strange syllables, Ursula felt the same electric charge of power in the air. Her spine seemed to quiver with it and her body began to tingle. At the same moment, the powder began to burn to produce a heady yellow smoke that stayed like a mist at ground level, gradually building up to head height. It did not disperse in the open air, as smoke should, but rolled around like dry ice getting thicker and more pungent every second. She didn't want to breathe it in, but there was no other air to breathe. Kai's voice at once seemed more distant and more resonant, as if he was chanting from the bottom of a deep well. Through the smoke she could see Macsen drink from the golden cup and pass it to her. He mimed for her to drink it, then pass it on. Some part of her was urging her not to drink it, to spill it on the ground, but the smoke drifted between her thoughts to confuse them. What could be wrong with it if Macsen had drunk it himself? The smoke itself caught at the back of her throat, drying it and making her thirsty. She took the heavy goblet from Macsen and gulped from it thirstily before passing it on. It burned the back of her throat like fire, but it didn't smell like alcohol. It smelled like perfumed honey. It was a strange taste, but before she could analyse it further she toppled over, insensible, her head on Macsen's shoulder.

It was dark when she awoke. She was cold. She was tied by her wrists, ankles and waist to something that was moving. There was total blackness everywhere and she was gagged. Her head hurt. When she moved it, a sharp pain like a hammer blow assaulted her.

33

She tried to reorientate herself. Did she hurt any-where else? Her bonds were chaffing her wrists slightly and her back ached, but she did not think she had been hurt anywhere. She was strapped to a horse. If she turned her head the very slight amount she could manage before pain overwhelmed her, she could just see through her peripheral vision moving shapes in front and behind her. She seemed to be in a convoy of horses, travelling at a walking pace through countryside. She could hear breathing but that was about all. No one spoke and the horses must have been travelling on grass because they made very little noise.

'My Prince.' The male voice, it might have been Kai's, was scarcely more than a whisper but it sounded loudly in the silence. '"Boar Skull" is stirring. He'll need to throw up.'

Just as the man said this, Ursula became aware of a powerful and building nausea. If she was sick in her gag she would surely choke. Strong hands untied and removed her gag. Two men lifted her bodily and carried her far away from the path of the horses. Ursula heaved and retched at the roadside, until she had nothing left to get rid of. The pain in her head made her sob. Someone handed her the golden goblet. She pushed it roughly away.

'Drink it! It's water. It'll not harm you.' It was Macsen.

She sniffed it. It smelled like water. She rinsed her mouth with it, then drank deeply. It was water. It helped a little.

'What did you do to me?'

'You drank of the Cup of Belonging – it is a rite for strangers, outlanders. It went wrong, or at least, it did not go as expected. Perhaps it was Kai. He does not know. Once or twice there have been outlanders, others like you, who raved. That's why you were bound. We could not risk that here. This is not friendly territory. Can you understand me?'

'Of course I can understand you! I am not an idiot. What was in that drink?' The sickness had not increased her respect for armed men. Her own recklessness alarmed her.

'Can you ride?' asked Macsen, ignoring her question.

'I told you I can't ride.'

'No, I mean are you fit enough to get on your pony? This is not a safe place to stop. I promise Rhonwen or someone will explain all, when we make camp. You are an enigma, stranger Boar Skull. I have drunk the Cup of Belonging many times in my life. It is the way we gain … information from those outside the tribe. Never have I gained so little from one of the circle or had such a headache for my efforts.'

Kai, "Red-head" and another man, Prys, "The Strong-handed", helped her back to the horse.

'I can manage. There's no need to push me, you great brutes,' she snarled at them. She felt weak and shaky. Her head still hurt. Someone had put her anorak on her, but the zip and buttons had not been fastened. She was cold. Had that honey drink been some kind of drug they had used to interrogate her? What had Macsen expected to learn from drinking with her? The familiar, small, hard kernel of fear in the pit of her stomach grew a little. She did not know how far she was from home. Her mother would be frantic with worry and nothing made any sense.

'You've learned the tongue of the Combrogi well, comrade Boar Skull,' Kai murmured in an undertone.

'We'll make a priestess out of you yet, Kai,' whispered Prys. Kai cuffed him roughly on the forearm. The two of them seemed to treat her with a certain wary respect. Why did they call her "Boar Skull?" What did they mean by the tongue of the Combrogi?

It was then that Ursula realised. No one had spoken a word of English since she had woken up. Since drinking the Cup of Belonging she found herself mysteriously able to speak and understand another language. It was so unlikely, it was almost easier to believe she was still unconscious or hallucinating some bizarre fantasy. The jarring motion of the pony beneath her, the cold and her continuing nausea were all too uncomfortable to be anything less than real. She fastened her coat with awkward hands and concentrated on staying on the pony. It bore neither saddle nor stirrups and it was a very long way from the ground.

Chapter Four

The Bear Sark

Dan concentrated hard to make sense of the words. It gave him something besides his fear to worry about. He was good at Latin but was unused to dealing with the spoken variety. The two men seemed to be looking for some people. Dan did not recognise the word they used to describe them. He got the feeling that he was listening to an altogether cruder version of Latin than he was used to. He desperately wanted to look up, to see who these people were, but he was afraid to give away his position. In spite of everything, he was intrigued. Who would be speaking in Latin? Why would anybody do that? The voices got closer. The voices stopped. Dan could sense their owners' presence not two paces away. He dare not look up. What if they had a gun? It was possible that these men had nothing to do with the appalling sight outside the hut, but his own fear and the dog's evident terror made for a persuasive counter argument. Dan was sure the men must have seen him. One of the men gave a short peal of laughter, mocking. This was it. Dan opened his eyes. He couldn't see anything but the tangled branches in front of him. He heard a rasping noise; he didn't know what it was. The dog responded at once. Growling deep in its throat it launched himself at the man, with a force that must surely have knocked him over. Dan raised his head and scrambled to his feet. In front of him was blood and confusion. He could see only the dog's head moving from side to side; something caught between its powerful jaws. A man in some kind of kilt was charging towards the dog with a long knife. Dan made no conscious calculations. The dog had not killed him when he could have done. It had warned him of danger. In his heart he had made the dog his ally. Somehow, more by an act of will than skill, Dan managed to lunge forward and thrust his heavy, borrowed blade between the dog's exposed flank and the long knife. There was a clang of metal as the two blades clashed and Dan felt the reverberation quiver up to the hilt of the sword. Standing up, Dan had a better idea of what was going on. The dog had one of the men on the ground. The object between its teeth was the man's neck. The dog was a killer! Dan had no chance to change his mind about defending the animal. He had committed himself. The man before him was serious. He clearly knew how to use a knife though he used it, unexpectedly, as a short sword for stabbing. For some extraordinary reason, he also carried a long body shield, shaped like the things riot police use.

Dan tried to use the weight of his own sword to stave off the attack. He did it desperately and in panic. The other man had the upper hand and looked about to use it, ruthlessly. Then the man spoke. Terror must have improved Dan's Latin because he had a pretty good idea of what the man said. It was something along the lines of 'I'll finish you off too, you young barbarian, you can join the red-haired trash.' The man with the long knife, fighting Dan, was the girl's murderer.

Something happened to Dan then. Terror deserted him, as did all thought. He found his place of quiet and it was full of blood. The huge blade in his hand weighed nothing; it was the extension of his arm. His arm was an extension of his will and his will was inflamed with a lust for vengeance. Time ceased. His opponent's movements slowed. The man thrust forward eagerly with his knife, his shield arm moved briefly as he shifted his balance and before he had time to raise his guard, Bright Killer was through the gap. Dan attacked in a frenzy of violence and kept on attacking long after the need had gone. His opponent, the girl's murderer, was not killed so much as butchered. Dan was so far from himself that he knew no mercy, only terrible, focused fury.

It was many hours later that Dan came to himself. He had

no memory of what had elapsed. It was a blank space, a skeleton too frightening to face, hidden in a locked cupboard in a secret part of his mind. The dog was licking his face. Both he and the dog were caked in blood. Something horrible had taken place in the bushes, not long ago. There were at least two bodies, so horribly savaged that they must have been killed by animals. Dan felt that both he and the dog were lucky not to have been involved.

He patted the matted hair of the dog's head. The dog nuzzled him in return. Dan was deeply grateful that the dog seemed now to be friendly. Dan would call him "Braveheart", after the film. He was surely fierce enough to keep Dan safe.

Dan felt no sympathy for these dead bodies, nor did his callousness seem strange to him. He was vaguely conscious of a need to wash, and a need to stretch his cramped muscles. The great sword was still in his hand. He was gripping it as if his life depended on it. He did not pause to wonder why he and it were so sticky with gore. He did not want to think about it. He forced himself to let it go. The imprint of the hilt remained in his palm. His arm ached a little as if he'd used new muscles. He stretched and walked over towards the mangled remains in the bushes. He wiped the sword on a red woollen cloak that lay some way from one of the corpses. Wrapping the sword carefully in its folds, he hefted it over his shoulder like an axe. He had lost the makeshift harness when he fell, hours before. He whistled to attract Braveheart's attention and, without a backward glance, moved on.

It was getting dark. The dog moved ahead of him, a dark shadow in an increasingly darkened wood. He could have done with his jacket. He couldn't for a moment recall where he'd left it and then he remembered the girl. That horror seemed days away now. His mind slid hastily away from the memory of it. He concentrated on the present. He was cold. His damp clothes were drying stiffly and gave him little warmth. If he could find a stream he could follow it to the town and maybe drink from it and wash in it as well. He was still worried about Lizzie and Ursula. He had been lost for hours and was still no nearer getting home. He walked on and toyed with the idea of running to get warm, but the ground was uneven and pitted with unseen obstacles. Bright Killer was a comforting weight over his right shoulder. From time to time he swapped it to his left shoulder, but he no longer found its weight burdensome.

At length he heard running water and followed the sound to a small stream. Braveheart drank eagerly and Dan followed suit. He washed his face and hands, but the water was too shallow and it was too cold to do much about his blood-stained clothes. His earlier concern about fingerprints seemed a lifetime away.

Braveheart sniffed the air and then stiffened his ears flat against his skull. He could smell something. A moment later Dan thought he could hear a distant unidentifiable noise. The events of the afternoon had changed him. He took cover and unwrapped Bright Killer, now dulled and smeared by his too hasty attempt to clean it up.

He had hoped for a car or maybe a truck, but there were no headlights and no engine noise. Something was coming he was sure. He could hear a rumble like faraway thunder. For the first time he gave serious attention to how he could explain his disreputable, bloody condition and, of course, the presence of an antique sword. He gripped it tighter. It was not wise to hold it but he was not prepared to hide it away until he was sure there was no danger. He stood closer to Braveheart, who was bristling with concentration, every muscle held taut, ready for action. There must have been seven mounted men, some kind of chariot and five or six other riderless horses bearing packs. They moved quietly for such a large band and carried no lights. What was going on round here? How many chariots and horses were there in Sussex? Why couldn't he run into somebody normal? A nice reassuring farmer in a Land Rover would be good. He just wanted to go home. Braveheart was tense but not growling. He made his decision. He hastily rewrapped the sword, lifted it onto his shoulder and jogged forward into open view. Braveheart matched his pace, running with him into clear view of the lead horseman.

'Hello! Excuse me, I'm trying to get to Hastings, please could you tell me if this is the way?'

Two things happened almost at once. He heard Ursula's frightened voice cry out, 'Dan!' and a large man ran toward him with a naked sword, not unlike his own. This was madness. Ursula was in danger now. He would not let them treat her like the red-haired girl.

He did not have much time to get Bright Killer out of its confining blanket, but he was sure Braveheart would not let the armed man get too close. He was right. Braveheart growled a low menacing growl and was poised to tear out the man's throat. From the corner of his eye he could see a second man, and a third approaching him from the other direction. He fumbled with the sword and worked it free.

A man was speaking – shouting, but Dan could not understand what he was saying. Why did nobody speak English? He felt hopelessly unprepared to stave off an attack from three grown men. He held the cumbersome sword awkwardly in trembling hands. Then he heard Ursula's scream of horror. With that sound he lost himself in the terrible clarity of his quiet place of blood. He and Bright Killer were one.

~ Chapter Five ~

Reunited

U rsula strained her eyes against the darkness. Dan! She thought she had heard Dan. Someone who could only be Dan was asking directions to Hastings in a polite English voice. Forgetting the oppressive silence in which they'd been travelling, she called out his name at the top of her voice. The sound was swallowed by the dark night.

Prince Macsen was taking no chances and had signalled his men Kai, Prys and Gwyn to surround Dan, their swords drawn, as if he was some kind of threat. The very idea struck her as ludicrous. What they might do to him terrified her. She screamed. She was so afraid they would hurt him. She heard someone shout then. There was a flash and clash of swords, vicious snarling and shouts of pain and anger.

'Please God, don't let him die!' was all she could think to say. If Dan was here she could not be too far from home.

Macsen was angry. His voice was low but, even though she could not hear the words, the tone was clear. He signalled, and men started to dismount, guiding horses into the bushes to one side of them. She could not see Dan. Was he still alive? Dread flowed like ice through her veins. Someone led her horse into the woods. Men busied themselves all around her. It seems they were setting up camp. A fire was lit and in the flickering light she saw Dan. Thank God! He seemed dazed and was being led, his hands bound behind him, towards the fire. He was walking, so the blood that covered him might not have been his own. A huge dog, about the size of a small donkey, with bloodshot eyes stood roughly muzzled by rope at his side. Dan was alive! Her relief was short-lived. The look in his eyes was not quite sane. Prys, Kai, and Gwyn followed behind Dan. All three men were bloodied and somewhat shamefaced.

Before she could move to talk to Dan, Prince Macsen was in front of her.

'You know this man?'

'Dan, yes he's ... another student. Is he hurt?' Macsen's language had no word for "classmate".

'He's not hurt,' said Macsen, 'but he's a cursed berserker, that's what he is and it took three good men to bring him back alive. He came very close to ending his days in that wood. Why did you not say that two of you came through the Veil? Are there more?'

Macsen's hard eyes searched hers challengingly. She found herself stepping back. She understood Macsen's words but they spoke of something of which she had no experience. Was the Veil the yellow mist? Was a berserker someone who was mad? Dan had never seemed mad before, or at least, not more so than the rest of the boys in her year. She had no idea what the man was talking about.

'Dan was behind me when I stepped through the mist. I don't know if he followed me.'

'Of course he followed you. He's here, isn't he?' Macsen let his irritation show.

Ursula could keep her own level tone no longer. She was scared and miserable, worried about Dan, her mother and her own safety. She wanted to go home.

'Don't shout at me! I don't know where *here* is. I don't know what you are doing here with your ridiculous swords and horses and creeping around in the dark. This is abduction. It's a … ' she wanted to say criminal offence but could find no word that meant the same. 'It's an … offence against the tribe,' she continued, resisting with difficulty an unhelpful desire to burst into tears. Macsen didn't say anything for a moment.

'The Cup of Belonging taught you little, Boar Skull. I have no time to fill in the gaps in your understanding or your courtesy. This has not happened before. The Goddess has a strange sense of humour. We ask for warriors and she sends us an ill-mannered whelp with a mind like a stone wall and a berserker, touched by the gods. It is my earnest wish that Rhonwen wakes soon or I will find myself setting hard hands on you to teach you some respect for a Prince of the Tribes. It is only honour of the Goddess that has stayed my hand so far, but I am not a patient man. Go to your brother but be wary, he is not free of the killing thirst. Ask him where he got his great hound from and his sword. I would know them anywhere. They belonged to a man of my people, Madoc ab Anwen. A man well known to me. If he has harmed one of my own, the Goddess will not protect him from my sword.'

Ursula felt Macsen's anger and frustration like a physical force around him, though his face remained impassive and his tone measured. For a split second she thought she saw it physically manifested as a nimbus of orange flame, then she blinked and it was gone. Her headache had returned. Dull pain ground her thoughts to fragments. It disrupted all her attempts to make sense of what was happening.

Dismissed by Macsen with a wave of his hand, she staggered over to sit next to Dan by the fire. He was something she was sure of, a fixed point in a world growing ever stranger. But Dan himself had grown strange. As she knelt down beside him, the beast on his other side growled and eyed her with a look that threatened extreme violence. She was afraid of dogs.

'Hi!' she said in her friendliest voice. Unused as she was to being friendly it did not come out well. 'Hello, Dan. Am I glad to see you!' Dan turned to look at her. She was more scared by the look in his eyes than by Macsen's anger. His eyes were blank now and expressionless. He looked at her without recognition. The Dan she thought she knew was not looking out from those lifeless eyes.

'Leave him. He'll come to. At least he's not one of the raving kind.'

It was Kai. He spoke roughly, but Ursula felt that he was trying to help.

'What do you mean? Do you know what's wrong with him?' Ursula found herself looking at the man who had drugged her, with appeal in her eyes. She did not like it. Kai winced and adjusted his position at the fire. His face was splattered by blood and he was ashen.

'It's not common even among the tribes, and the Goddess knows, we can be wild enough when the fancy takes us.' He smiled, but it was a grim sight. Although he was not old, many of his teeth were broken and the puckered edge of an old scar twisted his mouth into a gargoyle's grin. Kai by firelight was a frightening sight and yet Ursula was not afraid of him. She should have been. He had drugged her and attacked Dan, but something in her, something she couldn't explain, trusted Kai. He did not mean her harm. Of course, like so much else, her trust made no sense.

'But, by Lugh, he's fast on his feet, your Dan. If he had more practice with that sword, none of us could have taken him and I've been a warrior these twenty years. There are tales I could tell that would make the hair on your chest grow curly as a ram's horn. I knew a man, a bear sark, a "berserker" once. The most terrifying warrior I ever met and he was on my side! To look at him was to smell death, to hear his battle-cry was to feel death's cold breath on the back of your neck. That bear sark's anger was like a slow burning fire with damp wood, but when it caught, Lugh, he was like a forest fire, unstoppable – no thought in his head, just a mad, killing rage. He would kill his best friend soon as look at him, no idea what he was doing. He said it was like a red mist coming down and that was it! Great man in a battle as long as you could point him in the right direction, no fear at all. Felt no pain either … ' Kai turned and looked into the fire. He was holding his left arm and Ursula could see that there was a gash across his upper arm and chest from which blood was pumping out. His face looked sombre in the firelight. Why should Ursula feel sympathy? She thought instead about what he'd said about Dan. It did not fit at all with the boy she'd seen at school. Dan was clever, quick on his feet, on the periphery of lots of groups: smoking with the smokers, working with the workers, playing football with the hardest and the sportiest. He seemed to have no need for anger. He fitted in everywhere. Ursula had never seen him look ill at ease, or lost for words. She could have fallen for him, just for that alone if she'd been a different kind of girl. She'd never even heard of him being in a fight. She just couldn't imagine him mad with a killing rage. Yet he had survived an encounter with three armed men so something odd must have happened. There was a rustling behind her and as she turned to investigate, the pain from her head threatened to overwhelm her and her thoughts scattered. At that moment Rhonwen appeared at the fireside and Ursula felt her stomach knot. As in some part of herself she trusted Kai, in that same still instinctive part, she did not trust Rhonwen. She was her enemy. Ursula was sure of it.

Rhonwen did not look in Ursula's direction. But Ursula still had the sense that she was taking more notice of her than anyone else was at the fire.

'Kai,' Rhonwen said and a strange electric thrill ran through Ursula at her voice. 'Let me look at that arm before you bleed to death and put the fire out in the same night. We cannot afford to lose any more druid blood just now. Come to the tent, I want a word with you.'

Rhonwen's speaking voice was beautiful. It was low,

seductive and powerful. Ursula could sense the steely will beneath that velvet voice, so that the mildest suggestion became an ironclad command. Kai rose meekly to his feet, still clutching his arm and followed Rhonwen away from the fire. When he left, Ursula could see pooled blood where he had been sitting. He must have been in agony, yet he had managed not to let it show. Ursula's inexplicable respect for the man seemed justified.

'Ursula?' Dan's voice sounded very small and lost. 'Ursula, are you OK?'

Ursula turned to see a bemused but more normal-looking Dan, eyeing her with concern and relief.

'I didn't mean to upset you. I followed you, but I must have lost you in the mist. Who are these people? Have they hurt you? Do you know where we are?'

It seemed so long since she had stormed off in a temper into the yellow mist that it took Ursula a minute to realise what Dan meant.

'It doesn't matter about that,' she said quickly, embarrassed. 'Are you OK? You didn't look right … you're covered in blood.'

'I don't remember what happened. There are bits missing. I found a sword and a dead girl and the dog, Braveheart. He's great,' Dan's wan tone warmed with sudden enthusiasm, as he patted the giant beside him, 'and then I got here. I must have fallen and banged my head or something because it doesn't all fit together right … ' He looked at her with something like panic. 'Ursula, where the hell are we? I've run for miles and I can't even find the road and I've got to report the murder of a girl.' He paused and then said sharply, 'Where's Bright Killer?'

'Where's what?'

'My sword, I mean … a sword I found, I called it Bright Killer.'

'Macsen wanted to ask you about that.'

'Macsen?'

'He said he's called Prince Macsen. He's in charge. I think he knows the man who owned it.'

'I'm not surprised, there can't be that many people who take such an interest in antique swords. Why are they dressed like that?'

'I don't know. They're Combrogi. I think it's how they dress.'

'They're what?' Dan was not making this any easier. Ursula was embarrassed both by the extent of her ignorance and by her inexplicable pockets of knowledge. How did she explain a sudden grasp of the language? She was only in the second group for French and the third for German. Dan was in the top set for both – and did Latin. She continued doggedly.

'The Combrogi – it's what the tribespeople here call themselves. The trouble is I'm not sure where here is. I'm beginning to be afraid, look, don't laugh, right, but

I'm afraid we might have slipped back in time somehow. I know it sounds stupid.'

Dan didn't say anything. She wasn't even sure he was listening. She had thought he was himself again but he seemed very agitated.

'I need to find Bright Killer,' he said, as if she hadn't exposed herself to his ridicule with her bizarre theory. He tried to get to his feet, but was constrained by his tied hands. The dog nuzzled his cheek. Kai had returned from Rhonwen's tent and was by Dan's side at the first sign of his movement. From Kai's expression it was clear that he regarded Dan as some kind of wild animal. Perhaps that's what a bear sark was. The red gash on Kai's arm was gone. Ursula looked again. It must have been on the other side. With disbelief, she checked a third time. Kai had changed his jerkin, and there was no sign at all that he had ever been injured. Was it possible that Rhonwen had healed him? Surely it was not. Anyway, Ursula did not want to consider that mystery now. Rhonwen was not far behind Kai and her very presence made Ursula anxious.

Rhonwen looked at Dan with the same intense gaze she had fixed on Ursula but Dan seemed unperturbed by it. His need to find his sword was uppermost in his mind. Rhonwen scowled slightly. She said to Kai in her own tongue, 'It would be better if we did the rite for him too. He must be made one of us. He is too dangerous

53

otherwise. We might learn more from that one if I were to lead the ceremony,' she indicated Ursula with a disdainful inclination of her head.

It was Dan's turn to scowl. He understood nothing. He was unused to it. Ursula, on the other hand, found herself angry at being spoken about as if she were of no account. This woman would not put her through any rite. Whatever she had in mind could not be good, of that Ursula was certain. Ursula was determined to assert herself. She spoke up in Rhonwen's tongue.

'My brother and I want no ceremony. We want to go home, you have held us here long enough against our will. There will be people looking for us.'

Rhonwen looked both surprised and angry. Dan looked astonished. Rhonwen switched languages.

'I thought you said the ceremony was unsuccessful,' she said accusingly to Kai.

Kai looked uncomfortable. 'Aye, Lady, in part. I said the boy has not understood everything. He does not understand our ways, as should have happened in the rite, but he has learned our language. That is all. We learned nothing from him, but the true meaning of headache. He would not let us learn his thoughts.' He rubbed his head above the temples as if it still ached and said thoughtfully, 'I do not think the fault lay within the rite or the way I conducted it. There is something within the boy. He is unlike the others. We have called him Boar Skull. He hides his secrets in a harder head than I've ever come across.'

What Rhonwen intended to say next was drowned out by a sudden pounding of hooves, but Ursula sensed that it was unlikely to be complimentary. A rider galloped into camp and dismounted neatly at Macsen's feet. His tight economy of movement somehow conveyed a terrible urgency. Ursula found she knew his name. He was Caradoc-the-secret. He spoke in a voice so low that it could scarcely be heard even in the sudden silence of the watchful camp.

Macsen's own voice was hardly any louder but it carried like a clarion call of danger. 'No feast tonight. We will leave at once. Caradoc has found Madoc's daughter murdered, and slaughtered Ravens in the wood. Trouble will be here soon. This is not my chosen field for killing, comrades. We will move.'

The men who had been stretching their legs, watering the horses or warming themselves by the fire readied themselves within minutes. The fire was carefully extinguished and all traces of their brief stay disguised. Caradoc's small, stocky form slipped away to confuse their trail.

'What's going on?' Dan understood nothing of Macsen's words. Frustration lent a desperate edge to his tone.

Kai caught Macsen's eye. The Prince strode over to join them.

'Boy!' he said in English. And Macsen's hard eyes sought out Dan's bewildered ones.

Dan was grateful for words he could understand. 'Yes, sir?'

'There was a girl in the wood. Did you kill her? Is that where you got the sword?' The shocked and horrified expression on Dan's face was answer enough. He swallowed and looked back at Macsen with haunted eyes.

'I saw the girl. She had long red hair. She was already dead. I did not kill her.'

'The Ravens, in your tongue …' Macsen struggled for the word, 'Romans. There are two dead Roman scouts in the wood. Did you kill them?'

'I don't know. I don't remember. I don't see how I could …'

Macsen's face lost none of its impassivity but Ursula sensed his glimmer of sympathy for the wild-eyed boy.

'This is not the time for talk. I have seen you fight. I will give you your sword. I don't know what Boar Skull can do, but he is your brother to defend here. Don't look to my men to help you. We may have killing to do. Stay mounted if you can. We will ride. Whoever killed those Ravens may have brought death to us a little earlier than I'd have hoped. They were scouts. There will be others behind. We must ride fast. May the Goddess who brought you protect you now.'

With that he was gone, whispering orders to the men.

Kai untied Dan's bonds and gave him Bright Killer. Dan gripped it as if it was the only thing he understood. Perhaps it was. With steady hands, he cut through the dog's rough muzzle. He was growling. The noise was about the most threatening that Ursula had ever heard. Kai gave Ursula a sword too. It was plain in comparison to Bright Killer but heavy, longer and sharper than her mother's carving knife. It gave her no comfort at all.

Kai patted her shoulder and murmured, 'Taranis keep you, Boar Skull.' Then he was off.

There was much movement of men and ponies. Macsen was manoeuvring what Ursula assumed to be a cart. All was confusion. Ursula struggled onto her pony. There were no stirrups so Dan had to help her on. The sword got in the way. She was very frightened. Dan seemed quite calm and vaulted onto one of the spare horses as Kai and the others had. Ursula envied him his athleticism. She felt clumsy and uncomfortable. She held the sword's hilt awkwardly in her right hand. She was very afraid she was going to accidentally remove her horse's ears with her sword.

'Don't worry, Ursula, I'll keep you safe.' Dan seemed to have gained in confidence with the return of the great sword. The huge dog seemed happy to stand at his horse's side. Dan's tone was earnest, but she could not see his face. What turned him into a berserker? Would he turn on her?

Then, suddenly, the clouds parted around the moon and the ground was bathed in pale moonlight. Something silvery glinted in the woods. There was no time to run. It was the crested helmet of a soldier, an enemy soldier. The more she looked the more she saw. It was like counting stars in a cloudy sky. An arrow hissed past her ear. Someone or something let out a blood-curdling wolf's howl. Ursula did not know if it was Rhonwen or Braveheart. That seemed to be a signal for wild cries and ululation, a cacophony of aggression. The tribesmen had killing to do. They charged, hurling spears and insults at the enemy in equal measure, like drunken hooligans in some street brawl. The enemy stepped out of the trees to meet them. Ursula's heart almost stopped. They were not in parade ground formation, but there was no doubting what they were.

'Get behind me. Now!' said Dan in a tight, strained voice.

The enemy were Roman and there must have been fifty of them. There was the clash of metal on metal over and above the din of the wild Combrogi's battle-cries. The battle had begun.

~ Chapter Six ~

The Dragon in the Wood

Dan slid from his horse and planted himself before her, Braveheart snarling at his side. He had no shield, but then he wouldn't have known how to use one anyway. He held Bright Killer in his hands, ready. His heart was racing but he was determined to keep in control. The other Combrogi seemed to have abandoned their horses too. They were hurling themselves at the enemy as they emerged from the woods, screaming taunts and wild war cries as they went. He strained to watch their huge bulky shapes. He watched intently as if it were a game and he were trying to learn the rules. There did not seem to be any rules – there was just death any way the Combrogi could deal it. The Combrogi were all big men. Even bareheaded they towered above the Romans and their extra reach and height gave them an obvious advantage in hand to hand combat. They also fought very dirty. There was no code of chivalry here.

The Combrogi used everything, their brute strength, spear, sword, foot, shield and spear end. He watched as a bear-like warrior charged a Roman. He thrust his long spear into the Roman's unprotected sword arm, slashed at his belly below the breastplate, and then hacked the whole arm off with his sword, before retrieving his spear. Dan could hear bones crack. He could hear metal against metal, metal against wood, metal against bone, metal against flesh. He strained to see. The moon was shadowed now, but he was glad he couldn't see more. The dark silhouettes and the brutal sounds were enough.

How could the Combrogi run out there and start hacking away at strangers? It reminded him of the kind of madness that sometimes struck after a football match. The Combrogi were like football hooligans with swords. They gloried in the mayhem of a pitched battle. Where was he that this could be going on? Where were the police or the British Army or whoever stopped thugs in strange clothes brawling like this? Somehow, after this was finished, he must get Ursula and Braveheart back to safety. For now it was up to him to keep them safe. He did not know when he had taken mental responsibility for Ursula or indeed for Braveheart but he had and he would just have to do his best to make everything all right. He stood squarely in front of Ursula, who was still on her horse. A phrase flitted through his mind, 'Here I stand I can do no other.' It was how he felt. He could hear Braveheart's harsh breathing. He knew he was ready, anxious even, to join in. He hoped Braveheart wouldn't count as a dangerous dog and have to be put down when he got him home. He only fought in self-defence after all.

So Dan watched the Combrogi, watched what they did and recoiled from what he might have to do, if any-one came his way. Weren't the Romans and the Combrogi both his enemies? If they tried to hurt him or his friends they were. He felt small and ineffectual but he gripped Bright Killer grimly. He was glad Braveheart was ready and eager. The sword's weight and the dog's muscular presence made him less scared. He balanced the heavy blade and waited.

From her position on the pony Ursula had as good a view of the battle as was possible. The moon was cloud-ed again and it took time for her eyes to adjust to see the black forms against the black night. There was no sign of Rhonwen or Macsen. Dan stood in front of her like a sprinter at the starting block. That left only Macsen's men, Gwyn, Kai, Prys, Rhodri and Caradoc, to fight the Romans. Maybe there were less than fifty of them, maybe more. She could not judge. It was academic any-way. There were too many. There was no hope for the Combrogi against such odds. The wild ululation from Macsen's men seemed like whistling in the dark. Maybe they thought so too, for there was less noise now, just grunts and curses, hard breathing and the ominous clink of Roman armour as the enemy moved. There were cries too as men died. Men were dying there in front of her. It did not seem possible. Dark forms screamed and writhed and thudded onto the earth but it all happened in a kind of envelope of silence. The night, darker than any night she'd ever known, swallowed everything.

Ursula did not know what to do. She saw Kai spear a Roman, then raise his great sword to smash down through his opponent's neck. Moonlight briefly lit his face. It was contorted with effort and a grim kind of joy. These men who had taken her prisoner liked to kill. They did it well, or so it seemed, but no matter how many of the enemy they felled more kept coming out of the trees. She saw Gwyn aim his spear with ruthless accuracy into the unprotected face of Roman, then push him aside with his heavy wooden shield. Prys' shield had five or six spears protruding from it. He wielded it like some giant porcupine, as an extra weapon to turn aside the Roman shield and thrust his own spear home. She had to look and yet she didn't really want to see what these men were doing to each other.

The Romans shouted to one another, their voices drifting towards her out of the dark. They were shouting instructions, warnings, and directions as if engaged in some complex team game. In spite of the bloodshed inflicted by the battle-crazed Combrogi, they moved with almost mechanical calm and began to arrange themselves into battle formation. Five wild men, even five with the strength of ten, could not harry them into forgetting their discipline. Ursula knew nothing of battles but even she could see that the Romans were more than warriors. Individually the Combrogi warriors were a match for them but now the Romans had made themselves into a killing machine. Dan muttered under his breath. Braveheart growled. The war-hound's bloodied body quivered with the urgency of his need to join the battle, just waiting for the command that would unleash him, but Dan kept on waiting and somehow so did Braveheart.

The Combrogi on the ground only gradually became aware that they could not fight men in wedge formation. There was no room for single combat; there was no one to fight. There was only a wedge of trained men who knew that if they kept in formation they could not lose. The Combrogi retreated back to the waiting horses and carts. Prys ran towards Ursula, wiping blood and sweat from his eyes, licking his dry lips. Ursula could almost feel his contempt for her, for not joining battle. The air between them was colder for his disdain. He spat briefly in her direction and then ran past. She saw Kai and Gwyn too; they were breathing heavily, but from what Ursula could see, were unharmed. They exchanged brief grunted words that Ursula could not hear and Kai patted Gwyn briefly on the back. The dark stuff that stained their tunics was not their blood.

Their retreat left the Combrogi standing in a loose line, level with Ursula and Dan. Behind them were the horses and the carts. In front of them lay the woods and between them, the Romans, shoulder to shoulder, five ranks deep awaiting their orders. The Combrogi could have mounted up and galloped away. The Romans were on foot. The Combrogi would have stood a good chance of getting away, but they made no move. At any rate she, Ursula, should run away with Dan, now, before the Romans advanced. Her captors would not chase her, not with umpteen Romans on their heels. Ursula wanted to run, her mind told her it was a really good idea, but she did not know how to make her horse turn round. She was rooted to the spot by a frightening combination of incapacitating fear and incompetence.

Dan did not take his eyes from the enemy. In the dark she could not see his face, she only sensed the desperate focus of his concentration. He was not mad now, unless bravery was madness. He would not run. She knew he would not run. He would defend her, whatever happened. She could see that he really meant it when he'd said he'd keep her safe. It gave her a strange feeling to realise that he was prepared to die for her if need be. She was quite sure of it and yet he didn't even like her much.

She felt awed by his courage. She wanted to stand next to him not behind him so he would not need to feel responsible for her, but she was truly petrified. She could not move. It was not that her legs were jelly or anything it was just that they would not move. She gripped the sword she was given tightly and wondered if, when it came to it, she would try to defend herself or if she was stuck like this, like a rigid wooden doll that would just be chopped down, like a thing already dead.

She saw Kai adjust his shield out of the corner of her eye. Gwyn fastened his cloak more firmly and wiped his sword on the grass. They were going to fight again. Their intention was clear in every readjustment of their weapons. They were getting ready to die.

There was a pause, a new kind of quiet. Ursula's over-wrought senses heard only the small sounds of the panting men, the occasional clank and shuffle of the otherwise silent enemy. The five tribesmen coolly surveyed and weighed their enemy. It was almost over, but Macsen's men would not die cheaply. Even in defeat they were defiant, proud and strangely businesslike. Death was their business and they checked and readied the tools of their trade. The whoop of a war cry fearsome enough to curdle the blood startled them as it startled Ursula. A ringing, fluent outpouring of curses that promised disease, pestilence, dishonour and destruction on all the Ravens' brood unto the tenth generation sang through the silence and all hell and hope broke loose. It was Macsen, huge and magnificent like an avenging angel, with his unbound hair and lurid cloak streaming behind him as he charged forward into the middle of the Roman wedge, on a chariot drawn by two large, bay horses. His inspired men let rip their ululating war cries, boasting of the Ravens they had already dispatched. Spears raised they ran after him straight towards the Roman wedge. It looked like the most dramatic kind of suicide, six men against forty, but could the wedge stand against Prince Macsen? It would surely take more courage than Ursula could believe existed in the whole world. She could not bear to look. Then suddenly, when Macsen was within his spear's thrust of the front line, within range of Roman spears, the forest itself seemed to rear up and roar its displeasure. Ursula thought she had been afraid before, but this time her knees did turn to jelly and if she had not been mounted she certainly would have fallen. Braveheart whined and flattened his ears against his head. The Roman enemy were not so well drilled that they did not turn to see what made the awful sound. Towering several metres above the trees, flame red and burning with its own inner light against the dark sky, was a dragon. Its eyes burned with wild hunger. Something disgusting dribbled from its maw. It dropped its huge head in the direction of the hapless Romans and opened its huge jaw. The mechanical men, the Romans, began to scream and run from the protective wedge. At about the same instant the front line, distracted from their task at exactly the wrong moment, broke. Horses trampled forward and Macsen's men were behind taking full advantage of the broken and confused ranks. The dragon roared again. The whole night rang with the sound like a dry-throated lion's roar only somehow more threatening, more reptilian. A quick darting lizard's tongue flicked out and those legionaries not already cowering from the giant head now ducked away. Ursula felt that prickling sensation she had felt before, as if the air was filled with static electricity. She could almost hear the deep throbbing hum of power pulsing through her bones and she knew immediately it had something to do with Rhonwen. She blinked and was astonished and blinked again. As her eyes became accustomed to the bright glow of the dragon she could see it in a different way. It was no more than a puppet thing, an illusion of leaves and earth and swirling luminescent mist. The dragon was a creature of illusion and that illusion, she knew, was Rhonwen's. The Roman legionaries saw it only as a dragon, of that she was sure. They were fighting each other to get away. They were packed closely together and their panic made for disaster. There was too little room for any of the Romans to use their spears and their short swords did not have the reach to defend against the butcher blows of Macsen and his men. Macsen's well-trained horses reared and stamped while he and his men cut down their panicking enemy with ruthless efficiency. Even he was wary of the dragon and reaped his bloody harvest as far from its gaping mouth as possible. The Combrogi warriors' ululation no longer seemed like whistling in the dark as what had looked like a suicide charge turned into a massacre.

Unfortunately, too many of the panicked men raced for the horses as far away from the dragon as possible. Ursula did not know why they did not all run straight past her and Dan, claim a horse and ride away. They did not.

A man ran their way. He was a young soldier, wild-eyed and shaking, completely unnerved by the apparition behind him. He came so close Ursula could smell sour wine on his breath and salt meat. In other circumstances Ursula might have found him handsome.

'Let me through!' he smiled a little madly and plunged his short sword into what would have been Dan's belly, except that by that time Dan had moved aside and Braveheart had leaped for the soldier's throat. The soldier did not survive the encounter. Dan betrayed no emotion, merely pushing the body aside with his toe. Another man, seeing the death of his comrade charged forward, his mail glinting red in the reflected light of the dragon.

'I'll have you, hell-hound!'

Spear at the ready, he hurled it towards Braveheart's huge and snarling form. Ursula did not see Dan move. His reactions were always praised by the other boys at school in their endless post match autopsies, but she had never taken a lot of notice. She could only watch, wooden and unmoving as he moved with incredible speed to deflect the spear. She looked away as he thrust his bloodied blade into the Roman's throat. There were more. All the retreating Romans seemed too eager to join the fray. None sought to avoid the boy and the dog. Dan and Braveheart almost seemed to find a rhythm, like digging a garden or building a wall. For a madman Dan was very cold. He wasted no effort. He did not speak or cry out or threaten. His madness was of a cool and calculating kind. He just killed. There was ice in Ursula's own veins as she watched him. He was saving her, but she did not feel saved. She wanted to go home to a place where this did not happen, where men were not hacked, where limbs were not severed, where blood did not flow so endlessly and where death did not stare back at her so bleakly with unclosed youthful eyes. It was too awful for her to cry. She still could not move to save herself and if a Roman had fought his way past Dan she did not know whether she could have raised her own sword even in self-defence. Her hand was numb with holding it, as her knees were numb with the effort of staying on her horse. She just wanted it all to stop. Eventually it did. There was no one left for Dan to kill. There were bodies all around. How could a boy kill ten men, soldiers armed with shields and spears? None of it made any sense. Dan was slumped among the dead, uncaring. Bright Killer, bright no more, but clogged and sullied by blood and worse lay across his lap. His hand rested on the neck of Braveheart who licked his face wearily. Braveheart's whole head was wet with blood.

The dragon was gone and the only men still living were of the Combrogi. Bodies littered the ground. Then Kai began to sing.

Chapter Seven

Head hunters

Kai's rich baritone voice trembled with weariness as he sang. His face was all but lost in the gloom. Dark blood hid his features like camouflage paint, but he sang as if he were the only living thing left in the world. It was a song for fallen comrades, in a minor key, sombre and soulful. It was a lament for the lost beauties of the earth that the dead would never see again. It was a lament for the dead themselves whose own lost, brave beauty those of the earth would never see again. It was a song to honour a valiant enemy. Ursula felt a sob rise, but she was afraid that if she let it out she would descend into hysteria. Prys' face was stained with tears as he joined in. Ursula quickly counted the warriors, all the Combrogi were still standing. The tears were for the enemy.

The others were moving along the bodies. She couldn't see what they were doing. Surely they weren't looting the dead? It was worse than that.

Macsen rode towards her in his chariot. Even in the dark he seemed to glow with exultant triumph, a conquering hero, overflowing with the energy of victorious battle. In his left hand he casually held by the hair the decapitated heads of two Roman legionaries. Blood dripped on his cloak.

'You are still alive then, Boar Skull? Much good you did us out there. Does your brother live? I see *he* is a worthy warrior.' He eyed the pile of bloodied corpses at Dan's feet with respect.

Macsen then leaped lightly from the war chariot and tied the heads to his horses' reins by their hair and moved to check on Dan. It was as if he did such things all the time. Perhaps he did do such things all the time. Ursula swayed in the saddle. She could feel the world around her turning black. The thundering of her own blood was loud in her ears. She was very afraid she was going to faint. She could not look at the heads. She closed her eyes. When she opened them again everything would be all right. All the horror would only be a nightmare. None of it could be real. But even with her eyes shut she could smell things that had no place in her normal world. The world of history field trips and safe beds, mothers and comfort. She could smell male sweat and blood and excrement. She could smell damp horse, damp dog, damp wool and fear. She opened her eyes. She had not fainted but the world was as it had been. It was all still

72

there. Macsen was caressing Braveheart, whispering endearments, wiping flesh and gore from his muzzle.

'I should have trusted you Giff, my old friend, you would not have fought for just any man. You're a hound of the gods!' He looked at the slumped, insensible form of Dan.

'He is young. I would not have guessed he had the strength for all this,' he indicated the sprawled bodies again. 'The madness of the bear sark is well known. I have always heard that they could fight with the strength of ten. Now I believe it. He will be honoured among us for this. But you ... I did not think you a coward, Boar Skull. I'm disappointed. Rhonwen has found us no warrior in you. I will have to talk with Rhonwen about you and about the foolish risk she took just now ... ' His face looked suddenly grim, then cleared. He called out.'Gwyn! Bring water for Giff and a couple of cloaks for The Bear Sark, and mead. He is too weary to look to his own honour.'

With a hard look at Ursula, now shivering with shock and cold, he turned away to join the others. The moon was bright again and she could see them all cheerfully ransacking the corpses and hacking off their heads. Kai's song had changed. He sang now as a butcher might whistle when he prepared meat for his shop. It was now a lively song with a rousing chorus. Prys and Rhodri sang in harmony. Ursula could not hear all the words but it was something about threshing corn and reaping the heads of their enemies. It was a scene from hell.

The spasm of shivering that racked Ursula seemed to signal the end of her petrifaction. She managed to release the hold on her borrowed sword and slide gracelessly off her borrowed pony. Stiffly, she tried to force numbed limbs to move. She would have fallen but fear that she would land on a corpse lent desperation to her attempts to keep her balance. She staggered towards Dan's recumbent form. He was only a step or two away, just in front of her. She did not think about the danger. She should have. Braveheart or Giff, as Macsen had called him, growled warningly in the back of his throat. The warning was enough for Dan who snapped awake, wild-eyed. He reached at once, with reflexive ease, for Bright Killer.

'No, Dan! It's all right. It's me, Ursula, you know from school ... '

She hoped that reminding him of his own real life away from this slaughter might bring him back to himself.

She was not sure that he had heard her strangled whisper, but he did not kill her, so he must have done. He also did not put down his sword. It was hard to square Dan, the schoolboy, with Dan, the mad killer, even though she had seen the transition with her own eyes. He now seemed to be both people at once. He held the sword with an easy grip. It was, as it had been in the battle, part of him, an extension of his will, but he spoke like the schoolboy.

'I'm starving!' He looked at her with troubled eyes. 'Ursula, you haven't got any chocolate on you, have you? I'll pay you back. I'm so hungry I'm shaking. I feel like I've been racing all day. I'm cold too … ' he didn't finish. He suddenly noticed her face, which must have looked like she had stared into the pit of hell itself. He was all concern.

'Ursula, are you OK, you look terrible?'

'Oh, Dan!' she could not help it, she started to sob. 'Dan, this is a terrible place. I want to go home.'

She did not want to have to tell him what she'd seen him do. She desperately wanted him to be sane. In some deep part of her she willed him to be sane, to be with her in this nightmare so she would not be alone.

Dan moved to comfort her and suddenly noticed his own blood soaked state and the pile of corpses.

'What's this … ?' he began and then a terrible aware-ness shadowed his eyes and Ursula knew that this time he did remember what he had done. 'Oh my God! It isn't true. It can't be true.'

Braveheart licked his anguished face. The hound's breath was rank with the smell of raw human flesh. Dan did not push him away but hugged his huge neck with his free hand, as if it were a rock in a swollen river and he were drowning. He stayed with his head buried in Braveheart's flank for what seemed like a long time. Ursula had no comfort to offer him. How could she tell him it was all right? It wasn't. He'd killed six men, seven, or eight? She hadn't counted. He was fifteen, maybe sixteen years old and a murderer. He had killed in self-defence but it was still murder, unless it was justifiable homicide – or was that only in American films? Dan had been ruthless, terrifying, brutal and braver than she could ever hope to be. She had no words at all to offer him.

It was the sound of Gwyn's footsteps that broke through his despair. Braveheart stiffened at the approach. Dan was on his feet in a blink of an eye, sword ready, his face whiter than the moon. Braveheart bared his dagger-like teeth and gently growled. Gwyn very carefully kept his hands in view. He was carrying a wine-skin and a couple of thick woollen cloaks.

In a part of his mind he had never explored, Dan appraised the barrel-chested tribesman. He watched the way he moved, the way he favoured his right side, the slight awkwardness of his gait that betrayed a recent injury. He calculated where he would need to attack him and how hard. He ran through the possible moves in his head, taking into account the superior strength and height of the older man. Dan had fought him before. He was strong as a bull but his reactions were slower than

Dan's own. Dan was shocked by all that he now remembered he had done, but he had done it. He now knew he had done it. He could not undo it, however much he longed to. He could feel the violence that he had never known was in him. It was there but in his control. He knew where it was kept and how he could loose it. The quiet place of his school-days, his secret gift for total focus waited for him. Dan was very afraid that he had been mad. He remembered the red-haired girl and what had followed, the wild fight with Macsen's men when he had heard Ursula scream. He remembered it all. Madness was there waiting for him in that place of calm. He knew it. He felt it as a cold compulsion to destroy. He could lose himself in it at any time. He knew he had a choice, though. He couldn't be mad if he could choose not to be, could he?

The memory of those other fights gave him a grim confidence, just as it horrified him to the depths of his soul. He had spent his life avoiding fights. He hated violence. Even with his mates he looked away in the worst parts of films. Now, here he was, fifteen years old, a psychopathic murderer. How could it be true and how could it not be true? How could he face his sister, Lizzie?

Gwyn must have seen only Dan's confidence because beads of sweat gathered on his forehead as he met Dan's eyes. Gwyn's gaze was steady but Ursula could almost see his fear. The air around him seemed oily with it. Gwyn did not fear much and he did not like to be made afraid by a boy no more than half his weight. Ursula saw that too and felt compelled to break the silence. She spoke in English so that Gwyn gave her a deeply suspicious look.

'Dan, this is Gwyn, one of Prince Macsen's men. He's brought you mead and a warm cloak. You fought on his side.'

It was in Dan's mind to say that he fought on no one's side and that he remembered his previous encounter with Gwyn perfectly, but, as the shock of his new self knowledge grew, he began to shiver. A warm cloak would be good. He had never drunk mead. Mead too, seemed like a good idea. Exhaustion overwhelmed him and his knees almost buckled under him. The thought of going back to the place of madness now seemed repellent, impossible. He lowered his sword to let Gwyn closer.

'Here, take this!' Dan thrust the golden, sweat-slick hilt of Bright Killer into Ursula's unwilling hands. 'Tell him you speak for me and get us out of here, Ursula. I can't help you just now.'

He spoke through a muffling wad of exhaustion that insulated him from the world, from remorse and even from responsibility. He could not help Ursula tonight.

He wrapped himself in the proffered wool cloaks, took the wineskin and settled himself a few steps from the corpses, against Braveheart's back. Gwyn poured water into his cupped palm. The animal, seeing that the

78

man posed no threat to Dan, lapped it up thirstily before curling himself protectively around Dan. Dan took a deep draught of the warm sweet mead and was asleep. Gwyn gave Ursula a sharp look, both curious and hostile, and left them in peace.

It was all right for some. Just how did Dan think she was going to get them out of this situation? They should make a run for it really, but it was just not possible. Ursula felt tireder, colder and more wretched than ever before in her life. The ground was damp. Cautiously, Ursula moved next to Dan and Braveheart. Let the dog growl. She did not think he would attack a friend of Dan's. It was a gamble she was prepared to take. The huge war-hound opened an eye, but allowed her to settle next to her classmate. Dan stirred briefly and mumbled something about a blanket. He threw the loose end of the largest cloak towards her and sank back into sleep. More than a little self-consciously, Ursula laid down beside him under the cloak. It was warm. She stopped trembling. In the middle of a battlefield strewn with the desecrated bodies of the dead, Dan and Ursula slept under strange stars.

~ Chapter Eight ~

The Screaming

Acute cramp woke Ursula at dawn. Her cloak and hair were damp with dew. She struggled to her feet, trying not to wake Dan. Braveheart growled an acknowledgement of her existence but thankfully did nothing to attempt to terminate it. The scene was every bit as bad as she had remembered, but the heap of cadavers that had fallen to Dan's bear sark efficiency had gone, to be replaced by a heap of decapitated heads. She averted eyes that were drawn to the gruesome sight like a child's to a crushed bird on the pavement. As she moved, the dark-haired tribesman, Rhodri also moved. Had Macsen set a guard on them? She supposed that they were still prisoners of sorts. Yes, of course Macsen would have set a watch on them.

Macsen and his men were up and about. The horses and baggage were arranged in a circle surrounding Rhonwen's leather tent. It was a pale, grey morning and the small cookfire smoked badly in the damp morning mist. The ground had been cleared of bodies and a fresh mound of dark earth marked what Ursula guessed was a mass grave. It was a cheerless scene. Ursula wished she could have stayed longer in the oblivion of sleep. She massaged the muscles of her calves. Even as the cramp eased she still ached in every bone and her head hurt. The smell of death still permeated the moist air.

Ursula approached the fire cautiously and squatted down to bask in its meagre heat. No one took any notice except for Rhodri who watched her under the pretext of readjusting the pack on one of the animals. She felt like a criminal, which was strange, as she was the only one in the camp who had not killed someone.

Macsen and Rhonwen stood a little way apart arguing. Rhonwen looked as if she had spent the night in silken sheets. She looked unstained by battle or by the discomforts of the night. Ursula was suddenly aware of the mess she was in. It was another reason to dislike Rhonwen. Ursula strained her ears to listen. If she was going to get herself and Dan away from here she needed to learn all that she could.

'Rhonwen, my esteemed sister, I forbade you to get involved. I will not lose any more women to the Ravens. Especially not you.'

Macsen's tone was exasperated, Rhonwen's defiant.

'Without me it would be *your* neck that was looking a little light this morning.'

'The Ravens don't take heads.' Macsen was getting angry. 'They're so mighty they have no fear even of our warriors' ghosts. They have no respect for sacred mysteries. You should know that as well as I.'

'You know perfectly well what I mean. Without my illusion you and your men would have died a glorious warrior's death, and you would not be here arguing with me, plotting to fight another day. It doesn't seem to me that you're in any position to turn down help – even from a woman. A bit of gratitude wouldn't go amiss.'

Rhonwen's seductive voice was transformed into a harsh hiss of anger. Ursula glanced around and saw Macsen's men very busily not listening to this exchange. She had the feeling that few people spoke to Macsen that way. For a fraction of an instant it looked like Macsen was surrounded by an aura of vivid fury, that flickered like flame, then was gone. Ursula wondered if she was about to have a migraine. His voice was tight as if he reined in his temper as he had his horses.

'Rhonwen. That snake-tongued runt of a dog, Suetonius has slaughtered thousands of us. Who'll bear our warriors if all our women die in battle? We need King Cadal's help. He wants you as a living royal wife. He will not be too impressed with a dead one and we need him with us, Rhon. Especially now.'

'You mean especially now you've lost faith in my

magic. What about the dragon, eh? And The Bear Sark.' Rhonwen sounded petulant.

'One boy, Rhonwen. One boy and how many Ravens oppose us? And the other, Boar Skull, he is no warrior, though what he is I don't know and it seems, neither do you.'

Rhonwen's expression acknowledged the truth of this. She sensed that Boar Skull was dangerous but that was all. Macsen continued, his voice more reasonable, placating even.

'Rhonwen, I think you should forget the Veil. The Bear Sark is the first one who has been any use to us and it is not enough, Rhonwen. It was a dream and a brave one but this is not the time for dreams. I need men in battle and women in the marriage bed. You must go to the Sacred Isle, to Cadal. You will persuade him to loan me all his warriors and you must bear him many fine sons for the good of the tribe. If you would do that you would serve us now as well as the Iceni's Boudicca did in her time. I *will* have your obedience in this, sister, as my sword is my witness.'

Ursula felt herself colour at the reference to her uselessness, but she was chilled by Macsen's talk of marriage beds. For the first time she had some sympathy for Rhonwen. Macsen had clearly never heard of equal opportunities.

'And this is what our brother died for, is it?' Rhonwen

sounded desperate. 'So that those who can wield the magic of the land will waste it. I am the nearest thing you've got to a druid and you will not command a druid!'

Macsen's rejoinder was drowned suddenly by a scream that pierced the mist like a power drill, then another and another. It was Dan. Ursula did not hesitate she just ran towards him, terrified of what she might find. What would make a bear sark scream?

Panic made Ursula faster even than Macsen's men who followed her with drawn swords. Dan had his back to her. His arm was hooked around the neck of his giant hound, as if for support. He was staring at the heaped heads of Macsen's vanquished enemies and screaming. He appeared quite mad.

Ursula felt very cold inside. She was horrified by her own selfishness but her first thought had been, 'Don't let Dan be mad. I need him to be sane'.

Macsen looked at a loss. 'Knock him out someone, he will alert every enemy for miles around.'

Gwyn moved as if to comply but Ursula leaped in front of him. She had no weapon but her desperation and her determination. No one was touching Dan.

'Leave him alone.' Her voice came out as a rather pathetic girlish squeak. 'Don't touch him!' This time she sounded firmer.

Dan's screams fell on her ears like physical blows. She needed to stop him but she did not know how.

84

'Let me help,' Rhonwen's voice was silk once more. 'I have some gift for healing.'

'You will go nowhere near him!'

Rhonwen smiled and Ursula heard at an almost subliminal level the low buzz of her power, the electric tingle in her bones. Rhonwen was going to do something to Dan. She was going to get at his mind somehow, like they'd tried to get to Ursula through the Cup of Belonging. She had to shield Dan from this assault. He had saved her. Ursula had to save him. How?

Ursula backed towards Dan, keeping her eyes on Rhonwen. She did not dare touch him. Maybe he was mad enough to kill her with his bare hands. Ursula would believe Dan capable of almost any feat, superhuman or otherwise, since she had seen him fight. She wished she had a shield to place round him, like the great wooden wall that Prys had carried in the fight. Perhaps that would repel Rhonwen's power-filled will, as Prys had repelled the enemy's spears. She pictured the vast shield. She was probably one of the few women tall enough and strong enough to hold it and carry the weight of the wood with its huge bronze shield boss that was almost a weapon in itself. She had no such shield, only a burning desire to protect Dan. She fixed Rhonwen with her most granite-eyed stare.

'You will not harm The Bear Sark.'

Rhonwen's smile faded and Ursula felt the woman's

power flag a little. Rhonwen looked bemused. Dan's screaming did not falter.

'Well?' Macsen eyes challenged Rhonwen to prove her power.

'Oh Dan, please be calm. I can't keep them from killing you if Macsen gives the word.' Ursula whispered the words under her breath. She did not think Dan could hear her, but suddenly, unaccountably, he stopped.

Rhonwen immediately took the credit, accepting Macsen's approving nod with another irritatingly self-satisfied smile. Rhonwen had not done anything, of that Ursula was certain. Somehow her power had died too soon to get to Dan. Rhonwen's pale face was damp with sweat and Ursula was surprised to find her own body clammy with perspiration. Her head hurt so much she hardly dare move it, but Dan had stopped screaming and nobody had hurt him. Before she could enjoy the luxury of relief, Macsen spoke.

'Gwyn tells me The Bear Sark gave you his sword. Are you his Lord?'

He eyed her appraisingly. She knew important things hung on her answer, but she did not know what they were.

She was very aware of the hostility of the men towards her. In their eyes she was a coward or worse for not immersing herself in the bloodbath of battle. She thought rapidly. The men might kill her if they thought

86

her useless; if she was important to Dan they may be more likely to let her live. Ursula did not know what being Dan's Lord might mean, but it had to be better than being his dead schoolmate.

All eyes were on her.

'Yes, you could say that. I speak for him.'

Macsen nodded.

Rhonwen intervened while she had the chance. 'He should undergo the rite, Macsen. How can we be sure The Bear Sark will stay with us without the rite?' Her voice shook a little.

Ursula knew she was disturbed by the failure of her power. Bands of pressure tightened around Ursula's skull. Whenever she saw that woman, Ursula got a headache.

'I don't think the Ravens will accept him with open arms, Princess Rhonwen, not with a brace of their fine skulls on his bridle.' Kai still held his sword, uncertain of Dan's next move. His voice was amused.

'I would be more confident of your opinion, Kai, if you had not failed to perform the rite properly with this Boar Skull.' She shot Ursula a black look. 'This Boar Skull and The Bear Sark are more strange to this place than you realise. Those who call to me across the Veil cross worlds. They do not know us or our ways without the rite. They know nothing of our beliefs, our dreams. Why should they fight for us if they are not part of us?'

Kai looked embarrassed. Rhonwen was never going to let him forget that they had learned nothing from Ursula in the rite. She was never going to let him forget that Ursula had not been imbued with the values of the Combrogi in the rite. Rhonwen was not a forgiving woman.

Ursula cared nothing for Rhonwen's relationship with Kai, she did not notice the insult. Ursula felt sick. She believed the part about crossing worlds. Her very bones knew the truth of it. She had believed that at some level of her consciousness, perhaps from the first moment she had breathed this foreign air. She was not sure she dare tell Dan, if he had not heard it for himself. She felt something very like despair wash through her. Their situation was hopeless. How could she ever get them home now? Shock had distracted her from her surroundings for a moment, then she realised Rhonwen was still talking.

' … He must be brought to the tent and I will perform the ceremony …'

Gwyn again moved forward.

'No!' Every instinct in her rebelled against the very idea of the Cup of Belonging. The memory of the foul aftertaste in her mouth and the sickness after her own brush with the Cup of Belonging hardened her resolve. She did not know exactly what the rite did, but it was some invasion of the mind of that she was sure, some

88

sharing of the participants' thoughts. Dan's sanity was too fragile to risk.

'I will not allow The Bear Sark to undergo this thing.' Ursula said.

'You will not and who … ?'

Rhonwen got no further. At that moment Caradoc made another of his dramatic reappearances. He was breathless and dishevelled. He wasted no time on formalities.

'My Prince. It's as we thought. One of the Ravens did get away and on one of your ponies. He's heading straight for Deva. Even if the Raven did not recognise us, someone there will recognise your brand on the pony sure as day follows night. The legion will be heading for Craigwen in days.'

Macsen seemed to sag a little at the news. He sounded weary when he answered.

'It is well that we know it, Caradoc. By Lugh, I should not have come. Suetonius needed no reminder that we live still unconquered. He'll be after us now with a whole legion. Within days he'll have transformed this skirmish into a serious Combrogi uprising. He's only needed an excuse; now he'll get all the support he needs to crush us.' His sigh spoke of something deeper than weariness. 'We should have stayed at Craigwen. Rhonwen's dreams have brought us nothing but two lads. And if coming here were not bad enough I should never have brought our own ponies. It was so foolish but I know of none better for such a long, hard ride.'

He looked pained. Ursula did not really understand what was wrong but if it distracted everyone from Dan, she didn't care. Cautiously she touched Dan's hand. He did not flinch but he did not return the pressure. He had not moved since the screaming had stopped. She tried to see his face, but once more he had buried it in Braveheart's neck. The dog did not move, but stood offering what comfort it could, as if he understood. She hoped he was all right but could do nothing to help him now.

The Combrogi all looked grave at the news. Macsen seemed almost to physically shake himself.

'It's too late now for regrets. What's done is done.' He paused, struck by a sudden thought and a terse smile momentarily lightened his bleak expression. 'The Ravens will know fear if our stray legionary tells the truth. Seven against fifty – that should give them something to worry about. Now all we need is about a thousand more men and at that rate, we can rid this whole island of their black wings.'

It was true, as Ursula suddenly realised. If she could forget the horror of the battle and think of it objectively, it had been a stunning victory for the Combrogi.

'If the legion marches on Craigwen now we are finished,' said Rhonwen quietly, all her outraged pride forgotten. 'We are not ready for a siege. It will be a siege Suetonius will try.'

'It is not quite hopeless.' Macsen answered without conviction. 'Of course I would be happier to get the women and children away. The negotiations with King Cadal are well under way though he'll not take them without Rhonwen and most of my gold.' He flashed Rhonwen a meaningful look. 'We have not enough men and the preparations for a siege are only half done, but it is not hopeless. There are some people I know who may be able to detain the legion a little longer to keep them from your heels. Kai, I would have you ride back to Craigwen and make the necessary preparations. Word has been sent to the Carvetii, the Ordovices, the Novantae and the Damnonii. They have promised to send men to train together and learn something of the Raven tactics. Hane has been studying their ways for years and fought on their side once or twice when too young to know better. If anyone can forge a united fighting force from the tribes it will be him. You saw how they fought. It takes a dragon to break their concentration! If I can delay them, somehow keep them busy in the south till the winter, bad weather may also be our ally and we will have some time to prepare. The Ravens love a siege and if half the tales I've heard are true we will have to have some very clever tricks prepared to keep them from our throats.'

Kai looked worried. 'What of King Lud and the Brigantes? I thought …'

'Kai, we need them, but Lud's his mother's son. He'll take some convincing, I know. Let us do this night and the next enough to keep us living for the night after and the one after that. I will try to make it back by Lughnasa or failing that Samhain.' Macsen sighed.

'We will eat and then we should be on our way. Rest a while, Caradoc. I am sorry I cannot provide a more suitable victory feast. You, all of you, are the best. You deserve a five night feast for what you did last night.'

Macsen moved wearily back towards the fire, then turned to fix Ursula with his piercing stare.

'Boar Skull, I see you are not wholly without courage. You bother me. You will bear close watching. Bring us no ill, and your needs will be met. Look to your brother. The life of a bear sark tends to be brutal and brief.' He reached out and laid his hand on her shoulder in a surprising gesture of comradeship. 'Come, eat at the fire. You have a long way to travel.'

She seemed to feel the weight of his hand for a long time after he had removed it.

Chapter Nine

The Brother of a Corpse

Ursula was finding her already tentative grasp on the situation deteriorating further. She was very worried about Dan. She managed to get him to the campfire and even got him to take some dry biscuit stuff that the Combrogi produced. He would not touch the meat though. Ursula had been a little concerned about it too, until Macsen mentioned in passing that it was a rabbit that Rhodri had trapped in between keeping watch on Boar Skull and The Bear Sark. She ate it then, hungrily, and even gratefully. Dan would not. He looked at her with little recognition in his haunted eyes. He would not speak, but stroked Braveheart's head continuously. It did not augur well.

When she was not worrying about Dan she worried about her mother. She would think Ursula was dead. Her mother had seemed very fragile ever since her father had left. She was only now, after nearly three years, beginning to accept that he was not coming back. She loved Ursula and Ursula loved her with a fanaticism that was almost a burden. How would her mother cope without her? And what would poor Miss Smith feel like having lost two pupils in her care? Would she get the sack? She was surely too old to get another job.

Ursula stayed by the fire next to Dan and bit her nails as the men around her made plans. No one demanded her help.

There had been another row between Rhonwen and Macsen which seemed to end with Rhonwen promising to marry King Cadal, whoever he was, after she had helped Macsen in his mission to stir up trouble for the legion. There had been long discussions about who of the enslaved Combrogi in Deva could be relied upon to risk everything to buy Kai time to ready Craigwen. Caradoc spoke passionately that any of his tribe, the swarthy Silurians, would gladly die to see a Raven defeat. Unfortunately as far as anyone knew there were no Silurians in Deva. Kai wanted to ride to Deva himself and attempt to murder Suetonius in his bed, leaving Macsen to lead the party home to Craigwen. Macsen spent long hours persuading Kai that his courage would serve Macsen better in Craigwen and that Suetonius, as Raven Governor of the whole province, was not in Deva anyway but further south. Craigwen was much talked of. It only gradually dawned on Ursula that it was the name of Macsen's fortress home in the north. Macsen was very sure that he was uniquely qualified to infiltrate the occupied territories and cause trouble. In the end no one challenged him and the talk turned to plans; how best to burn down Deva or start a slaves' revolt to distract the legion from a march on Craigwen. None of it made any sense and, as none of it seemed likely to get Ursula home, she allowed all the talk to wash over her. She was distantly grateful for the imminent departure of Rhonwen, if not of Macsen. The visceral dislike she felt for her appeared to be mutual.

The only time she roused herself from her shocked stupor was to prevent Kai tying the heads of the men Dan had killed to the bridle of his horse. Kai was upset. Apparently it denied Dan the honour due to him. It was clear that he believed that the taking of these heads was very important. He explained to Ursula that the shades of these Romans would serve Dan in the afterlife, and would help him in battle. To leave the heads with their bodies would risk their retribution in the afterlife, if not before. Ursula tried not to recoil. Respect for the religious beliefs of others had been inculcated in her from her earliest childhood. Privately she thought Kai was even more dangerously insane than Dan. He believed absolutely in the power of the ghosts of the dead. More than anything else she just wanted this whole horrible experience to stop. She wanted to go home. She was quite unequal to the task of expressing the depth of her revulsion when it came to carrying dead people's heads around with her. She only just managed to convince Kai that it was not the custom in her country to behead the dead. He was more easily persuaded that Dan might very well start screaming again if he saw another Roman skull detached from a Roman legionary. Kai did not want Dan to start screaming again.

Ursula rode her horse with all the grace of a bag of cement riding bareback. None of the Combrogi had saddles. Bright Killer was stowed behind her along with the sword Macsen had given her, which she was yet to use. The only good news was that her headache had lifted. It was only one discomfort less to worry about.

Kai had hesitated to allow Ursula to ride next to Dan. He was obviously afraid that they might try and escape. It was only Ursula's dull-voiced assertion that she knew of nowhere to escape to and the fact that Dan didn't look like he could fight his way out of a paper bag at that moment that persuaded him. Dan's irritating natural balance enabled him to keep his seat with apparent effortlessness. His face remained closed and grey, but his eyes did not seem as blank as they had before. She did not think that he looked so much mad as wounded. Braveheart walked at the horse's side. He was not a lot shorter than Dan's pony.

When Dan finally spoke the shock combined with the numbness of her rear end was almost sufficient to knock her off her horse.

'So, where are we then?'

'Dan! Are you all right?' She turned her head as far as she dared without upsetting her precarious stability. As far as she could see he was not frothing at the mouth or exhibiting signs of dramatic madness. His face, like his voice, was unexpectedly calm.

'I suppose so. I'm sorry about the screaming. It was those heads. I … It made me realise what I'd done. It was so barbaric. It was like waking to a nightmare and realising you were some kind of monster. At home they will put me in prison. I won't be able to look after Lizzie and she'll grow up thinking I'm this violent psycho. What with my dad and everything … who will keep her safe? I couldn't take it. I think I'm OK now, though.'

There wasn't a lot to say. It was not the moment to explain that she thought they would never go home, but Dan had a right to know.

'Dan, I did find something out,' she began, searching for a gentle way to tell him that they were lost in another world. 'But it's not good news. Rhonwen said… '

'Rhonwen – the woman. Did you fight with her? When I was lost in the … Well, when I was screaming. I knew I was screaming, right, but it wasn't me. It was like I was somewhere else. I saw her coming towards me. She was holding her hands out as if to help me, but the look in her eyes ... It was like she wanted to eat me or something. I know it sounds stupid. But you were there, and you had this huge shield and you held it in front of me and she couldn't come any closer. She wanted to. She was very angry but you stopped her. And I heard you say really loudly, as if you were shouting inside my head, "Dan, be calm. I can't keep them from killing you if Macsen gives the word." Then I wasn't in that place any more and I could stop screaming. I thought it was a dream but it was more real than that. It was as real as this, but different.'

Ursula swayed on her pony. How did Dan know she had thought about a shield? Could her thoughts have turned back Rhonwen's power? It did not seem likely, but then how likely was it that Rhonwen could have brought them through a mist into another world? Once again she was at a loss for words.

'I don't know what happened. I wanted to help you but I didn't know how, or at least I didn't think I did.'

There was silence for a minute apart from the sounds of the other men, their horses and Braveheart's even panting. Ursula tried to make sense of Dan's experience, failed and decided it was the least of her worries. Maybe thoughts had more power here.

'Dan, I don't think we're on earth any more. I mean we're on a world that seems like it, but either we've gone

98

back in time or we're somewhere else. Rhonwen said she'd brought us through the Veil, you know that yellow mist, from another world. I don't know but I think it's true. This doesn't seem like home. The air feels different and that illusion Rhonwen did with the dragon, it's like a kind of magic and ... '

Dan said nothing for a minute. Ursula stopped burbling and tried to watch him from the corner of her eye. What if Dan was not the only one who was intermittently mad around here?

'Do you remember in year seven we did some stuff on Roman Britain with Mrs Enright?' he said at last.

'Yes. So? Did you hear what I said? We're on another world. Why are you asking about Mrs Enright?'

'She talked about the Celts, they were the people the Romans invaded. They were wild and warlike and there was a Celtic queen, Boudicca, who fought the Romans and nearly won. They almost repelled the invasion but then the Romans got more troops or something and the Celtic tribes fought among themselves and gave the Romans an advantage. Mrs Enright said that the Romans talked about the Celts as if they were savages, but they were actually quite a developed culture – they had druids and great jewellery and stuff. Well, I think the Combrogi are ancient Celts. Now either we're both mad, or we've got mixed up in some horrible re-enactment of history or we've gone back in time. If I believe I'm mad, I might just as well forget everything because nothing can make sense. So let's forget that.' He swallowed hard and his voice came out as little more than a whisper. He was not really half so confident that he wasn't mad. 'Those heads were real, Ursula, there was no trick. I really killed all those people. We've not seen a coke can or an electric light. I think we've gone back in time. I just don't see how.'

It seemed more credible when Dan said it. He was much more logical than she was. It didn't quite explain the magic, of course, but it was possible that magic had once existed. After all, even their own time was full of the idea of magic if not its reality. The idea must have come from somewhere. Why not from a time when the magic was real?

Her speculation was interrupted by a low growl from Braveheart. Kai, riding ahead of her suddenly halted. Kai turned fluidly on his pony to whisper to her. 'Shh, the hound's heard something. Someone may be following us. Get off your horses quietly and get behind those rocks there.' He pointed to some rocks at the side of the track.

'Take your blades and be ready.' He made some rapid hand signal in the air and the rest of the small band immediately began making preparations for a stand. Spears and swords and shields were only seconds away so it did not take long for the small convoy to be fully armed and ready. Dan hesitated to hold Bright Killer but took it, gingerly. Braveheart, still listening intently, wagged his tail. He liked a fight.

Ursula moved stiffly to the cover of the rocks. 'Please, not more death,' she prayed.

No one made a sound. A bird sang somewhere and insects buzzed, but the men and animals managed an almost preternatural quiet. Dan was sweating. She could smell him. They huddled together with Braveheart, behind the rock. He still wore his blood-stained shirt under one of the cloaks Macsen had given him. He looked and smelled like one of the winos that slept rough under the railway bridge at home. She was sure that she must reek too. She would have liked to have cleaned her teeth.

Someone was coming. Kai signalled and the men readied themselves for ambush. Then Braveheart leaped to his feet and ran towards the approaching stranger. Dan made a dive to stop him but was too late. With a curse, Kai went after the war-hound, his sword ready. Dan was almost as quick.

'No! Dan don't!' Dan was gone. The element of surprise already lost, the men emerged from the rocks to see Braveheart fling himself at the figure of a boy leading a large horse. There was a body on the horse. It had left a trail of blood that was as good as an arrow pointing to their whereabouts. Fury and fear flitted across Kai's face.

He feared that a spy had trailed them. His sword was raised. With one blow he could have separated the boy's head from his shoulders. He'd had enough practice. Braveheart bared his teeth. The warning growl in his throat should have warned Kai that he was prepared to rip his throat out. Gwyn's spear was aimed at Braveheart's chest. Nobody moved.

The boy could not have been much more than eight. He was dirty and ragged though probably no more so than Ursula herself. He carried a spear, which he gripped, ready to defend himself. The knowledge that he stood no chance was written all over his terrified face. Surely Kai could not kill a child? Dan was not about to find out. He flung himself between Kai and the boy. Bright Killer flashed.

'Tell him I'll kill him if he lays a hand on the boy.'

Ursula scarcely needed to translate. Dan's intention was clear enough. Kai took one step back to put himself out of the reach of the sword. Ursula noticed that it gleamed again. Dan must have cleaned it after the battle, she thought irrelevantly.

'Who are you?' Kai said. He did not lower his weapon, but he seemed disinclined to fight Dan. The boy looked too frightened to speak. Dan put a hand on his shoulder and the child flinched. Dan gave him an encouraging smile. Something of Dan's confidence must have communicated itself to the boy. He relaxed fractionally.

'I am Bryn ab Madoc of the Coritanii tribe. This is my father; he was killed when killing many Ravens who ambushed us. They came yesterday and killed Gwynfa, my sister, when Da and I were out. We were looking for Prince Macsen, who was my father's friend. Giff knows me. He was my father's war-hound. I thought he was dead too.' Unshed tears shone in Bryn's eyes but his voice was firm.

Kai regarded him thoughtfully. Then Bryn noticed Bright Killer gleaming in Dan's hand and shrunk away from him.

'That's my father's sword!'

'Dan. Where did you get the sword?'

Ursula's voice sounded harsh.

'I told you. I found it in a shack in the wood. There was a dead girl outside with red hair.' He paused as the still clear memory ambushed him again. He swallowed hard.

'I took it, to defend myself in case the killers were still there. Braveheart found me there.'

Ursula translated this. When she mentioned the red-haired girl the boy's composure faltered. Kai made up his mind. He believed the boy. He was one of their own.

'This man is worthy of your father's sword, Bryn ab Madoc. He has killed many Ravens and avenged your sister's death in rivers of blood. We will bury your father for you. You may travel with our protection if you wish it.' The boy nodded, losing the battle to contain his tears. Dan, who had understood nothing of what had been said, understood all he needed to. He put his arm round the child who immediately got to his knees. The jumble of words that he mumbled was almost too fast for Ursula to follow. She shrugged at Dan's inquiring glance.

'He's binding himself in a blood oath of allegiance to your man, The Bear Sark,' explained Kai. 'I suggest he accept it. If he is who he says he is, which I don't doubt, he has no one left. There are almost no free Coritanii left. He has no tribe, no place. He will make an honourable – ' he said a word that Ursula could only translate as meaning something like body servant or squire. 'The boy believes that The Bear Sark saved his life when he protected him just now. The Bear Sark avenged his sister. Bryn will die for him.'

Ursula did her best to convey this to Dan who looked predictably horrified. He nodded his assent to the boy's oath with obvious discomfort.

'Does Dan … I mean, The Bear Sark need to do anything else?'

'Only death will break a blood oath. Bryn has sworn it. Nothing else needs to be done.'

Great, thought Ursula, in two days Dan had acquired a sword, a dog, a servant and a reputation she suspected that many others had literally died for. All she'd acquired was a fine collection of bruises. If this was a new world, she and Dan seemed destined to keep to their old world's status – golden boy and loser. Resentment took the edge off the realisation that Kai, whom she thought she liked, would have happily murdered an eight year old boy.

~ Chapter Ten ~

Alavna

Ursula was surprised at the trouble Kai took to bury Bryn's father with honour. She had thought that the Combrogi were inured to death. They seemed to cause it with grim regularity.

The men helped lift the bloody body from the horse and carried it to a nearby stream. He must have died from his wounds just before he reached them because Gwyn said he was not yet cold, and the stiffness of death had not yet frozen his limbs. While Kai carefully washed the body, Caradoc disappeared to muddy the tracks the boy, Bryn, had left. The others dug a deep pit close to where the stream widened to form a small pool, near some trees. It was beautiful and still and Kai explained to Bryn that it would be sacred ground beloved of the gods, being close to both a grove and a pool, like the holy places of the druids. Kai dressed the corpse in the best clothes that could be found from the packs they carried with them. The dead man's own clothes were burned. Kai pinned his own brooch to the fine, green woollen cloak they had found for him, while each of the men gave something of value to the dead man. Gwyn gave a spear, Prys his spare shield, Rhodri a ring and Caradoc a slender gold torque. Kai hinted that the dead man might need his sword, but Ursula did not even suggest that to Dan. Instead she offered the sword she had borrowed. Dan gave his watch. For some reason it no longer worked, but it had a silver metal strap and looked good.

They laid their large oval shields on the ground and lashed the four together with thick rope to make a bier on which they laid the body. Gwyn, Rhodri, Prys, and Caradoc acted as pallbearers. The boy helped the men to cover the body in earth while Kai sang of the dead man's deeds in so far as he knew them, of his courage and his willingness to embrace death for his people. They buried the severed heads too, though they cast one or two as an offering into the pool. Ursula was deeply grateful to be rid of them. In the heat of the day the stench was becoming overpowering.

Bryn was very happy about the burial, especially the heads, for the spirits of the dead Ravens would serve his father in the afterlife. His father had killed nearly as many men as there were heads, he was sure. His eyes glowed with bright pride to see his father so well accompanied into his new life. Braveheart howled once, when the first clod of earth landed on his master's body, but afterwards seemed well content. He stayed close to both Dan and Bryn, which was not difficult as wherever Dan went, Bryn followed at his elbow. The men did not treat him as a child, nor did he behave much like one. He was grave and attentive. In this brutal world it seemed there was no opportunity for childhood.

After the burial, they journeyed on in sombre mood. Dan was thoughtful and distracted. Afraid of where his distraction might lead, Ursula attempted to teach him the language. She didn't know where to start. She knew the language of the Combrogi as she knew her own; so she had no ready made lists of verbs or declensions to offer him. In the end he asked questions and she gave him the answers. He listened hard to the conversation around him and tried to talk to Bryn. It kept Dan's mind off darker thoughts and he made astonishing progress.

With typical Dan-like confidence he decided to speak only in his new language, unless he needed help, which Ursula would supply. Ursula had tried that once with a friend. They had decided to only speak French, but had been forced to give up after ten minutes when the topics of the weather, their names and birthdays, were exhausted. Dan, predictably, had no such difficulty and, on the occasions when he did get stuck, Ursula only needed to think the word for Dan to know it. It happened more than once and gave her a strange feeling. Was Dan developing the capacity to read her mind? The thought made her shiver.

They journeyed for several nights. Ursula got confused as to how many. Each day was the same. They rode all day except for breaks to water the horses, attend to calls of nature, and of course to eat. Ursula had a tendency to "comfort eat" as her mother described it, but here when she most needed comfort, there was little of interest to eat. The food was plentiful but tasted terrible and they ate the same thing every day. At first light, Rhodri, who was the best camp cook, apparently, secured a large iron cauldron over the fire and prepared a salted porridge of oats and other grains. Without sugar or honey to sweeten it and without milk or cream to improve the flavour, only hunger enabled her to eat it. It was like eating thick, salted wallpaper paste. At midday they ate dry oat biscuits and dried salted meat. When it was too dark to ride any further Rhodri concocted some broth with root vegetables and barley. They drank only mead or stream water and Ursula found herself day dreaming about a nice hot cup of tea, and a bar of chocolate. The waistband of her trousers felt loose.

At night the men took turns to tell tales or sing songs when they were not on watch. Dan, Bryn and Ursula were not trusted with a watch so slept for most of the hours of darkness. Ursula's bruised body ached from all the riding and all the falling on to hard ground. She was not a natural horsewoman.

She slept for around ten hours each night, Braveheart at her head, Bryn at her feet and Dan lying next to her. Macsen had taken the only tent for Rhonwen.

The songs the Combrogi sang round the fire were almost all about war and feasting, about gods or heroes or ancestors or possibly all three. She found the riding so exhausting that she kept drifting off into sleep during the singing. Perhaps that was why the songs pervaded her dreams, which were often violent and bloody. Sometimes she dreamed of Macsen and Rhonwen, whose green eyes seemed to haunt her with generalised malevolence. She dreamed of the Veil a lot, of the yellow mist choking her, or of stepping through it into deserts or seas. Most nights, some way or another, she dreamed of the infinite variety of ways she could die. Not one of them was pleasant.

In spite of this, Ursula was less frightened than she had been since she walked through the Veil. She rode without the imminent sense of danger that had kept her whole body racked by an inner tide of adrenalin. The men, though wary, seemed more relaxed too. Caradoc still scouted ahead and then covered their tracks behind them. He rode so far and fast that he had to change ponies several times in the day, though he himself seemed tireless.

They avoided towns and rode through unspoiled

countryside. They rode over ancient wooden pathways to cross marsh and bog, through woodland, over hills and through rich farmland. It was spring, Ursula thought, though nature had never been one of her interests. She could feel the energy of new life welling up through the ground. It seemed to travel up through her own spine, like sap rising. It filled her with a wild excitement. She pulsed with it. She felt more alive than she ever had at home, more aware. She was fascinated by the sights and smells of the land and the beauty of it all. If she had only known that her mother was all right and had been able to change her underwear, she would have been happy.

Dan's grasp of the Combrogi tongue had developed to the extent that he could hold quite complex discussions. Ursula was not altogether pleased about that. He said some very provocative things, too loudly, as if he no longer cared much for his safety. He was worried that they were on the wrong side.

'I thought the Romans were the good ones, the ones who brought civilisation, law and justice. All I have seen of the Combrogi is their lust for death.'

Bryn spluttered red in the face. Ursula suspected that some rule or custom kept him from contradicting his liege lord. Dan really had no right to talk of other people's lust for death, but he was right. They found themselves among the Combrogi who had drugged her, tied her to a horse, threatened her and killed virtually every civilised Roman they had come across and then cut off their heads. She turned to the child.

'Bryn ab Madoc, Kai would have killed you. Where I come from to kill a child is a terrible evil. It is hard for us to see that the Combrogi are not evil if they could do such a thing.'

Bryn blushed a deep scarlet and looked like he wanted to spear her. Braveheart, picking up on his anxiety, growled. Braveheart did not entirely trust her. Bryn looked at Dan, as if for permission to speak, which irritated Ursula greatly.

'I am not a child. I am Dan's squire. Had Da lived I would have served him and learned the ways of war as a man. I know enough of them now to kill you, Boar Skull. You are no warrior, big as you are ... '

The boy cocked his spear at Ursula's face. Ursula's fear rose like bile to her mouth.

'That is enough, Bryn. Ursula, I mean Boar Skull is my ...' Dan groped for a word and came up with Ursula's usual fallback description. 'Brother ... You owe her respect. I mean him respect.' Bryn laughed at the mistake, with all the heartiness of an eight year old and let his spear drop. Man or not his sense of humour was exactly what Ursula expected of an eight year old boy. At that age her mother had not even let her get a knife from the knife drawer. Ursula shot Dan a warning look.

Whatever Queen Boudicca had done, Ursula suspected that like Macsen, these men wanted their women as far from action as possible, bearing babies. She remembered just enough history to know that childbirth was a very risky business before modern medicine. There was little Ursula could be sure of in this world, but she was absolutely sure that here she would rather be a boy.

Dan muttered, 'Sorry!' in English. Ursula was not listening. There was trouble ahead.

Above the tree line they could see a plume of dark smoke rising. The unmistakable stench of burnt flesh travelled downwind towards them.

Gwyn, his face pale and his eyes dark with just contained fury, rode towards Dan.

'Beyond is the settlement of Alavna. We were to have stopped there for supplies. This is something Kai would have you see, strangers.'

He muttered 'Raven lover' under his breath to Dan. Ursula knew it as a bitter insult. Gwyn dug Dan viciously in the ribs with the hilt of his sword. It was swiftly done and Gwyn's look defied him to retaliate. Dan winced but kept his face impassive. Ursula felt sick. Something very bad was going to happen. Would they be killed now as potential traitors because of Dan's big, too clever mouth? She knew what the smell meant and she had no stomach for what she might see. Two bodies more would likely as not make no difference. She was trembling. She hoped that they would not let Bryn watch. He was still a child. Children should be protected. She clung to that thought; without such a belief she too would be a savage.

That thought stayed in her mind as they rode through what was left of the village. But no one had been able to protect the children of that place, though it was clear that many had tried valiantly to do so.

There are things too terrible to be contemplated, too dreadful to be remembered and yet which should never be forgotten. What had happened in that village was one of them. Many of the bodies were charred beyond recognition, but the Ravens had shown no compassion to any, babies, children, pregnant women, old men. There had been torture too. Prys said they did it for fun and as a message for the other Combrogi. Such action was not unknown in Ursula's own time. Then they called it ethnic cleansing. Until that moment she had not known what those words meant. Ursula did not think she could ever be cleansed of the memory of it. Scrawled on the lime washed wall of the one of the few remaining buildings were the words "Legio II", the second legion. The civilised Romans even had graffiti and they wrote it in blood.

Dan was weeping openly, as were the Combrogi warriors.

'What price the Ravens' laws and justice now?' Gwyn said, but his sneer was muffled by the sob that caught in his throat. Ursula couldn't cry. She tried to shield Bryn and stop him from looking, but he had seen his father and his sister killed. This was his world and Ursula could not protect him from that.

They all helped to bury the dead. It had to be a mass grave. There was no time to do more. There was always the risk the legion might return, that they might know that Macsen's men would return this way.

At the graveside, when Kai had said and sang all he could in the circumstances, Dan surprised Ursula again. He knelt at Kai's feet.

'I am sorry I spoke as I did on the road. Four nights ago I killed Ravens because I could do nothing else. Kill me now if you will, but I swear to you that I will kill all the Ravens I can for what they have done today. For this and for Bryn's sister, the red-haired girl and for his father, Madoc. This is an abomination.'

Kai and the others looked as taken aback as Ursula. Dan's grasp of the tongue was still incomplete but in using the word for 'abomination' he had used the strongest word he knew. It was an obscenity, but then so was what they had witnessed.

Kai wiped his face with his cloak. They all looked the same, faces blackened by soot, streaked by sweat.

'Oaths that bind the soul are serious things. You are a stranger and stranger to us than any of the others Rhonwen called through the Veil. You are a Bear Sark.

You will kill because it is your nature. You have no choice. We are all bound by this, all of us, together, by what we have seen here. We shall carry the name Alavna always with us and we will each of us avenge this,' he hesitated for it was a vile word, '"abomination."' All the warriors drew their swords and stuck them one by one in the earth of the grave mound.

Kai was first. 'I am Kai Alavna ab Owain. By my name I swear to avenge this.'

Bryn was next. He looked so very small next to Kai but he was indomitable. He had no sword but he stuck his spear defiantly in the soil.

'I am Bryn Alavna ab Madoc. By my name I swear to avenge this and the murder of my kin.'

Dan and Ursula were last. Dan thrust Bright Killer deep into the ground with all his force.

'I am Daniel Alavna ab George. By my name I swear to avenge this.'

Ursula had no sword or spear. She knelt on the damp earth and kissed the soil. She did not know what else to do. Could she kill anyone? Should she? Even for this? Here, there was only one answer.

'I am Ursula Alavna ab Helen. By my name I swear to avenge this.' She was her mother's daughter. Worlds away she was still that. The oath hung heavily on her. She was committed. She was Combrogi now.

~ Chapter Eleven ~

Craigwen

They rode swiftly after that. They were anxious to put miles between them and the legion's scouts. But they all knew that however far they travelled they would never leave Alavna.

The ride was uneventful, though to strained nerves the flurry of wings as they rode past a bird's nest or the snap of a branch underfoot was an event to provoke a nervous reaction. Dan was trying hard not to think of Alavna, of the small body of a child of Lizzie's age. He was trying to get Ursula to talk. He needed distraction. No one silenced him, so he guessed that they must be far enough away from enemy scouts to be reasonably safe.

'You're very quiet.'

'Well, those are the first words you've spoken since Alavna.'

'Are you OK?' Dan knew it was a stupid question.

'Not really. Are you?' Dan shook his head.

'Since we've been here I've felt weird. Haven't you?'

'Ursula, for a lot of the time we've been here I've been berserk.'

Ursula looked embarrassed. 'Sorry, I didn't mean …'

'It's fine. I'm trying not to think about it.' Kai's words, 'You are a bear sark. You will kill because it is your nature, you have no choice,' echoed rather hollowly in his head. He was not a machine. He had choice. He chose not to think about it. 'What do you mean?'

'Well, I feel sort of plugged in to this world, sort of connected. I feel things more. I don't know if it's that cup I drank from, or if it was the Veil or if it is the land itself, but I … Well, like, I'm quite convinced that just around the corner there are a load of men waiting to jump us.'

Ursula's normally rather expressionless face was contorted with embarrassment. She did not like exposing herself to ridicule. She felt that she was being ridiculous.

'No, I don't feel that …' Dan said slowly. 'I feel even more disconnected than usual I …'

As they rounded the corner, there was a whoop and then the blood-chilling war cry of the Combrogi. Three armed men sprang out at Kai and Gwyn, the leading riders. They had their swords ready. Dan's heart sank. He did not want to go to that place again. He did not want that compelling liberating rhythm of killing. This time he would have a choice and he would not go there. As long

118

as they did not touch Ursula, or Bryn or Braveheart. His sword was already in his hand. That much was already automatic. He pulled ahead of Ursula and Bryn and, for the first time, wished he had a shield and knew how to use it. He could feel the disconnection. It was like slipping into another gear. It was happening more quickly and more easily every time. He felt the beginning of the terrible calm.

'Dan! It's OK. They're Macsen's men.' Ursula's voice shattered the calm and brought him back. 'It was beginning to happen, wasn't it?' Dan nodded. Sweat was breaking out on his forehead. 'You weren't even angry, were you?' Again he shook his head. Then he remembered something. From what seemed like a long time ago he dredged the memory.

'Ursula! The men were there, like you said.'

'Dan, I'm scared. I think something is happening to me. I feel like I'm changing, not just because of Alavna. It's like your bear sark thing only different.'

Dan did not understand exactly but her distress was very clear. He leant over and squeezed her hand.

'Dan! I'm a man, remember. Don't hold my hand!'

Ursula's outrage was almost funny. It was more like the girl he'd liked at school.

He grinned, but Ursula did not smile. 'You will help me, won't you?'

'What do you mean?'

'You know ...' her exasperation was clear. 'You know, do all that boy stuff.'

'What like peeing standing up?' At that even Ursula laughed. 'I'll make you an oath.'

'No, not an oath!' Ursula interrupted him. But it was too late. The air was charged with the portent of it. Dan's oath to her was unsaid but not unthought. She could feel it binding them. It was a magic as real as the power that conjured Rhonwen's dragon but less visible. Poor Dan, he was bound by his nature as a bear sark, by his oath at Alavna and to his loyalty to Ursula. He had little freedom left, but he could not see it. It worried her that she was so sure that their oaths did bind them here. It was yet another proof that the place was changing her in subtle ways. She put her concern aside. Events were moving quickly. People were arriving. New people bringing new dangers. She had to concentrate.

Kai was signalling. They had mastered the Combrogi battle hand signals on the ride. Dan dismounted, but did not drop his sword. He resisted the urge to help Ursula down from her horse. Dan took his responsibilities seriously. He watched her impartially. Could she be a boy? The question was more – could she be human, at the moment. There was not a part of her clothes or face that was not covered in soot, grime, muck or blood. They walked together towards Kai and his new companion, one of the three men who had attacked them. Bryn and Braveheart followed a pace or two behind.

'I am male, I am a warrior, I can do this,' Ursula muttered under her breath, grinding her teeth. She was a good four inches taller than Dan anyway and strongly built. Like an actress, she seemed to make herself seem even bigger, squarer, with those words. She had lost weight on the ride, enough to show off the sharp angles of her face. It was a well-made face, finer than you might expect. She might be beautiful one day if she gave up scowling and tooth grinding and covering her face in blood and grime. Today, yes, she looked like a boy and an extremely disreputable one. She was good at adopting an aggressive stance too.

They stood in front of Kai's companion. Dan was not afraid. He held Bright Killer as if it was part of his arm, and had, to be honest, forgotten it was there.

Kai flashed him a look and Ursula whispered, 'Lay down your sword or you'll get us killed,' in deeply irritated English. Dan obligingly laid Bright Killer down.

'Finn, these are the men Rhonwen brought through the Veil. This is Finn the castle steward.' Kai waved at Ursula and Dan as if proudly displaying his prized cattle. He must have been seeing them with different eyes because both looked too weary to be very impressive.

'You travelled for four nights' ride on the whim of a princess for two ... boys. Is this all she got for her dreams

121

of drawing a great army through the Veil at Cenn Croech?' the man, Finn, seemed to spit contempt. Kai ignored his tone though he answered his question.

'These two were called through the Veil by the Princess Rhonwen near Cenn Croech. This is Ursula Alavna ab Helen, known as Boar Skull. He has courage, if no skill at weapons and he buried the children of Alavna with his own hands and kissed the earth on their grave. I, Kai Alavna ab Owain vouch for him.'

The others of their convoy were gathered round.

'This is Daniel Alavna ab George, known as The Bear Sark. He has killed more Ravens than I have counted and could kill an army if someone taught him how to hold that sword right. He buried the children of Alavna with his own hands and planted his sword deep into the soil of their grave. I, Kai Alavna ab Owain vouch for him.'

Finn looked extremely taken aback. Then, to his even more evident astonishment, each of their companions vouched for Ursula and Dan. It was a big thing it seemed, like adoption. Bryn explained it to Dan while Kai and the others talked about Alavna. It meant that if they did anything wrong and injured the tribe in any way, their companions had taken the responsibility. If anyone killed or injured them, their comrades would avenge them. Ursula did not know the full import of Kai's words, but she still shivered as they were spoken. She did not need to know exactly what was meant. She could feel all the promises thickening the air.

They walked on into full view of the fortress, which stood on a cliff above a sparkling sea. They walked across the grassy plain of the valley, shadowed by steep-sided hills on either side. News had travelled quickly and what seemed like hundreds of people then arrived to gawp at them or to welcome Kai. Someone took the ponies and they moved in a small bubble of empty space, maintained by the frown on Kai's face. No one jostled them, but the frank stares of the people made Ursula feel like an exhibit in the zoo. Dan could hear her teeth grinding as they began the steep climb to the fortress gates.

The fortress itself was built largely of stone. It was not exactly a castle of the Romantic kind with high turrets and round towers. It was simpler than that. It had solid, high, curved walls within which other buildings huddled. It was surrounded by a ring of deep ditches, hewn from the rock and filled with sharp pointed stakes. Most significantly of all, the cliff it crowned was so steep, Dan almost had to use his hands as well as his feet to climb it.

It should have made Dan feel safe, but the occupants seemed scarcely less hostile than Ravens. Dan felt his spirits sink.

~ Chapter Twelve ~

The Great Hall

Finn was enormously proud of Macsen's fortress. It had been built by a Raven engineer who had switched sides rather than be branded a thief. Unfortunately for him, his thieving was inveterate and he had ended his days skewered by a Combrogi spear, before the completion of the fortress. He had been an innovative engineer, a genuine genius, but because he had never been entirely trusted, Macsen had ensured that his own men make slight alterations to his plans. The result was, apparently, a brilliant fusion of Combrogi workmanship and Roman ingenuity. Not that Dan cared. He wanted to be rid of the reek of death that clung to his hair and clothes and he wanted a little bit of peace.

They were led through the main gates, through a paved courtyard towards the great hall, a rather squat Romanesque basilica within the circle of the all enclosing wall. There were other stone and timber buildings within the wall whose functions Dan could only guess at. At a nod from Finn, servants led the travellers towards one of these, the Roman engineer's innovation, a Roman style bathhouse. Being dirty did not usually bother Dan. His mother had cared a lot when she was alive and he'd never quite understood why. Now he was more desperate for a hot bath than at any other time in his life. It was then that Ursula shot him a look of pure panic. She would not go through the door, but hovered awkwardly in the courtyard. He realised then that a bathhouse would probably involve communal nakedness. How could they get out of this one? A servant was already helping Kai to strip. His naked torso was all but completely covered in blue tattoos of an intricate intertwining leaf design. He was very heavily muscled. Dan wondered how he had ever managed to fight a man like that and, as he remembered, injure him. Aware suddenly that staring at another man's chest might not be acceptable behaviour, he quickly averted his eyes.

'Kai,' he began, 'my lord Boar Skull is not accustomed to …' to what? He was without inspiration. He began again. 'In my world, we do not usually …'

Kai was looking at him with amusement.

'Rhonwen's other outlanders were afraid to unclothe their puny bodies in the company of men!' Kai laughed broadly and the others joined in. Kai leavened his remark with a gentle clap around the shoulders which would have knocked Dan over, had he not braced himself. These were men who had vouched for him; they had a right to mock him he supposed. Gwyn alone looked contemptuous. Dan forced a grin.

'There is a private room you may use for your own purposes.' Kai winked. 'A servant will attend you!'

Prys began a raucous and extremely vulgar song. There was the general spirit of a post rugby match changing room. He would really have liked to stay. For Ursula's sake he followed the servant. The relief on her face and her smile when he explained that there was a private bathroom transfigured her. She could definitely be beautiful, if she was clean and smiled more often.

They took turns to bathe and Ursula refused the attentions of a servant, though she did have the presence of mind to ask for bandages to bind a chest wound, that she claimed to have received on the road. Dan had been worried. He could not remember her being injured until he realised that she would need to bind her chest if she was to look like a convincing man. They were brought fine new clothes to wear. Dan felt a little bit of an idiot in diamond-patterned blue and yellow trews, bright blue tunic and green and blue plaid cloak. He was also given a fine leather scabbard for Bright Killer. The sword was a little too long for him even with a proper scabbard.

Clean and shiny, he looked very young indeed. The servant had brought a rawhide leather breastplate to wear over his tunic, but it was too big and hindered his movements. He gave it to Ursula. She was dressed in oranges and reds. She looked nervous and was grateful for the breastplate. She would have covered herself completely in armour if she could. Ursula had also been lent a fine sword to replace the one she had given to Kai for Madoc's burial and a gold torque, befitting her status as The Bear Sark's Lord – though no one was too sure of either of the outlanders' status. Dan thought she looked scary, which pleased her. She was worried that she moved too much like a girl, though Dan could not see it as a problem. She carefully watched the way he walked, but found his rolling swagger unnatural and too difficult to copy.

'Well, try walking like Kai then. He's nearer your height anyway.' Ursula concentrated very hard on picturing Kai in her mind and pulled back her shoulders, threw out her chest and tried to copy the swing of his massive forearms and equally solid legs.

'That's brilliant!' Dan had never realised that Ursula could be such a magnificent actor. She seemed in a moment both bigger and more masculine.

'I don't know if I can do this.'

'You did it on the road. What's the difference?' Dan really didn't see it as such a big deal. After the first slip-up he'd even started thinking of Ursula as a boy himself. 'It's not as if you were a girlie girl in the first place.'

'And just what do you mean by that?' she snapped back with another of her glowering scowls and an icy flash of suddenly cold blue eyes.

Dan knew enough about Ursula to consider an emergency subject change.

'Hang on a minute. I don't think your sword belt is quite right.' Ursula permitted him to adjust it. The servant who had arrived to usher them into Finn's presence coughed politely. Dan hoped that he had not seen Ursula practising her walk. They both followed the servant across the courtyard to the Great Hall. Ursula's scowl had deepened to thundercloud proportions and Dan could hear her grinding her teeth. He wished she did not withdraw into herself when she was afraid. Dressed in his outlandish garments, without the perverse comfort of his mad, bear sark persona, he felt nervous too. He reached for his place of calm madness, just to check it was still there. If it was, he could not find it. Before panic unmanned him completely, Braveheart bounded towards him. Bryn, clean and clothed in suitably handsome clothes, followed with all the dignity of his new rank of squire. He looked at Dan's fine clothes with obvious pride and satisfaction. Dan did not want to let him down. With one hand on Braveheart's head and the other on the hilt of Bright Killer he followed the servant inside.

The Great Hall was a large oblong room with a low rafterred ceiling and a series of small high windows. The late afternoon sun scarcely illuminated the room and the deficit was dealt with by a series of torches fixed to the wall by finely worked bronze holders. The room was a riot of colour, noise and scents, not all of them unpleasant. Richly decorated fabrics covered the hall and floors in a kaleidoscope of shifting patterns. It looked like a film set of some alien court. The room was filled with men and women, lavishly dressed and adorned with heavy gold jewellery. Everyone was talking and gesticulating at once, like a huge party. But it was a party that expected trouble. There was an electric tension in the room, an excitement that almost shaded into fear. The splendour and the strangeness of it overwhelmed Dan. Ursula looked very uncomfortable, though she brightened when she saw a number of the women were as tall as she was. Her pale blonde hair was not so extraordinary here either. Dan could almost see her doubting the wisdom of adopting a male role. Perhaps it might not be so bad to live as a woman. Certainly the servants moving among the throng with goblets of Roman wine and mead treated the women with as much respect as the men. The proud bearing and confident conversation of the women there gave no indication that their place was inferior in any way.

There was little furniture in the room, indeed almost

none. At a signal, which Dan missed, the assembled people sank gracefully to the ground, sitting on furs and rugs. They carried on their animated chatter without pausing for breath. There was one low leather sofa, low backed and short-legged. It was the only furniture in the room. Finn indicated that Kai should take it. As Macsen's second-in-command he took precedence over the steward while Macsen himself was away harrying the legion. Cleaned and scented and dressed in fine clothes Kai looked every inch a barbarian warlord. He wore a breastplate that shone like silver, if indeed it was not silver. His red hair, combed and oiled, hung in two complex plaits down his back and his long moustache drooped almost to the level of his chin. The rest of his face was freshly shaven. He spoke clearly and well of what had befallen them on the road, of Rhonwen's success in raising the Veil and adding two warriors to their number but most of all he spoke of Macsen's plans to defeat the Ravens at Craigwen and of the need for the women and children to leave for Ireland. King Cadal had confirmed with Finn that they would be cared for under the usual terms.

There was a pause and a general low hum of whispered concern. Many of the gathered men and women exchanged glances. Dan saw a young warrior touch hands briefly with a red-haired girl as tall as Ursula. Even here inside the stone walls of Craigwen, lives were at risk. Everyone looked grave. Kai continued, 'Let us not pretend that the Raven is other than a savage bird, that has scavenged on our tribal feuds too long. It has grown fat on our past mistakes and it is not so fat that it has grown foolish. Prince Macsen has studied its ways. We will fight and we can win but we must be prepared for what will come, for the death of many among us before the fight is won. We will be besieged by the legion, of that there can be no doubt. We will fight the better for knowing that our women and children are safe. Women of the Combrogi, you are our hope. If we shall fail, from where else can a future come but from your strong wombs and from your proud hearts? It will be your duty to keep our ways and honour safe there on the Sacred Isle, against the day when the Combrogi can walk freely again on the Island of the Mighty.'

Kai paused again and met the eyes of the assembled throng. For the first time Dan was aware that the survival of an entire people was at stake. The presence of the two strangers paled into insignificance besides the life of their tribe. Dan felt his earlier nerves to have been a vanity.

Finn spoke in the silence that greeted Kai's words.

'King Cadal will send his warships tomorrow soon after dawn. Princess Rhonwen will join the other women when she returns. Prince Macsen wishes all our warriors to train together under the leadership of Hane. If our old style of fighting cannot destroy the Ravens we will learn new ways. What the Ravens can do can not the Combrogi do better? For tonight we feast.'

He clapped his hands and servants bearing low wooden tables, more wine and food rushed forward to ready a feast. Prys guided Ursula, Bryn and Dan to sit with their companions of Alavna. Everyone began to chatter and laugh again, but Dan felt there was a brittle edge to the laughter, a desperation to the humour. Even so, the Combrogi knew how to feast. Eat, drink and be merry for tomorrow or maybe the next day, we die.

~ Chapter Thirteen ~

Warriors of Craigwen

Dan's quiet place of blood and madness remained lost to him. In spite of having drunk several glasses of mead, Dan could not sleep. They had all lain down to sleep where they had feasted, though men and women had been leaving together all night to go elsewhere to say their goodbyes.

He kept probing the place in his mind where he thought he'd kept his madness. He worried at it as he had worried at the gap in his teeth when he had a tooth knocked out at rugby. The gap still remained; his madness did not. He did not want to be mad exactly, but to be in such an inherently mad situation without its protection worried him more. Is this how Ursula felt? To his surprise he found he did not like to sleep indoors either. The smell of so many bodies, however frequently immersed in the Roman baths, bothered him. There was a smell of grease and stale alcohol. Indoors even the distinctive smell of Braveheart's damp hair bothered him, as it never had outside. Carefully he disentangled his cloak from that of his companions. Ursula touched his hand in the darkness.

'Are you going outside?' The men around them were more or less insensible with drink. They stirred only to belch or worse and did not appear to notice Dan and Ursula's clumsy attempts to creep away. They were the ones without wives who had drunk ale and mead until they had passed out.

Once outside in the clear star-filled night Ursula spoke.

'I dreamed I saw Rhonwen last night. She and Macsen were in a town. It looked like a Roman town. She started a fire as a diversion, to help Macsen. It must have been part of his plan, you know, to keep the Ravens there under pressure so they wouldn't set off at once for Craigwen. Well, the fire began as an illusion, like the dragon, but she lost control. I could kind of feel how it happened. The power twisted somehow out of her grasp, and the fire became real. I could see her face and her eyes and her mouth open wide, screaming for help. In my dream I knew what to do to make it stop, but I couldn't quite do it. It was terrible – her face. She was horribly burned. I think Macsen put out the fire but I don't know. I don't think I'll ever forget her face. Dan, do you think you can dream true things, like you know I might be clairvoyant or something? I am sure it was real.'

Dan wanted to put his arm round her, but he was sure there must be sentries watching.

'I'm sure it was a dream. You probably drank too much mead.'

'No, it's awful stuff. I had the servant bring me water. It's so sweet I'm sure it must rot your teeth.' Surprisingly, everyone she had seen had quite good teeth, but then hardly anyone she had seen had been much above forty.

'Well,' Dan continued, 'you've never been clairvoyant before.'

'And I suppose you were always a berserker before?'

'Fair point, but I may not be a berserker again either. The madness – I could kind of feel it before, it's gone.'

Ursula looked at him very hard. There was enough moonlight for them to see each other clearly. She looked at him as if his head were transparent and she could look inside.

'Trust me – you're still a berserker, still mad.'

She didn't say it like a joke. He was sure she believed it and, bizarrely, he felt comforted. He didn't believe she had become clairvoyant, of course, but he trusted her instincts. He felt relieved and exhausted.

'Ursula, it was just a bad dream. Let's go back inside. Everyone will be up at dawn. Who knows what we'll be asked to do then?'

*

They were asked to help. To carry endless boxes and leather bags of things to the waiting ships. The bay was shallow and the Irish sailors came ashore in small coracles of stretched hides. It was not an easy landing place because the rocks that surrounded the bay were particularly dangerous and broke the waves to form strange tides and eddies. The spring tides were vicious and the coracles came ashore surfing on white waves. They seemed fragile craft for such precious cargo. Loading the coracles took care and it was midday before everything and everyone was on board. Women comforted crying children by telling them of the heroic journey they were to undertake, but there was not one who didn't look tight-faced and anxious as they stepped aboard. Dan wanted Bryn to go but he was so outraged at the mere suggestion that Dan backed down. Dan did not want to start an argument about manhood, but he did not want the responsibility of Bryn's life in his hands, when it came to a fight. It seemed, as in so much else, that he had no choice.

When all the women, the children, the bags, a strong box of gold as surety, and even some small domestic animals were all safely stowed aboard the small fleet, the warriors lined themselves up on the shore and beat their shields with their spears. It was a defiant gesture but a sad one. The Celts were not ashamed to cry and many of the men were damp-eyed as they waved the children away. Dan wondered if Ursula regretted her choice. She was committed now to playing the role of warrior and, when the fighting came, wielding a sword with the rest of them.

The fortress felt rather forlorn when the women and children had left. The warmth and welcome of the place such as it was had left with the women. Craigwen was now a barracks. It became clear that Dan and Ursula were not the only strangers to enter Craigwen. Since Kai's return fifty or so additional tribesmen had answered Macsen's call and arrived with their retinues to train under Hane. Dan and Ursula felt rather lost. Bryn, with an instinctive grasp of the fortress protocols, managed to bring them food and news of new arrivals. It meant little to either of them, though the food was welcome. It was late afternoon when Kai sought them out.

'Ah! Boar Skull and Bear Sark. You have found food I see. I have spoken with Hane and we agree it would be good for you to train with "Macsen's men", the ones from other tribes Macsen invited to learn Raven techniques under Hane. It will be tough for you. Usually our lads start at Bryn's age, but you will have to pick up what you can. The best men haven't come. Macsen will be very disappointed. I fear no true warrior of the Combrogi will admit he ever has anything to learn.' He sighed heavily. 'Anyway we of Alavna will train alongside the others of our tribe, who will obey Macsen whether they like it or not, and you will learn how to use that sword of yours the right way.' Dan got the distinct impression that Kai was looking after them. He looked embarrassed and would not look at them directly. 'I will be blunt. Not all the warriors we have been sent are of the best quality, there's more than one troublemaker among them. It may be hard for you. If the Cup of Belonging had allowed you to share an understanding of our ways it might have been easier but it didn't. You are very old not to be warriors of the blood. Some of the younger men resent The Bear Sark's reputation. They will know that you, Boar Skull, did not fight the Ravens by our side. They will not make it comfortable for you. You will sleep in barracks with the others. I will help if you are in fear of your life, but for the rest you must cope as you best can.' He looked at Ursula. 'Boar Skull, I think your brother hears you even in his Bear Sark mood. Keep him from killing our allies if you can. I don't trust them and there are a few I could name whose skulls would better decorate the gatepost than their necks but still we are bound by ties of hospitality. I would not shame Prince Macsen by having Combrogi blood shed within these walls. We are to meet in the courtyard. May the Goddess keep you. I fear you will have need of her kinder face.' Kai's grin was broad enough but he was clearly worried.

It did not take very long to see why. Six warriors had travelled eight nights in all to bring Ursula and Dan to Craigwen. Nobody believed they were worth it, and everybody set out to prove it. Hane was the embodiment of every mean-spirited drill sergeant cliché that ever breathed on celluloid except that he was broader even than Kai and real.

Ursula was not very fit. Every one of the men there, whatever Kai's opinion of them, had trained as a warrior from the age of eight. They may not have used a gym to weight train, but their every muscle was as hard as endless exercise and a rich diet could make it. They were nearly all tall too. It was not hard to identify the trouble-makers of whom Kai had so kindly but awkwardly warned them. The biggest was the smallest man, Huw, the Prince's cousin.

Ursula had avoided every games lesson she could for the past four years. She was probably a stone or two overweight, even taking into account the natural puppy fat a girl of her age ought to carry. It was not going to be easy. She gritted her teeth and focused on what she had to do. What she had to do was ignore the almost continual jibes of the men round her. She had to ignore the pain. She had to force her body to obey her sullen will. She made a mess of every exercise. She dropped her practice sword at regular intervals. She failed to do a single press-up.

'Come on then, outlander! Show us what you've got. My ma's mule's got more balance than that. If you were the best, by Lugh, I'm glad I don't have to meet the rest.'

It was like school only worse. This time her attackers were each of them capable of killing her as easily as they might wring the neck of a rabbit for the pot. Huw was particularly vicious. He was furious that his father had sent him to be trained further and his anger had to find an outlet. With an unerring instinct for the weakest in the pack, he chose endless bullying as his outlet and Ursula as his target. His whispered insults were in her ear for the whole of that first day. In the first hour of training she missed home so desperately. If will alone could have raised the Veil, she would have done it. After the second hour she had begun to distance the pain in her body from her mind. By the third hour, when she was bathed in sweat and even Hane glowed with a hint of dampness, her arms seemed to belong to someone else except for the pain in them which was definitely hers. She kept lifting her sword above her head and counting to fifty, jumping and leaping and twisting as she was bidden. She ignored the men around her, apart from Hane who was issuing orders. She concentrated only on doing as she was told. Exhaustion seemed to break down her natural resistance to the power she had sensed since the moment she had walked through the mist. She felt a tingling in her spine, like pins and needles, travelling up her back and making her scalp prickle. 'Give me strength,' she prayed. 'Don't let me cry or fall over or let myself down.' The mockery had subsided a little as Hane had them all doing exercises that were new even to the Combrogi. Ursula hung on and found a little bit more strength, a little bit more of the sap-like energy of spring. It might have been her imagination but if it was she didn't care. Something kept her upright; something allowed her to keep moving. She did not want to give Hane, Huw and the other brutes more to mock than she had to.

Dan found the first day's training little more comfortable than Ursula. He was fit, but only by the standards of a twenty-first century schoolboy. By the standards of the Combrogi he had a long way to go. The exercises were not as unfamiliar to him as to Ursula, but battle used different muscles from football. His upper body strength was pitiful. It was a testament to the power of his madness that he had ever managed to wield Bright Killer for so long in battle. He spent much of the first day's training being surprised: he was surprised that everyone else bar Ursula was so much fitter than he was. He was surprised that even the ancient Celts did press-ups, he was surprised that his approximation of a man-like grip on Bright Killer was completely wrong. The Combrogi did not grip their swords with their whole hand. Hane had to show him several times before he got it right. It immediately improved his control of his sword, if not his effectiveness at waving it round his head, jumping over it or doing any number of the manoeuvres that Hane set them. He was not sorry when the first day's training ended and he could crawl into the barracks and sleep.

The barracks was another story. It was a long wooden cabin with open unglazed windows, covered with wooden shutters. There was a central fire that smoked all night and kept the air thick with acrid woodsmoke. There was a dirt floor. The men slept in their cloaks on wooden pallets, arranged in two rows on either side of the room. It was draughty, damp and smelly. The only light came from the fire. As the Combrogi were capable of building from stone and even had the underfloor heating favoured by the Romans in the Great Hall, Ursula could see no purpose to the discomfort. By the end of the day she was too tired even to complain.

She would have preferred to sleep as she had on the road, close enough to Dan and Braveheart and Bryn to share their warmth, and to feel the comfort of another living thing close by in the loneliness of the unfamiliar world. Instead she slept on her pallet, next to Dan. More than once she found faeces on her pallet and once the flayed carcass of a rabbit. She was not the kind to complain and she tried not to let Dan see what was going on. It was bad enough being an outcast in her own world without adding to the ignominy by proving she was an outcast in this world too. Dan still had Braveheart with him and slept with his arm around the great hound's neck. Ursula was pleased that he had not had to join the pack of dogs that slept near the stables. Prys said it was because his unusual size made it difficult for the other dogs to accept him. She completely sympathised and made more of an effort to befriend Braveheart. Not that it mattered; he was too clearly Dan's dog. Bryn slept on Dan's other side and helped him dress and generally looked after him. Ursula tried not to mind.

She ate what was offered in the Hall. She drank watered ale, which was disgusting, but quenched her thirst. At night she slept the sleep of the almost dead. The first night she did not believe she was capable of doing any of it again the next day. She was, of course, given no choice. At least she had no more precognitive dreams, or none that she remembered. She dreamed instead that she lay cradled within the earth itself. It yielded to her aching body as if it were a bed of the softest down and gave her restorative warmth and comfort.

~ Chapter Fourteen~

Strong Magic

By the third day the Combrogi themselves were in rebellion. Not of course at the living conditions. Ursula had learnt that the barracks followed the model of most of the village homes. No, the Combrogi rebelled at the manner and type of training Hane and their loyalty to Macsen obliged them to undergo. Macsen believed that the traditional Combrogi tactic of raining spears and stones down on the enemy and then charging forward en masse to engage in single combat was ineffective against the Ravens' highly trained fighting force. He wanted them to fight as an army. He wanted them to fight like their enemy. More than that Hane was busily acting like the enemy, insulting them at every turn.

'A Raven soldier could spear you at ten paces and have you on a spit like a sucking pig, if you make that mistake too often.'

'Hold your shield higher, man, do you not know the

meaning of "up"? It is where you will not fall when kicked off these battlements.' Gwyn found it particularly difficult to tolerate this approach as he was Macsen's champion. He had apparently saved Macsen's life in battle and would fight first against an enemy if single combat were called for. It was a status of which both Ursula and Dan had been unaware.

After the first day Dan, having less to unlearn than the warriors, found it physically taxing but relatively simple to do what Hane asked of him. He concentrated hard and even received grudging praise from Hane. His easy manner and evident skill kept him out of trouble with the others. Ursula found it much harder, but as her strength grew so did her skill. She partnered Dan, who was patient with her. No one else but the comrades of Alavna would even look at her unless it was to trip her up or catch her a hard blow across the back of her legs with the flat of their swords.

It was after Hane had been particularly scathing about Gwyn's footwork that Gwyn finally exploded. 'This is Raven training. It demeans us to use their ways.'

Hane was no fool and he needed to show Macsen some tangible result of his training methods or he would lose the Prince's support. Without Macsen's support the warriors he so enthusiastically humiliated would tear him limb from limb. Hane smiled a mirthless, charmless smile.

He spoke in a gentle voice.

'Gwyn, if you doubt my methods, I will show you the exact extent of your vulnerability. If you do not work as a team the very weakest of the enemy can overpower you if they work as a unit. I'll prove it with the outlanders.'

Ursula felt herself blush. She needed no precognition to know that this could not end well. Dan didn't want to meet Gwyn's eyes.

Gwyn swaggered towards them. He laid down his wooden weapon and picked up his own sword. Dan took up Bright Killer, never more than a footfall away. Ursula picked up her own weapon. She was sweating so profusely that it slithered in her hand. Her heart raced. She knew what Gwyn was going to do. Gwyn knew more about Dan than Hane. Gwyn had observed him turn berserker to defend Ursula in the battle of the dragon. He had seen how Dan was prepared to defend Bryn on the road to Alavna. Gwyn had the measure of Dan. Ursula was not even sure Hane knew that Dan was a true bear sark and not just nicknamed "The Bear Sark". The fortress was full of such names.

She could see that Gwyn was envious of Dan's reputation, he wanted to prove that he was still Macsen's champion even against a berserker. All Gwyn had to do was threaten Ursula. Concern for his friends was the major trigger for Dan's madness.

Whoever won this, it was not about to be a test of

team techniques against the glory route of single combat. This was single combat on Gwyn's terms. If it made Hane look foolish all the better.

Ursula knew the strategy would work. When she looked at Dan she could see his madness, curled like a cobra, feigning sleep, ready to strike. Could she hold Dan back from it as Kai believed? She was by no means sure.

Although no one on earth could have persuaded the Combrogi away from the long sharp-sided swords they had always used in favour of the Raven's short stabbing gladius, Hane had insisted they act defensively as a team, each member protecting the other. As long as you remembered to give your partner room to swing his long sword or launch his spear such a tactic did leave you less exposed than usual to an enemy weapon. Combrogi lines could never be as tight and as strong as the Ravens'. The Combrogi needed so much more room to fight but it was one step in a new direction. Ursula took up the defensive position, protecting Dan's right side. Gwyn faced them, an irritating smile on his face.

'If you try to attack the man on your right, see how his partner can block you and then launch his own attack,' Hane called out, oblivious to what was going on here.

Predictably Gwyn ignored both Hane and Dan and launched straight into an attack on Ursula. She blocked the first thrust of his sword by luck alone. She heard

Braveheart growling in the background. She saw the second blow coming for her unprotected side and ... suddenly Dan had dropped his shield and was there. She stepped behind him. Her shield would only interfere with his freedom of movement. Hane was bellowing for them to stop, that the exercise should not be done that way. The Combrogi ignored him as thoroughly as Gwyn had. The men were yelling at each other and taking bets.

Ursula did not know which way she would bet. Gwyn was experienced, taller and massively strong. Dan was so quick but nowhere near as strong. She willed strength into his right arm and felt the strange humming tingle that had always accompanied Rhonwen's use of magic. She did not know if it made any difference.

It was Dan's speed that was remarkable. When berserk he was totally fearless of course and did not burden himself with any thought of defensive strategy, but more than that, time seemed to slow down for him. Gwyn's moves were swift and practised but there seemed no gap between thought and action when Dan fought. Gwyn raised his sword to deliver a crippling blow to Dan's unprotected shoulder. Gwyn used his shield to protect his own exposed side. As he reached to deliver his blow Dan switched his sword to his left hand and sliced under Gwyn's raised arm. Had Bright Killer had a point Dan would have stabbed him. As it was the slice was more debilitating. Gwyn dropped his sword and his guard. In the time it took Ursula to exhale Dan had Bright Killer at Gwyn's neck. The shouts of the men were suddenly silenced. The assembled warriors waited.

'No!' Ursula's voice was loud and clear. Dan would hear her. 'This is Gwyn of Alavna. You will not kill him.' The cold light of certainty died in Dan's eyes. He seemed to return to himself.

'Lay Bright Killer down.' Ursula kept her voice low but commanding. Dan did as she ordered. Ursula fought the urge to hug Dan. He had saved her life again. Gwyn would have had no scruple about injuring her very seriously, to prove his supremacy. She did not think he would have killed her outright, but in a world without antibiotics, it might have amounted to the same thing.

Hane endeavoured to take control. He sounded shaky. He had seriously underestimated both Gwyn and Dan. He had foolishly expected Gwyn to attack by the book and Ursula and Dan to neatly turn the attack aside. He had not expected this near fatal encounter.

'We will overlook this breach of discipline. We will break now and resume when I bang the gong.'

Gwyn struggled to his feet and bowed stiffly in Dan's direction. His eyes burned with some powerful emotion. Ursula hoped it wasn't hate.

'Are you OK?' Ursula asked Dan softly.

'I turned berserker, didn't I? Did I kill anyone?'

Ursula had a firm but unexamined conviction that

149

Dan should face up to his Bear Sark nature. She had perhaps watched too many daytime chat shows about 'learning to forgive yourself' and 'confronting your dark side'. Whatever the reason, she was not prepared to let Dan sink into voluntary amnesia.

'You know what you did Dan, think about it.'

Dan wrinkled his face.

'I injured Gwyn under his sword arm. His shield was in the wrong place. I switched sword arms. I can play tennis with either hand, I suppose it's the same. You stopped me killing him. I heard your voice in my mind like a rod of heat melting the ice. I did what you said. I don't know how I heard you. I didn't hear anything else.'

'You went bear sark very fast,' said Ursula, changing the subject. Did he read her mind? Or did she speak to his?

'It's quicker each time, like a gear I kind of slip into. You were right, it hasn't gone away.'

His feelings about his madness were decidedly more ambivalent now. At least it was keeping them alive.

'Thank you for stopping me from killing Gwyn.'

'Thank you for stopping Gwyn from killing me.'

They grinned at each other.

'Ursula, did you try to help me in any way?'

'No, I got out of your way I thought …'

'No, I mean did you, this sounds stupid, did you try any, any magic?'

Ursula felt herself blush again.

'I thought ... I mean I wanted to help and Gwyn is bigger than you and I ... kind of wanted to send you strength. I know it's so fantastic and unlikely that I could ...'

Dan silenced her when he showed her Bright Killer. The imprint of his fingers was buried deep into the metal, as if the hilt had been made of wet clay.

'Next time, not quite so much, eh?'

Ursula felt cold. It was true then. Something strange was happening here. Unless she too was mad and imagining this extraordinary scenario, in this world she could perform magic.

~ Chapter Fifteen ~

Changes

The men treated Dan with new respect as a man among men, not as a promising boy. They treated Ursula with decidedly more caution. They didn't seem to like her any more than they had before. She did not have the knack of being liked, but as a man who commanded the man who bested Macsen's champion she had a kind of status. The small presents left in her bed ceased. Huw kept his distance. Needless to say Ursula resented it. She did not want to survive only in Dan's reflected glory.

There were no further challenges to Hane. Although Gwyn's humiliation was not Hane's fault, or indeed Dan's in any real sense, Hane was somehow connected with it. The warriors learned what he had to teach them and gradually came to recognise that there were some benefits to the new ways.

*

Time passed. The summer harvest festival of Lughnasa came and went. Macsen did not appear but then neither did the legion. That at least was a good thing. There had been word. Kai and Finn seemed to know what was going on. There were rumours of a great fire at the army barracks at Deva which had destroyed half the town. Hundreds of slaves suspected of being involved had been slaughtered. It was rumoured that King Donicca, Macsen's uncle, was injured in the blaze and that Rhonwen too had been hurt. Ursula did not wish to listen to rumours. She did not want her suspicions confirmed. She did not want to have powers of precognition. She had no energy for more than the daily grind of survival. It was a constant battle against exhaustion and her own physical awkwardness.

They had a day off training for the festival and the remaining servants did what they could to produce a feast.

All the men from the outlying region came along – the farmers who paid for their protection with grain and meat and who would move inside the fortress walls when the legion came. Ursula had not realised at the time but the women and children from the whole region had gone to King Cadal. Without their women the men got very drunk and danced and sang. As the night became more drunken, the songs became more maudlin and Ursula got more homesick. Otherwise there was little change in the routine of train, eat, sleep, train. Kai made sure they had adequate clothes for all occasions. They got to use the baths regularly and no one commented when Ursula chose to bathe alone. At least, although they commented a great deal, it was never in Dan or Ursula's hearing.

Ursula dreamed of the Veil very often. She dreamed she managed to raise it and she and Dan stepped through it, but they never stepped back into their own world and time, only ever into places where endless wars raged. She woke sobbing from these dreams every few nights, but if the other men heard her, again they said nothing. She thought of little but home and rest and of course, magic. Every day she felt the magic in her growing stronger. She felt its power running through her into her sword arm. It was a good thing she was using so much energy or she feared she would explode with the pressure of it building up inside her. She felt a kind of excitement in every nerve ending. It was like some repressed internal electric storm. It heightened her perceptions: sounds were sharper. Her vision was more precise. Each thread of wool on her cloak seemed to her clear and distinct. Other people's emotions clouded the air with a colour of their own. She learned to ignore it because it frightened her. She was truly beginning to fear her own brand of madness; the delusion that she had power. A part of her did not, could not come to terms with the magic that pulsed through her. She threw herself into the training until even the men noticed her fierce passion to succeed. And she was getting stronger. She felt herself becoming steel-sinewed and iron-handed. Her rather flabby body was becoming a well-oiled working machine. She delighted in it. If this was what fitness felt like she rather regretted never having tried it before. Her speed and co-ordination improved too. She was a coiled spring of energy just about containing the forces pumping around inside her. Dan was proud of her, she knew. He glowed with it when he looked at her. She was getting very good at fighting. Strangely she had quite a good temperament for it. Unlike Dan who became his sword when he fought, Ursula was cool and calculating. She watched and weighed what the others did and she copied them. She lacked Dan's instincts but she could learn. She learned well.

It must have been late October when Kai approached her in the courtyard. He and the other warriors of Alavna had left her and Dan much to themselves. Ursula knew that Kai did not want to make things more difficult for her than they already were. The Combrogi were highly attuned to subtle gradations of status. Kai had high status. Ursula, who was not even a warrior and an outlander, had low status, very low status. If Kai had shown particular interest in Boar Skull, the others would have taken out their resentment on her. It came as something of a surprise to Ursula to find that she thought of Kai as a friend. She was glad to see him. He spoke to her casually. Ursula was careful to show him more respect than she ever had on the road.

'I have had word from Prince Macsen and the Lady Rhonwen. They will be here by the festival of Samhain, as the first leaves begin to fall. There are some things you need to know. Macsen's uncle, King Donicca, has died. He was taken by the Ravens two years ago and Macsen has been running his lands. Macsen's father, Huw's father and King Donicca were brothers. It is the custom here that a new leader will be chosen by the King's mother, Queen Usca, from all her grandchildren. Huw is a contender.' Kai paused to gauge her reaction. Ursula tried hard not to show one. 'I have noticed that Huw is not a chosen drinking companion of yours,' Kai continued, diplomatically. Kai obviously knew more than she would have liked about Huw's earlier persecution of her. Ursula found herself blushing. She did not want Kai to see her as a victim. 'Look, Boar Skull, whatever Usca decides there is going to be trouble. She will be coming from Ireland as soon as is seemly. Huw may well try to impress her by starting something. I do not believe he would dare to do so with me, or any of Macsen's closest men. I have little regard for the man but he is not completely without sense. He won't risk fighting The Bear Sark. But he might call you out, Boar Skull. That's what

156

I came to tell you. Watch your back. If he challenges you do not kill him. We cannot risk a rift within the tribes right now.'

'But I …' Ursula began.

'I have watched you, Boar Skull. Some change has happened. Rhonwen has chosen better than she knew in you. You have the heart and liver of a warrior. Trust me. I have druid blood and see further than you might think. You could take Huw and most of "Macsen's men". We were not sent the best, remember, just those trouble-makers the tribes wanted rid of. We will have to hope they send us more and better warriors before the second legion turns its full attention on us. Keep that Boar's Skull of yours cool and use whatever you have to not kill him, if it gets to that.'

Kai looked at her in such a deliberate way that she wondered if he knew about the magic. Once more she speculated about what had happened in the rite of the Cup of Belonging. She had trusted Kai since then; there was a connection between them. In spite of his barbarity, she trusted him still. He was worried. That emanated from him clearly enough. She would heed his warning. She couldn't help feeling proud that he thought her a warrior. That would be something to take back home with her, if she ever got back home.

She told Dan what he had said.

'I think he's right. You're getting really good. You're

very strong. Is it magic?' He glanced meaningfully at the distorted hilt of Bright Killer. He had not tried to have it repaired as it now fitted his grip as if made for his hand, though it was a little more difficult to use with his left hand.

'I don't know. I should be strong. Hell, I'm big enough. I perhaps didn't want to be strong at home because, well, girls aren't ... Oh I don't know, Dan. I never saw that there might be any advantage to being huge ... I just wanted to be someone else, I think.'

Dan didn't say anything for a while. He was thoughtful.

'Ursula, at school you know, it wasn't that you were tall that was the problem. It was the way you looked at everyone like you weren't interested in them. People were afraid of you. I think they thought you were stuck up. I didn't, I mean, I always thought it was tough to be so different and big and that you had to be like that not to be bullied. It's good to be tall and ...'

He gave up, afraid of Ursula's response. Ursula was still not the easiest person to talk to about such things. But this time all Ursula could see was Dan's earnestness and his desire to make her feel better. He was always honest and well-meaning. She felt the prickling of tears. She really did not want to cry.

'Thanks, Dan,' she said quietly. It took a lot of self-control for her to say that. She hated criticism of any kind. It made her want to turn in on herself and reject the critic along with the criticism. She knew Dan was not trying to hurt her. No one had ever taken such risks to protect her. He cared about her. That was important. It made the criticism bearable. Had there been other times when people had tried to offer friendship with advice and she'd rebuffed them? She thought of her father. He was always giving her advice. It was a pity he hadn't stuck around long enough to help her accept it. She felt familiar anger return. She didn't need him or his love. She could survive without it. She pushed such unwelcome thoughts away.

'We'd better get back. Training will start again in a minute.' Ursula hesitated. She wanted to give something back to Dan for his embarrassed kindness. She was not good at being nice. 'Dan, you know before, when you wanted to promise to take care of me and I didn't want you to. It was because here, oaths bind, with a kind of magic that ties up destinies. We are bound to Kai and the others because of Alavna. We are bound to this place by that promise. I don't know how I know, but it's like when I knew you were still bear sark. I know that's how it is and I want to promise you something. I'll fight for you too, Dan. You have been a good friend to me. I don't know how, but I will try to find a way home.'

Dan smiled. It was a very shy, pleased smile. Checking that no one could see them he kissed her lightly on the cheek. She stepped back in surprise at the same moment that he stepped back in horror.

159

'Ursula, you've grown stubble!'

Ursula touched her cheek. It was true. She looked at her own forearm. There were no mirrors in the barracks. She had been joyfully unaware of her appearance for months. Now that she came to think about it no fifteen year old girl should ever have a forearm like that.

'Dan! What's happening to me?'

Dan looked very uncomfortable. She was not sure he'd looked at her much recently either.

'I don't know. We've both got bigger with all this training and the food. I've never eaten so much meat ever.' It was true Dan had grown. He was nearer her height now. Bright Killer, hanging in its scabbard, now no longer threatened to scrape the floor. His slightly skinny, runner's frame had filled out with all the heavy labour of combat training.

Even so she could see by the look in his eyes that he was shocked now that he really looked at her.

'I look like a man, don't I?'

'Ursula, you're trying to look like a man.'

'I'm not trying that hard right now. Well?'

'Well, yes, if I didn't know you, and I didn't know you'd bound yourself … um, I'd have thought you were a boy, well, yes a man, a strong, fit man.'

Ursula had almost stopped listening. When had she stopped binding her breasts?

Chapter Sixteen

Politics

The news of King Donicca's death was widely known by the end of the day. The warriors talked of him with affection. Huw and some of the others disagreed and thought his decision to stay as a slave in the Raven domain unmanly and perverse. They declared rather ostentatiously that they would rather slit their own throat than wipe the backsides of the Raven enemy. Prys spoke out in his defence and Ursula trusted his opinion more than Huw's. It also struck Ursula as rather disloyal of Huw to be so rude about his father's brother.

Prys was blunt. 'Huw, you are not worth that man's toe-nail clippings. He knew he could damage the enemy more if he were alive and in the enemy's own town than if he were dead on some lonely hillside. How do you think Macsen has successfully kept the legion away from us all this time? The old king had a few tricks up his sleeve and you can bet he taught Macsen more than a few of them.'

Huw did not attempt to attack Prys for his insult. Ursula found it hard to blame him for that. Prys looked like a bear and fought like one. The others watched carefully and drew their own conclusions. Prys had to be pretty sure that Huw would not be chosen King to speak of him so casually. Either that or he didn't care. Ursula suspected that he didn't care. Prys was Macsen's man. Speculation about the new King was rife but there were few bets placed on Huw being made King.

Preparations began at once for another feast. Representatives of all the surrounding tribes involved in Macsen's tentative tribal alliance would come to hear the judgement of Queen Usca, Macsen's venerable grandmother. She had left for Ireland with the other women. King Cadal intended to bring her back to Craigwen on Macsen's return. That way Cadal could discuss tactics with Macsen and collect his promised bride, Rhonwen. The men claimed that it was possible that a crowning and a marriage might all take place at once. They said it matter of factly and Ursula divined that it was because no one was sure that there would be enough of the Combrogi left come next spring to make such ceremonies possible. The end of their world felt very close to these men. The possibility of failure haunted them. Ursula felt it. It was not exactly fear; it went deeper than that. All of them would fight to their last drop of blood to keep their world alive, to keep the life of the Combrogi. All of them knew that it might not be enough.

Ursula found herself wondering what would happen if Huw were to be chosen as King. She was also vaguely disturbed by the thought of Rhonwen's face in her dreams. She had gathered from the talk of the men that Macsen had indeed set fire to much of Deva to force the legion to remain there through the winter. They had been obliged to rebuild the destroyed barracks. Macsen had also made sure that there was enough concern about a possible slaves' revolt for the local aristocracy to demand that the legion remain to protect them. The legion was busy trying to stamp out any symptom of an insurrection among the Combrogi slave population. The men were bitter about the Combrogi slaves. Huw was not alone in believing that it was better to be dead than to serve the Raven enemy. It seemed that Macsen and Rhonwen had succeeded in delaying the march of the legion on Craigwen, but if Ursula's dream was true Rhonwen, at least, had paid a price. Ursula remembered the look of terror in those green eyes as the flames engulfed her. Ursula could not forget Rhonwen's terrible recognition that the magic had gone wild and out of control. Ursula could not forget her scarred face. If the dream were true would Cadal still marry Rhonwen? Her beauty had been ravaged by the flames. What would happen to the alliance, to all those women and children if Cadal did not marry her? She would have liked to speak of it with Dan but she was avoiding him as much as possible. Every time she looked at him she saw the discomfort in his eyes.

She saw herself as he now saw her. It had been so good not to know what she looked like. It had been such a relief to be free of the tyranny of her own image. She did not want to think about what she was becoming. She had checked herself over carefully in the bathhouse. She had become very muscular it was true. She had lost weight and that had made her breasts smaller. She was still a woman, though, just a very strong one. Her legs and arms, which were all she could easily see without a mirror, looked more like Kai's than her own. She shed a few tears in the privacy of the bathhouse. She had wanted to lose weight for years. Now she had, she looked even less attractive than before. It should not have mattered. She was after all trying to look like a man. Ridiculously it did matter. It made her more of a physical freak than ever.

Craigwen was not a place for self-pity. On hearing the news of Macsen's return Hane redoubled his efforts to school them in Roman fighting methods. Ursula had no free time to think.

King Cadal arrived with Queen Usca, the first truly old person Ursula had seen. She did not look stupid enough to choose Huw or one of the other cousins over Macsen but then how could anyone tell. Her face was wizened and what had been a tall frame was bent by arthritis, but her eyes were shrewd and almost the same green as Rhonwen's. Ursula sensed power in them and she kept her distance. Over the next few days there was a steady stream of arrivals. The most respected warriors of the other tribes had come for a council of war with the new leader, whoever he should be. They were as different from "Macsen's men" as it was possible to be. Ursula found herself sympathising with Hane. If he'd had men like this to train instead of the likes of Huw what a fine force he could have made.

The visiting Combrogi looked magnificent. Gold torques decorated every throat, every arm and every sword. Even their horses' bridles were richly decorated with gold. Their clothing was of the finest cloth. Their armour was of polished silver and elaborately embossed leather. Some had winged helmets, others wore Viking-like horns, and almost all had the long drooping moustaches favoured by Macsen's guard. The barracks was full to overcrowding with guests and in spite of the imminence of winter and the near certainty of siege, Finn slaughtered as many cattle and sheep as were needed. Cooks baked as many oatcakes as would be needed by an army and barrels of ale and mead and costly imported wine were opened for the warriors. The Combrogi loved excess. This was to be a wake for the dead King, the investiture of the new King, a council of war and the festival of Samhain. It was the day on which the Combrogi believed the dead walked again on the earth.

For the first time Ursula and Dan also heard the talents of a true bard. At the festival of Lughnasa there had been singing but of an amateur kind. King Cadal's Irish bard was treated with as much honour as the Queen. When he first strummed his travelling harp Ursula knew why. It was like the magic in a way. Under his clever fingers and under the influence of his compelling voice things changed. Not only did he paint elaborate pictures in words and music he actually mixed the colours of the auras in the room changing the emotions, weaving patterns with the threads of feelings in his audience. Perhaps only he and Kai and Ursula saw what he did but everyone else felt the effects. He made sad men happy and quiet ones loud. He made Huw magnanimous and the sullen Gwyn playful. He knew what Dan was and gave him wide berth for which Ursula was grateful. He exchanged one look with Ursula and gave a start of recognition. For her he gave a virtuoso display of musical manipulation. He played his audience like he played his harp and they didn't even know. It was disturbing really but fascinating. She saw Kai watching her curiously. She kept her face impassive. She was sure that Kai suspected her of magic.

It was a few nights later that Macsen arrived. As he had

promised when he had left Kai and the others on the road, he was back for the festival of Samhain. Ursula was obscurely comforted by that. Macsen was dusty from the road and nursed a terrible gash to his arm. He too had paid a price for the success of his mission. He was pale with fatigue. Ursula hung back from the welcoming party. She could feel pain in the air. It was a soundless wail that set her teeth on edge. Someone was suffering. She did not want it to be Macsen. Then she saw Rhonwen. It was just a glimpse. Ursula did not want to meet her. Rhonwen's cloak was grubby from the journey, but she still wore a splendid gold brooch to secure it. She carried herself as gracefully as ever and her long black hair hung loosely down her back. In the months since her disfigurement she had somehow had a silver mask fashioned to cover her scarred face. From behind its smooth surface her green eyes glittered dangerously. It covered her whole face from hair line to chin and emulated her cold beauty perfectly. It was a sculpted replica of Rhonwen's features, its silken smooth surface broken only by two elegantly curved nostrils and two upwardly tilting eye holes. The effect was deeply disturbing. Now Ursula knew undeniably that her dream had been true. Until that moment she had pretended that the rumours might have been false. Now she knew that behind the mask lay the wreck of Rhonwen's beauty, horribly disfigured by fire. That was the pain that hung in the air.

It was Rhonwen's pain. It grew. It felt like screaming in her ear. She saw Kai wince and the bard pale. There seemed no way to block it out. Fortunately Rhonwen herself chose to muffle it somehow, and it quietened to a whimper. The men all looked taken aback when they saw her. The rumour of her terrible injuries spread as fast as the flames that had injured her. They were practical men; their thoughts fixed on survival. One thought united them, as Rhonwen must have been aware. What of the alliance with Cadal?

Cadal himself came to greet her. She had heard the men talk disparagingly of him as one not to be trusted, more interested in gold than honour, but to his credit he did not flinch at the sight of the silver mask. He knelt at Rhonwen's feet and offered her the traditional words of betrothal. The whole castle held its breath for the reply. Rhonwen's silver tongue was silent. She merely nodded graciously and it was left to Finn to stall Cadal and whisk him away to a private audience with Macsen.

There were no women to attend Rhonwen. Queen Usca had only brought one serving woman. Kai spoke briefly to Dan and then courteously asked Bryn to assist the Princess Rhonwen. It was not what Bryn wished to do but he could not refuse Kai, especially as he was clearly acting on Macsen's wishes.

Ursula had forgotten the headache that had plagued her since she had crossed the Veil. It always seemed to occur when she was near Rhonwen. It was as if the presence of Rhonwen's magic disturbed her thoughts, put pressure on her skull. With Rhonwen's return that headache returned. It combined with Ursula's dull awareness of Rhonwen's own pain to make Ursula very short-tempered.

It did not help that no one else seemed to be aware of it or at least did not speak of it. Both the bard and Kai looked strained and Ursula wondered if their apparent sensitivity to magic also encompassed sensitivity to this terrible projection of pain. She did not like to ask. She was not at all sure that she wanted anyone to know that she thought she could hear silent screams. It made her own sanity all the more suspect. It was one of those many times when she longed to be home, safe with her mum. She was so tired of the pain and the fear, the hard, unforgiving nature of the Combrogi life. She was in no mood to deal with Huw when he made his move.

'Hey Boar Skull, you looking for your little bear sark? Very close friends, aren't you?'

He was surrounded by his coterie of hangers-on. There were many more of them since the death of the King.

'You're not quite so impressive without your tame madman to defend you, are you Boar Skull?'

It occurred to Ursula that he might have been trying to rile her, but her general irritation was such that she didn't really care. Maybe a good fight would clear her head and if it did not, she knew it would feel almost as good to shut Huw up for good as it would to be free of the headache. With a warrior's unerring instinct for a fight, men were gathering at the tension in the air. She knew they were a hair's breadth away from taking bets.

'Do you want to try your luck?' She towered above Huw. She could feel the earth's strength surging in her veins. He would be a fool to try his luck, but the Combrogi had no rules against being a fool. Maybe Kai was wrong and Huw was such a fool.

It is possible that Huw hadn't looked at her too hard lately, because now that he paused to weigh her up as a serious opponent he blanched visibly. It was still true that she had only been training for months rather than years, but the hard, fit body that faced Huw belied that fact. Boar Skull had been the most incompetent warrior Huw had ever seen. He'd seen servants with much greater natural talent. Boar Skull had quietly endured the taunting and the other things he'd done. Huw had thought him a coward. The boy that looked at Huw now did not look like a coward or indeed much like a boy. It was a warrior that faced him with an expression as impassive and as immovable as rock. Huw had made a mistake but he could not back out now without a huge loss of face.

Huw drew his sword. Ursula found that she was not afraid. Had anyone pulled a knife on her at school she would have been a gibbering wreck. A sword was nothing more than an extremely long knife honed to a sharpness that a butcher would envy. She was a little surprised at her lack of fear and by the ease with which she had pulled out her own sword in response. She found herself eager to prove herself a man with one part of her mind just as with the other she was horrified at her casual acceptance of a level of violence a civilised person should abhor. Maybe she was no longer a civilised person. Maybe she had been desensitised by months of training and the sights she had seen since crossing the Veil.

Huw started to dance around her dodging and feinting. She watched him cold-eyed. She had no shield to hand so that was one less thing to worry about. Huw was very nervous. She could smell his fear as strongly as she could see its hectic glow around his body. She remembered her conversation with Kai. He had asked her not to kill Huw if he challenged her. She would try to do as he had asked, but she was suddenly coolly aware that what she had been learning were the techniques of death. It was hard to restrict injuries when you were wielding close to a metre of razor sharp metal. This was no playground fight. If she wanted it to end in no more than humiliation for Huw she could not slash at him with her sword. She surprised herself by what she did next. As he dodged she raised her foot and tripped him up. As he recovered she punched him hard in the jaw. She had only seen that move in old films and was surprised at its effect. Her hand stung with the impact but her timing had been perfect. All her considerable force had been transmitted through that punch. Huw was knocked out cold.

'He has bad manners for a boy of royal blood. He is lucky I did not think it fit to kill him.' Ursula spoke very deliberately. There was no greater sign of contempt than to call a warrior of the Combrogi a " boy".

She was not even breathing hard, though she felt quite shocked by what she had done. It had been a calculated alternative to killing him. She, Ursula, had considered killing someone. It was a terrible thought. She had not done so but she knew that the choice had been a real one – she could have killed him. That's what she had been doing with all this work, learning how to kill. It was something to keep her awake at night and this was the first time she had really understood what Hane's training had done to her. She, like Dan, was a potential killer now. It was not a happy thought.

To her surprise more than one of "Macsen's men" clapped her on the back approvingly. Huw was not a popular man. She caught Kai's eye and he grinned at her. If Huw was made King she might have to leave Craigwen in a hurry, but then if Huw were made King she would not be alone in that.

Chapter Seventeen

Warrior Making

Dan's response to the news of Ursula's encounter with Huw was not what she had expected. While he was pleased that she had come out of it well, he was very disturbed that he had not been there to help her.

'I'm a big girl now,' Ursula complained in irritated English.

'Shhh! Don't say that here. Do you want to be sent off to Ireland with Rhonwen?'

Ursula's headache had not eased. She could also still feel Rhonwen's pain, a dull ache like scarcely bearable toothache. She did not want to think about Rhonwen.

'My dream was right you know.' Ursula forgot her irritation. 'She was burned in a magic fire. I don't know how she did it. Before with the dragon it just seemed like a dragon. It wasn't real.'

'It seemed real enough to me.' Dan was not sure what Ursula was getting at. Her talk of magic and dreams disturbed him. In this strange world he relied on Ursula being normal. That she was not "normal" any more was a fact he consistently tried to deny to himself.

Their conversation was interrupted by the arrival of Kai and Gwyn. They were both dressed formally in their most magnificent and warlike best. They had washed their hair in lime so that it stood out from their heads as if sculpted in marble. Dan and Ursula automatically adopted a "ready" stance. Kai approved.

'You have both learned Hane's lessons well. He is re-commending that you both be accepted as warriors by the tribe. You will be the first outlanders to have lived so long and also to have proved worthy. We hope it will be to Macsen that you give your allegiance. Queen Usca is deliberating now.'

Both Dan and Ursula looked as taken aback as they felt. They had been with the Combrogi long enough to recognise the honour for what it was and to be overcome with it. To be made a warrior here, through their own effort, was like being given an Oscar or the Nobel Peace Prize. Warriors were born and raised and trained from childhood. They were not made of fifteen year old out-siders. Ursula spoke first.

'Kai, we accept! It is an honour. We are proud that you think us worthy. What if it is Huw who is chosen?'

'Don't worry. Not every King lives to rule. Queen Usca chooses. Often as not the tribe decides. Go to the

174

bathhouse and scrub yourselves clean. Bryn will bring you oils with which to anoint yourselves and special garments. At the moment of oath-taking you must appear before the King naked and then Rhodri will tattoo you with the sacred symbols of our people. My servant will fetch you when we are ready for you.'

Ursula had heard nothing after the word naked. She found herself colouring to the roots of her hair. It was like a nightmare. She was to appear naked before several hundred men. Instead of being accepted as a warrior she would be rejected and sent away from Dan, and Kai and Bryn and Braveheart to another place where she didn't know the rules and where everything she had tried so hard to learn would be useless. She gulped hard to prevent the tears from falling. Kai could see them shining in her eyes, but he might have thought them tears of pride. Dan did not risk looking at her until Kai had gone.

'God, they are barbarians – they will kill Huw if it suits them without batting an eyelid. What are we doing here? Why are we so pleased to be warriors?'

'Dan. Right at this moment I'm not interested in Kai's ethics. I have to appear before Macsen or worse, Huw, naked. What am I going to do?'

Dan looked at her blankly. 'Oh, I see what you mean. Can't you maybe plead extreme shyness? It worked with the bathhouse. They've never made you bathe with the others. They know our customs are different. Maybe we can say it's the ultimate dishonour for us to be naked in front of several hundred warriors or something.'

It might work. Ursula found her breathing was returning to normal.

'Dan, I don't want to go to Ireland. How can I get us home if I'm so far away from you? I don't want to have to be someone's wife and have babies and everything. I'm really scared.'

Dan looked at her. He couldn't bear to see her so upset.

'Even if you do have to show yourself naked you've proved yourself, Ursula, as a warrior. There aren't enough warriors. They might not make you go. You're not Combrogi, not really.' She could see him running through his mind the possibility of several hundred male warriors without their women knowing that Ursula was one. Dan blushed.

'You might have to kill a few before they left you alone.'

'I don't think Macsen would risk that. I think he'd send me away.'

'Don't worry about it. We may get away with it. I'll think of something.'

They walked to the bathhouse with heavy hearts. The Great Hall was filling up with warriors waiting to hear the judgement of the Queen.

Bryn had been loaned back to them for the ceremony.

He was very keen to tell them of Rhonwen's face, which he had seen without its mask. Ursula silenced him and made him explain what she had to do with the oil and everything necessary for the rite. Reluctantly Ursula bathed and anointed her body with it. Bryn had long ago ceased offering to help her. She got herself ready alone. At one point there was a huge roar from the Great Hall. Queen Usca had made her decision. She was no fool. It had been Macsen she had chosen as King. So it was to Macsen that Ursula would have to appear naked. It was a terrible, horribly embarrassing thought. She wanted to go home very, very badly. She could not even bring herself to imagine the humiliation she was about to undergo. There was no escape. When Kai's servant came she struggled to pull herself together. She decided on a strategy. She would be proud. She had played a man's game and won on men's terms. She was a warrior. She would not let herself down. She had proved herself any man's equal. What was wrong with being a woman anyway?

Dan watched her anxiously. Ursula had never looked less like a woman. Macsen and Huw and the others were in for a shock. She had her granite face on. Her blonde hair was oiled and scraped away from her face so that nothing detracted from the sharply defined planes of her face. She made a handsome-looking man, high cheekbones, firm jaw, piercing green eyes. Her muscles had bulked out quite incredibly in the months they had been with the Combrogi. Could she have always have had them? Had they just been hidden under fat before? It didn't seem likely. This world had done strange things to them both.

He and Ursula walked side by side to the end of the Hall. It was Macsen and Queen Usca who now sat together on the couch. Rhonwen, Cadal, Kai, Rhodri and Hane knelt next to them and the rest of the Combrogi sat in their characteristic lotus position in front of them. Dan and Ursula felt and looked terribly conspicuous walking through the seated mass. All eyes were on them: the outlanders who could fight like Combrogi warriors: Boar Skull and The Bear Sark. Bryn had tried to restrain Braveheart but he did not have the strength. There was laughter as the great dog broke free and squeezed himself between the outlanders. The loyalty of the late Madoc's Combrogi war dog only enhanced the status of the new warriors. There was general agreement that this time Rhonwen had done well. And if there were only two, they were better than nothing. They proved that outlanders could survive on Combrogi soil and even thrive, if they had the good sense to submit to the discipline of the tribes.

It seemed a long walk through the seated men to Macsen.

Kai prompted them to kneel.

Macsen looked impressive in his regal finery, even his

leather breastplate was gilded with elaborate swirls. Seated he still looked enormous to Dan. His eyes were warm and he whispered, 'You are welcome, Bear Sark, and you too, Boar Skull.' He then spoke formally to the assembled company. 'It pleases me that my first act of Kingship is to take the oath of these outlanders who have served the Combrogi well since the Princess Rhonwen called them through The Warrior's Veil. Let them show themselves ready to serve as warriors in traditional warrior dress.'

There was laughter at that, for once all the tribes had fought naked apart from their tribal tattoos. It was not useful when fighting armed and armoured Raven legionaries and the custom had more or less died out. Two servants helped Ursula and Dan disrobe. It was unnerving. Even Dan felt uncomfortable. He felt very exposed. To be naked, among so many elaborately clothed people! He felt acutely self-conscious and very un-warrior like. Ursula was like a block of stone. She was as much lost inside herself as ever Dan was in the midst of his bear sark phase. He shot her a worried glance. She did not acknowledge it. He tensed himself for the moment of truth. Neither of them had attempted to argue their way out of the ceremony. When it came to it, it was not something you could do. Dan waited. He held his breath, anticipating Macsen's cry of surprise. None came.

Rhodri stepped forward to paint Ursula's muscular forearms with the winding serpent of the tribe. Dan stared at Ursula in frank disbelief. The person standing next to him was as much a man as he was himself, if not more so. Ursula's face was closed and impassive. It did not seem as if she was really there. Dan did not know what to think.

'Stop!' It was Rhonwen's voice of command. 'This is no man.'

Queen Usca responded with a low chuckle.

'He'll do well enough for me!'

Macsen looked at Rhonwen in confusion. Ursula looked at Rhonwen with very cold eyes.

Macsen spoke in an undertone. 'What are you talking about? Kai, I fear my sister is unwell.'

Rhonwen's voice was edged with hysteria. 'This is an illusion.' She pointed a quivering finger at Ursula. 'This person is not a man.'

The men who'd trained with Ursula laughed at Rhonwen outright. The servant turned Ursula to face the assembled warriors for them to judge for themselves. There was a general foot-stamping, spear-banging assent to Ursula's masculinity. Several men began to make vulgar remarks concerning Rhonwen's experience of men but were inhibited by Macsen's icy glare.

Rhonwen stood up. Her green eyes flashed from within the silver of her impassive mask.

'I am a priestess of the new magic and I say this is an illusion.' If she was trying to prove it, she had no impact. Ursula remained a solid muscular male presence. She was unperturbed by Rhonwen's accusation. Was she even aware of it? Ursula seemed unlike herself in every way. Dan did not know what to do. Had Ursula always been a boy even at school? He thought back. Ursula was a girl in his own world of that he was sure. Here? Here he was sure of nothing. He remembered the stubble on Ursula's face when he kissed her and lapsed into confusion.

The room was in uproar. Respect for Macsen kept the laughter low but there was still a certain amount of spear banging and wisecracking among the warriors. Good mead was flowing and the warriors were in celebratory mood. The Combrogi had respect for their own rituals but Rhonwen's claim was too outrageous to be taken seriously. Kai was whispering to Rhonwen to sit down. The bard, who was seated nearby, had his hands clamped to his ears and was grimacing horribly. Kai looked uncomfortable. Rhonwen seemed intent on revealing what would not be revealed. She raised her arms as if to invoke powerful magic, then unexpectedly turned and ran from the room.

Silence descended on the assembly.

Macsen took control.

'We are here to accept the oaths of Ursula Alavna ab Helen, known as Boar Skull, and Daniel Alavna ab

181

George, known as The Bear Sark. Do you accept them as warriors of our people?'

There was a general roar of assent and Ursula and Dan bound themselves once again to a fight that was not theirs.

~ Chapter Eighteen ~

The Warrior Maid

Dan steeled himself not to flinch as Macsen signalled for the tattoos to be drawn on the exposed skin of the new warriors. Quite what his father would make of Combrogi body art on his return home he could not guess. He saw Rhodri, the tribal artist, out of the corner of his eye. He was checking the point on an evil-looking needle in readiness for his work. He reached forward to begin engraving Ursula's forearm. As his hand brushed her flesh, he cried out and leaped backwards with a curse.

'By Lugh! He's on fire!' He was breathing hard. When he raised his fingers to show Macsen there were raw red weals on his fingertips. His fingers were burned.

Ursula did not appear to have noticed. She did not move. Her face remained totally expressionless. She was as still as a rock. There was a smell of scorched flesh. Standing next to her Dan was suddenly aware of the dry heat emanating from her. What was going on now?

'Don't touch him!' The bard pushed his way to Macsen's side. 'I have heard of this happening. It is a kind of a fever – it will burn anyone who goes near him. Get him out into the cold. It is all you can do.'

The bard's voice was pitched low so as not to disturb the revellers in the Hall. Few people were still watching the ritual tattooing. It was a slow and lengthy process, a craftsman's work not a spectator sport. Most of the men were busying themselves with serious drinking. King Cadal and Queen Usca were deep in conversation. Macsen nodded tersely.

'The light is better in my chamber, Rhodri, we will continue this work there!" Macsen's voice was deliberately loud. There was some good-natured hissing and jibing at this unconventional move, but no one took a lot of notice.

The problem was to get Boar Skull out of the Hall. Ursula was totally unresponsive.

'Ursula!'

Not by the flicker of an eyelash did she indicate that she had heard.

Kai silently passed Dan his clothes.

'Make a show of putting these on. Keep Boar Skull from view." He mumbled. Then Kai unsheathed his sword. Dan's heart leaped. His own hand was on Bright Killer's hilt.

'Easy Bear Sark! I'll not hurt him but I'm not such

a fool as to touch him with my bare hands.'

Kai prodded Ursula lightly with the flat of his sword. The heat it conducted made him curse and wrap the hilt in Boar Skull's cloak. Ursula responded by moving forward. Unfortunately, for ease of defence there was only one entrance to the Great Hall. It was at the other end of the Hall. Macsen and the bard moved with one accord. The bard unslung his small harp from his back and began a popular ballad to an heroic ancestor of Macsen's. Macsen fell in behind him. Kai tried to steer Boar Skull to follow. She moved grudgingly, with the distracted look of a sleepwalker. Dan made an elaborate show of struggling into his garments to attempt to disguise Kai's actions from anyone interested enough to be bemused. Braveheart, Bryn and Rhodri completed the procession. Dan felt more than a little ridiculous but it got them out of the overcrowded Hall. The cool silence of the courtyard had never been more welcome. In the darkness, Ursula glowed with a red heat. Dan found he was trembling. It must have been shock.

Macsen was disturbed.

'Bard, Kai, what is going on? What caused my sister to act like that? And what is wrong with Boar Skull? I need Rhonwen to cement the alliance with Cadal. I do not have time for whatever this is.'

'There was a battle.' It was the soft low voice of the bard. 'This young warrior is in truth a young woman and

185

a powerful magician; more powerful than Rhonwen. Rhonwen tried to reveal the illusion. She could not because it is not an illusion. This woman has made herself a man. Only she can undo what she has done. It is an astonishing feat of power. Rhonwen tried to enter this one's mind. You have well named her Boar Skull. She is too strong. Magic is all Rhonwen has now. She cannot bear to be weaker than a girl, an outlander.'

The bard paused. Kai nodded.

'The bard speaks truly. I believe he is right. I could not have said it so well. I sometimes ... feel the magic. This is no illusion. Boar Skull is a man but by will not nature.'

Dan nodded. 'She was a girl in my world. She copied you, Kai. She tried to look like you so no one would send her with the women. She did not want to be a wife or a mother. She was afraid.'

Kai grinned and glanced at Ursula's sculpted semi-naked form. 'I think she flatters me.'

Macsen looked thoughtful. He did not register any surprise. 'If she has the gift of making things really change, not just seem changed, we need her more as a magician than we ever would a warrior. It is a hard power to master, as Rhonwen will tell you. What of this fever? Is that born of magic too? Do what you can for this warrior maid. I have to return to the Hall. This is a crucial moment for our plans. I have to persuade the tribal leaders that our only hope is to unite against the Ravens. Is there any news of Lud of the Brigantes?'

Kai shook his head. Macsen sighed. 'We need the Brigante tribe. They have more warriors than any other and they understand how the Ravens fight.'

'They ought to, they've fought for their interests often enough.' Kai's response was tart.

Macsen shot him a warning look and headed back into the Hall.

The warrior maid stood naked and unmoving where Kai had left her. It must have been November, though the Combrogi did not call it that. It was cold. The sea mist that shrouded Craigwen at this time of year made it seem colder still. Dan shivered. The red glow from Ursula's body began to fade.

'What happened to her?' Dan asked.

The bard answered distractedly. 'The fever? Oh, that is nothing, she overreached her power, that is all. She changed her true form and repelled Rhonwen's attempt to coerce her. It happened to the druids sometimes. That will not harm her. It is the shock that worries me, the fact that she does not know where she is. The fact that she hasn't spoken.'

'Can we take him er … her inside now?' Kai's voice was anxious. The moment the red glow faded from Ursula's skin he threw his cloak round her. 'We don't want his death from exposure. It's a raw night tonight,' he explained to no one in particular. The bard nodded. Kai guided Ursula's still uncooperative form into Macsen's chamber.

Dan wanted to touch her. He wanted to shake her. He needed to try and bring her back from wherever she'd gone. She had brought him out of his madness. He must find a way to do the same for her. He could not lose her as he had lost his mother. He had been too young to save his mother. He could not protect Lizzie any more. He had to be able to save Ursula. She was lost, he knew. She did not know what she had done. Poor Ursula.

Dan sat down heavily on the pallet heaped with furs that was Macsen's bed.

'Have you ever known anyone go into a shock like this?'

Kai seemed very upset. 'It happened with the other outlanders. Once or twice after we tried the Cup of Belonging. They could not accept that they were not where they belonged. They reacted like this and usually died before many nights. They would not eat or drink and we could not help them. I would not have had this happen to Boar Skull.'

The bard had strapped his harp on his back the minute they had left the Hall. He wore it like others wore their shields. He unstrapped it again.

'I may be able to get through to her. I have a magic of my own. She recognised it.'

He began to play. The tune seemed vaguely familiar to Dan, though he could not identify it. It soothed the tension from his strained limbs. It loosened the taut muscles of his neck and shoulders. It wound itself round his heart-strings and made him want to cry. He could not manage here without Ursula. She was his rock in his madness. He lurched across the small room towards her. He began to whisper to her. He held her stiff hand and murmured.

'It's OK, Ursula. Everything will be OK. Come back, Ursula. I need you here. You bound yourself by oath, remember. You said you'd fight for me, Ursula, and get me home. A promise binds in this world, you said so.' Dan felt a slight movement in Ursula's stiff hand. The music kept to its hypnotic pattern, swirling around with all the complexity of a Celtic design. It was like a design carved in sound, a mandala, forcing his thoughts into a pattern. It was pushing him towards that other place, the place he did not want to go. It was taking him to the cold place. He was slipping into it. Ursula!

'Dan!' It was Ursula's voice. Her strong hands were at his shoulders, shaking him. 'Don't you dare turn bear sark!'

He almost cried with relief. She knew him. She was all right.

He shook himself. The music had stopped. Kai was looking at Ursula with undisguised relief.

'Boar Skull, are you all right?'

'Yes. I wasn't. It was awful.' Ursula sounded frightened. 'I was in this numbing, grey place but Dan was turning bear sark and he called to me.' She paused and sighed, shakily. 'Ages ago I promised him I would fight for him. When I said it I was thinking about helping fight the madness when it comes and he doesn't want it. I remembered the promise and then the greyness went and I was back, here. I'm all right now, I think. I'm cold.' Rhodri passed her a drinking horn of warm mead. For once the sweetness was welcome. She was helped to the warmth of the bed. Kai had a quiet word with the bard and with Rhodri and Bryn. What had happened to Boar Skull was not to be talked about. No one argued and they left. People didn't argue with Kai.

'Ursula, they know.' Dan sat with her, almost overcome with relief that she was no longer stone.

'Know what?'

'Know that you've made yourself a man.'

'Oh that.' She said it coolly as if the discovery had not thrown her into a near catatonic state.

'It was a bit of a shock,' she smiled weakly. 'I didn't know I could do that and worse I didn't know that I had done it. Rhonwen tried to reveal me but she couldn't. She wasn't very happy about it. Where is she? My headache's gone, has she?'

'She ran out. Ursula, can you make yourself a girl again?' Dan's voice was anxious.

'Why?' Ursula's voice was flat.

Dan was taken aback. 'Well I just …'

'I'd like to bathe and just relax for a minute. Does Macsen know?'

Dan nodded.

'He's not going to send me to Ireland?'

Kai interrupted. 'If you are stronger than Rhonwen, the King will not have you out of his sight. His family has paid dearly for the power of the new magic. He wants a say in the use of it. He will find a way to use you and your magic.'

Ursula nodded wearily, though Dan was sure she had as little idea of what Kai was talking about as he did. She dragged herself to her feet. She had made herself into an Adonis of a man. She wrapped herself in the ritual garments unself-consciously and headed for the bathhouse alone.

'What do you mean "paid dearly for the power of the new magic"?' Dan asked.

Kai sighed. 'Bear Sark, I am unused to women becoming men and nearly dying in the process. I am going to sit here quietly with my drink. Strange things often happen at Samhain but it is some time since I have seen anything as strange as this.' He noticed the worry in Dan's face.

'Don't look so apprehensive. I don't think what happened to Lovernios, Macsen's brother, has anything to do with Ursula, but ask the bard. I only know that after the Ravens killed most of the druids, there was some attempt to perform the most powerful ritual. Lovernios was involved. Macsen won't speak of it.'

It was at that moment that Ursula returned. She had emerged from the bathhouse a different person. Both of them stared at her silently.

'What?' She had blushed scarlet at their attention. She had lost the incredible musculature, though she was still strong-looking for a woman. Her face had softened. The angles were as sharp, the high cheekbones, the jaw, but she looked different, prettier. The body wrapped in the ritual white bleached tunic was definitely female. Dan and Kai both looked embarrassed.

Kai leapt to his feet. 'I should get you something else to wear, Ursula.' The name came uncomfortably to his tongue. He had only ever called her Boar Skull.

'Kai, I'm still Boar Skull. I can go back to being a man again if it's easier. I know what I did to make it happen. I willed it so. I was desperate to be a successful warrior and to be strong. I can will it again, if you want it. I can will lots of things now.'

Ursula closed her eyes and in front of Kai and Dan transformed herself into an exceptionally pretty redhead, with a cascade of shoulder-length hair. The face remained Ursula's, just plumper. The expression in her green eyes was wicked. Kai looked very uncomfortable. Dan was simply staggered. When Dan recovered his equanimity he was struck by a sudden thought.

'Ursula, didn't you use to have blue eyes?'

'Of course. I still have.'

Staring into her emerald eyes as strangely-coloured as Rhonwen's, Dan found himself quite unable to argue.

~ Chapter Nineteen ~

The Bard on the Battlements

Dan went in search of the bard to thank him for helping to recover Ursula. He was vaguely conscious that he had been skilfully manipulated into almost turning bear sark. Somehow the bard had realised that Ursula would respond to Dan's need if not to her own. It was strange. Ursula's face gave so little away. Dan sometimes doubted that she even liked him and yet it was her loyalty to him that had been strong enough to save her. Ursula confused and bemused him at every turn. He had to get away from her for a while. She was trying out a variety of female forms to the amusement of Kai. She did not seem able to make herself physically smaller but she was perfectly capable of changing shape quite dramatically. Dan found it hard to recognise his mate Ursula in the various female guises that had appeared in front of his eyes. He did not like what those forms made him feel. He did not want to feel those things for Ursula, or maybe he did. He was confused. He had grown to rely on Boar Skull, his training partner, his friend. He hadn't thought too much about Boar Skull's gender, it hadn't mattered. He was disturbed to find it mattering a lot.

In the Hall Macsen was receiving oaths of allegiance from other tribal leaders. The drinking horns still circulated and there was a notable mellowing of mood. Gwyn and Prys stood behind Macsen as bodyguard. There was no sign of Rhonwen, though Cadal still sat next to Queen Usca on Macsen's couch. The bard was tuning his harp alone at one side of the room. Dan was greeted and welcomed by several warriors as he made his way towards the bard. 'The Bear Sark is it? I hear you are quite a fighter. We'll have to test you against my champion here one of these days.'

'Bear Sark, drink with us. Now you're a warrior you'll have to learn to drink like one.'

'Ah, it's our tame madman. Well done, Bear Sark, we're glad to have you with us!'

'What, no tattoos yet? What is that fool Rhodri thinking of? You've earned them. Make sure he doesn't forget to do them. The old ways are still worth something.'

Dan was comforted by the warmth that engulfed him. The older grizzled warriors greeted him as a high achieving nephew. Rhodri and Caradoc were as pleased by his new status as if Dan were their own brother. They were proud of him and it was a good feeling. He reached the bard after much hearty back-patting and arm-clasping. He felt quite choked by it. His own family, well, his own father anyway, had not been in much of a state to praise him for a long time. If it were not for the painful thought of his sister, Lizzie, who needed him, and whom he had abandoned, he would have been happy to stay with these hard-living barbarians. The Combrogi knew death waited for them, was never further than a sword's blow away. Because of that they made every second count. Emotion was never far below the surface. What they felt they acted upon.

The bard looked up at him expectantly. Dan spoke. 'I came to thank you for bringing Ursula back. I owe you a debt, if my sword can serve you?' It was the way they said things here, but the bard held him back with an admonishing hand.

'You are already too many times oath-bound, Daniel. It is no wonder you can only be free in your madness. I want no oath from you. You have already given the only oath that counts to the Combrogi. I am not like Ursula. I can weave only simple magics but I can see what I can see. You and she could save us. There is a deep bond between you. Together you amount to something, something that might save us. If only you stay together. She has mastered the magic of her own body. Not even the druids could do that. It is time she tried to change the world.'

196

Dan had begun to trust his instincts and his instincts urged him to trust the bard, even though Dan had no idea what he was talking about.

'I want to understand more … about this magic. Can it hurt her? Kai spoke of paying for the power. He spoke of Macsen's brother, Lovernios?'

The bard's eyes darkened at the name. 'I fear to talk of dead druids on such a night as this. I have to sing for Queen Usca now. Meet me at the battlements when I have finished.'

Dan nodded. Something in the bard's tone frightened him. Did the dead really walk here at Samhain?

'I will meet you …' Dan paused. In a world where names were so important it seemed impolite to style him merely "bard". 'I do not know your name.'

'I am called Taliesin. I will speak with you soon.'

He returned to his harp and Dan knew he was dismissed. The name stirred a memory, but he might have heard Kai or one of the others talk of him.

It was cold on the battlements and eerie. Dan had chosen to stand a little way from the watch on the seaward side of the fortress. The great breakers of an autumn sea crashed against the rocks of Craigwen. In the darkness the white crested waves formed ghostly shapes in the dark night. He wished it were not Samhain.

'Daniel?'

'Here, by the wall.'

'The shades are out in force tonight.'

'You can see them?'

'Of course. You can't?' Dan shook his head, grateful for his lack of perception.

'You wanted to know about the druid Prince, Lovernios, Macsen's brother?'

'Yes. No, well, I don't know. I just want to know more about magic. Is Ursula in danger from it?'

'Everyone is in danger, my friend. It is the human condition.' He paused as if gathering his strength together. 'Few people know about Lovernios. It was the secret we kept from the Ravens; our hope for the ultimate victory. Only time will tell if we were right. What do you know of the druids?'

'They were priests, magicians?'

'You are almost right.' Taliesin opened his arm to embrace the whole scene, the open battlements, the wild seascape in a dramatic gesture. 'Everyone knows that this, all of this, is just one world among many. Worlds touch in places and the walls between them are thin. Tonight the world of the dead and the living meet as you could see, were you sensitive to such things. The druids found some of the ways between these worlds. Rhonwen talks of a veil between worlds. The druids talked instead of bridges. The world of the gods and the spirits of the trees and the pools of this land cross and recross this one and those who have learned how can walk the bridges between them. For the druids all the bridges they knew were toll-bridges. You could cross but only if you paid. They paid in blood, rarely theirs, and in other things – gold sometimes. The sacred groves were places of bridges and if you paid the toll the right way you could cross or allow the spirits to cross over to this world and do your will.'

It was fortunate that it was too dark for the bard to see Dan's expression of frank incomprehension.

'Of course if the toll was a sacrifice it had to be done the right way. There are seven hundred sacred cuts alone. They varied with the age and sex of the victim.'

'The druids sacrificed people?' Dan was all attention and horror. Taliesin was surprised by his surprise.

'Of course, blood fuelled the magic of the druids, it was its price. Blood and gold were the roots of druid power. The Ravens disliked the power the druids exerted. Their word was law. Macsen would not have had this trouble uniting the tribes if there had been enough druids behind him. Even warriors faltered at a druid's word, for they had power in the world of the dead as in the living.'

Dan found that his mouth was dry. The Combrogi practised human sacrifice. He shivered and not just from the cold. He was not sure he wanted to know more.

'What has this to do with Macsen and his brother?'

'The Ravens destroyed all the holy places, Mona and Llyn Cerrig Bach and the sacred groves. They slaughtered druids by the thousand. They took the gold and in months destroyed the knowledge of centuries. I know little of the druids' mysteries. I do know that Prince Macsen's brother, the druid Prince, was the last hope.'

'What do you mean?'

'You must know that the Ravens came here for conquest and for wealth. If we did not oppose them and gave them their taxes they would let us be, but the druids had wealth and power and the Ravens were afraid. The Ravens bought allies where they could. Our friends the Brigantes have long been client kings. The Ravens fought those they could not buy: the Silures and the Ordovices. They were nearly defeated by Boudicca of the Iceni and the Trinovantes. Then, after they sacked our most sacred place, Mona, the Ravens killed 80,000 men, women and children at the place they call Mancetter. The harvest failed. There were few left to gather what little there was and many of us starved. They were desperate times. Macsen was too young to fight and lucky enough to be far from the worst of it, but he remembers. We all remember. Those who could escaped to Ireland. Those few druids who still live are there, too old now to do much. Lovernios hid in Ireland, but as the situation got more desperate, he devised a plan to save us. I should not have been allowed to be involved, but I was young, too young to be a druid and unmarked by the ritual signs. I helped get Prince Lovernios to this island. Too many people, whose names I must not say, died to get us to Lindow.' His voice cracked with emotion.

'The Ravens were killing anyone from the rebel tribes, all warriors, boy children, anyone who might have touched the hand of a druid. We picked a sacred place that was almost unknown, as far as possible from occupied territory, but close enough to the old roads. It was Beltain. It had to be Beltain, a day of sacred power. We had baked oakcakes and burned just one, the old symbol of the chosen. He who picked the burned piece would be sacrificed.'

Taliesin stopped. The chill wind had dropped.

'Even the spirits of our dead remember and are listening.' He stared at something Dan could not see and smiled a wan smile. 'It was bravely done. Macsen has something of his brother's greatness.' The bard's eyes shone with tears. Dan could see them in the dim moonlight. The night was suddenly very still, as if the whole of Craigwen, even the tide and the moonlit cliffs, waited on Taliesin's words.

'It had to be Lovernios because he was the best of the Combrogi. He was physically perfect, fully trained in the druidic ways, gifted and of royal blood. He gave himself gladly. He was killed in the most sacred way. I cannot tell you how, it touched on the mysteries and anyway I cannot bear to remember. It was not painless and it went on for a long time. He never cried out and when it was over we laid him in the holy pool for the gods. Those involved scattered and waited for the gods' response. We could find none. The Ravens tightened their grip. Reinforcements came and they have hunted us like animals ever since. If we are not enslaved and shipped abroad to fight for the Ravens in other lands, we are killed unless we pledge loyalty to the emperor and deny our gods. I heard of Alavna. You were there. I do not need to paint you a picture.'

That was true enough. Dan was too familiar with the retribution of Ravens.

'So what happened then?'

'Nothing. We had hoped that the gods would respond to such a sacred sacrifice. But the gods of this land were deaf to us. They did not rise up to oust the Ravens from this Sacred Isle. For the Combrogi there has been only despair until now.' The bard stopped, as tears choked him. 'Dan, I'm sorry, I can talk no more of these things tonight. The spirits of so many of our dead crowd around me. Go to Ursula. Don't let her leave Macsen's chamber until the dawn. I would not have her see what I can see tonight. Such sadness! Such waste! We will talk again I promise.'

The bard picked up his harp and as Dan turned to leave he could hear its plaintive strains. He was no wiser really. He still did not know what the bard's tale had to do with Ursula. He did not waste time in speculation. He hurried to Macsen's chamber and the warm glow of the firelight. The knowledge that the unseen ghosts of the Combrogi dead haunted the night was enough to make the hairs rise on the back of his neck. He gripped Bright Killer firmly. It was a futile gesture. How could he defend himself against the dead?

~ Chapter Twenty ~

King Cadal's Demand

It was not necessary for Dan to defend himself against the dead. He returned to Macsen's chamber without incident. Ursula was sleeping on Macsen's pallet when Dan returned. Kai stood guard. He offered Dan a drink of warm watered mead which Dan accepted gladly. They drank in companionable silence.

'Our Boar Skull is full of surprises,' Kai said at length. Dan looked at her sleeping form and found it impossible to see any sign of the warrior Boar Skull.

'She fights well though,' Dan said, wanting Kai to know that even as a woman she was worthy of respect. He had misunderstood the Combrogi yet again.

'Combrogi women have always been great fighters. It is courage that buys victory not vast strength. It grieves us all that our women could not fight beside us now. It does a man good to fight for his land with his wife beside him. After the slaughter of Mancetter when so many

Combrogi died King Donicca ruled that he would protect our women if nothing else. It is wise but if I am to die in battle I would rather spend my last night on this earth in the arms of my wife than alone. She would say the same too if you could ask her.' Dan had not known that Kai had a wife. Kai looked sad. In an effort to cheer himself up he changed the subject.

'Watch that Boar Skull girl of yours. You will have a fair few good men to kill if she makes a habit of shape shifting like she just has. Combrogi blood is hot enough to give her trouble and she has not the sense a woman should have.'

Dan feared Kai was right. It was a novelty for Ursula to be beautiful and with her newly discovered power she could certainly be that.

Macsen's unceremonious entry ended their conversation.

'There's no sign of Rhonwen, and Lud of the Brigantes has not arrived. We need him and we need her. She may have gone to Lud herself. She was talking about it on the road. We've heard rumours that he intends to break his word to me about backing us. It would be too easy for him to follow in the footsteps of his treacherous vixen of a mother Cartimandua and stay with the carrion.' Macsen nearly spat his disgust.

'What am I to do with her?' he indicated the peaceful form of Ursula.

'I'm not sure I can keep her here. Rumours are bound to surface about what she is. Why did Rhonwen not realise she had this power? Did you know? There is so much we could have done with the power she can wield.'

Kai looked grave.

'I glimpsed something in the Cup. No one has ever resisted the sharing of it all before, but no I was suspicious of her but I did not guess why. I am sorry, Macsen. I did not think of it.'

Macsen waved an impatient hand. 'What's done is done, Kai. I shan't waste more thoughts upon it, but I won't hide from you our situation. If Rhonwen does not agree to marry Cadal and breaks faith we are in trouble. I don't think he's going to break his end of the bargain, even after what has happened to her. Cadal is a better man than I thought or he is playing a game I've not fathomed yet. But without the support of the Brigantes it's looking very tight. The legion has been training hard. Everyone knows what's at stake. If they overcome us then the tribes are finished. These Ravens have some fine tricks to defeat a siege. I've learned much these last few moons and I'm not confident we can do it. I'm not sure the tribes have grasped the desperation of it.'

Macsen's handsome face was taut with fatigue and tension. Nervous energy poured out of him with his words. He could not keep still. One pace of his long legs brought him to Ursula.

'It is a pity to wake her. She is very young, don't you think? Perhaps if Cadal would take a sorceress rather than a princess priestess?' Dan's look of horror was reflected briefly in Kai's face.

Macsen sighed. 'No, you are right. He would not and she will be more use to us here if she can learn more of the magic in time.'

Dan did not like the way Macsen spoke of Ursula as if she existed only for his convenience. It was the way his father sometimes spoke of him and of Lizzie. He could feel the cold anger begin to grip him. He fought it. This was not the time.

'Prince Macsen.' It was hard to speak. The cold madness drew him and he could feel himself slipping. 'Ursula has bound herself by oath to you but she is her own man.' Or did he mean woman? Thoughts were becoming frozen in the ice. 'Give her some respect.'

It was the bard who saved him. He had entered the room a moment behind Macsen. Something had changed. Even through the growing coldness he could see it. Taliesin had left behind his melancholy of the battlements and was all business. His soft voice disrupted Dan's steady descent into his killing place.

'My Lord, King Macsen, King Cadal has asked me to beg you to find the Princess Rhonwen. He is concerned for her safety and wishes to return with his bride and Queen Usca on the next tide. This time of year the sea can be stormy and my weather sense warns me of imminent bad weather. It was only the urgency of our need to confer you in your Kingship that caused him to sail at such a dangerous season.' The bard's great dignity made his words seem more gracious than they might have done.

'Yes, of course.' Macsen visibly searched for courtesies he did not feel. That he was under serious pressure was evident to Dan and must have been as clear to Cadal's perceptive bard. 'We are grateful for King Cadal's haste in accompanying my esteemed grandmother across such dangerous seas at this time. I will leave at once to search for the Princess Rhonwen, though if she is on her way to King Lud of the Brigantes, I will not find her quickly. King Cadal must know that Rhonwen's mission is to help us defeat the Ravens. It is a noble cause and she is fearless in its service. She will not fail to return to him. She is honourable and has promised her consent to the marriage.'

The bard bowed and left with a swift, concerned glance at Dan. Dan was trembling from the closeness of his brush with madness. Macsen appeared unaware or at any rate unconcerned by Dan's condition. Macsen spoke abruptly to Kai. He seemed to lack the time or the strength to speak in anything other than a rapid staccato.

'Have the girl ready to ride by next watch. I will take her with me and Gwyn, Huw and Prys as my honour guard. I dare not leave Huw here either. Who knows what mischief he could ferment among our reluctant allies. It's a bad time for me to leave but I have to keep Cadal happy. Our women and children depend on his goodwill. Kai, old friend, I need you here to make preparations. I have not told you the worst of it yet. I have just had intelligence that the Ravens are on the march. Suetonius has sent orders. He cares more for finishing us than for ensuring the security of Deva. They will be here before the winter. We have weeks not months to prepare. If the men are not too far gone in their cups, we must have a Council of War before I leave. Oh, Kai! It is too soon. We are too few. I'm not sure we can survive this.'

Macsen's face was a study of anguish. Kai put his hand on Macsen's shoulder in a gesture of comfort.

'Every man will fight, Macsen, with everything he has. You can ask no more of us than that we will gladly give. It will have to be enough.' Macsen nodded and clasped Kai's proffered arm, then swept from the room. Dan had the strong feeling he had forgotten that Dan was there. Kai had not.

'I don't trust Huw with either the King or with Boar Skull. And as for King Lud of the Brigantes,' Kai made a derisory sound, deep in the back of his throat. 'He has only ever supported the interests of King Lud of the Brigantes. He would only give us aid if we were certain to defeat the Ravens. The odds are not that good. Huw is not without friends in the Brigantes camp. He has nothing to lose by trying to gain credit with them. He has none here. A young warrior who followed the royal party may find himself with an opportunity to serve the King, especially if he had an experienced tracker like Bryn or Braveheart. I will arrange for you to borrow my war horse and make sure that the watch will let you out. Bryn will know what to do for the rest.' Kai's gaze was steady. 'This smells wrong. I don't know what Rhonwen is playing at. This is the wrong moment for Macsen to leave. The men need him here.' He caught Dan's uncertain glance at the still sleeping Ursula. 'Don't worry, I'll make sure Ursula leaves here as Boar Skull. If she knows Huw is her travelling companion she'll need no persuasion.'

'Taliesin said for her to stay here until dawn because of Samhain.'

'So the bard has been haunted this night too, has he? Don't worry, Macsen will not need her before dawn. He has much to do.'

Kai's concern for the King shocked Dan. Was he missing something? What exactly did Kai expect to happen? Was Kai expecting treachery? Kai was busy instructing servants. With more unanswered questions than ever Dan left to sort things out with Bryn.

~ Chapter Twenty-one ~

The Druid's Gift

It was in fact late afternoon by the time Ursula, Huw, Prys, Gwyn and Macsen rode out from Craigwen. Rhonwen had taken a couple of horses with her but no servants. Macsen was furious at her foolhardiness and struggled unsuccessfully to hide his anger from her prospective husband. It was to be devoutly wished that Cadal valued bravery and decisiveness in a bride.

Macsen's War Council had been brief enough. All Combrogi were instructed to move to the fortress and prepare for siege.

As Kai had predicted Ursula needed no persuasion to reconstruct herself as the muscular Boar Skull. If anything she had made herself even bigger, and struggled to fit into her leather breastplate. She had to be strongly discouraged from growing a warrior's moustache on the grounds of serious implausibility. Those who did not know of her power would not believe that even Boar Skull could have grown a moustache overnight.

Dan watched her leave with a sense of foreboding. He was not looking forward to more time on the open road. He would be alone but for Bryn and Braveheart. He felt responsible for both of them and very unequal to the task of keeping them and Ursula safe against unknown dangers. He was also worried about the increasing ease with which he turned bear sark. He mounted Kai's best horse and slipped quietly away from the fortress with a very unhappy heart. He had no trouble leaving. Kai had, as he had promised, warned the watch.

It was difficult to leave Craigwen due to the steepness of the natural cliff on which it was built. It was a bit of a scramble. He fell off his horse once or twice and grazed his knees, which made Bryn giggle. Bryn was more or less born in the saddle. There was no way he would ever fall off his pony. It was not an auspicious beginning to Dan's first task as a warrior.

There was someone waiting at the foot of the escarpment. A horse whinnied and Dan reached for his sword. Braveheart flicked his ears back against his head and sniffed the air. Surely the enemy had not come this close? Would a Raven scout stand mounted in daylight in full view of the fortress? Dan made Bryn get behind him. The boy's excitement was obvious. He was totally fearless because he was with The Bear Sark. He was eager as a puppy and his exuberance just made Dan more acutely aware of his responsibilities.

Dan dismounted. Leaving the reins in Bryn's willing hands he walked to the mounted man. He had not fought a mounted man before and part of his brain calculated angles and sword lengths. He did that all the time now even when at rest. Perhaps that was why when he fought he didn't need to think about such things consciously. He pre-programmed himself with his constant awareness of tactical possibilities.

The man was not tall. He was swathed in a dark cloak so it was hard to tell what weapons he carried. Dan decided to take control.

'Who goes there?' It was the Combrogi challenge. Literally translated it meant "Who is it that stands at the entrance to my lands?"

'There is no need to attack me, Daniel Bear Sark. It's the bard, Taliesin. Kai thought you could do with company.'

Dan trusted the bard. After their conversation on the battlements he felt close to him but Kai's worries were contagious. If he was wrong about the bard's trustworthiness then he had hesitated for what he knew was long enough for a spear to gut him. No spear came.

'Why did Kai not speak to me?'

'Kai trusts us both, Daniel. He told you to speak to me, did he not? You need fear nothing from me. I am King Cadal's man. If anyone should help look for Rhonwen it

213

should be me. Rhonwen is part of Cadal's bargain. He wants her bloodline in his children's veins. Her magic is a gift he wishes his sons to be blessed with. I am here to see her found. I have no quarrel with Macsen. If he can defeat the Ravens then all of us live to see another day.'

Dan was not sorry to travel with another man. He did not know if the bard could fight but at least he was another adult. Dan knew exactly the moment he had left childhood behind and entered adulthood. It was the moment he had found Bryn's sister. He feared another moment like that, like Alavna. He did not want to meet it alone except for Bryn and Braveheart.

' "OK" as they say in my country. We will travel together, but if there is a fight stay out of my way. I know you know, but I am a true bear sark. I have not killed an ally yet, but it could happen.'

The bard nodded. 'I know what you are, Daniel. I can help you if you like. A bard learns many things in a long training. Things we do not sing of. You may be grateful that I found you. There are few of us left since the Ravens can't tell the difference between bard and druid and have killed the lot of us off.'

Dan signalled for Bryn to join him and mounted his horse.

'You never told me what all that stuff about Lovernios has to do with Ursula's magic.'

'I was trying to. Some of us believe that the power

Rhonwen uses is a gift of the gods. Maybe it was bought with Lovernios' blood or maybe it was given as a result of his self-giving; that is something of a theological debate among the ageing druids in Ireland. It doesn't matter. It is the gift that is important. When the druids heard about Rhonwen raising the Veil they sent me to persuade Cadal to help Macsen so that I could investigate. Cadal is keen to help. If his children have magic he will be the most important chief in all Ireland. We none of us want to believe that our druid Prince sacrificed himself for nothing.'

'So?'

'Rhonwen has power, but I don't think she can save us, but she brought us Ursula and I think with your help she can.'

'But … how?'

The bard said nothing. Dan carried on.

'How does she have the gift, though? How do you know it is the same as Rhonwen's?'

The bard sighed. 'It is hard to explain. I just know it and Kai knows too. Kai was never a druid but many in his family have been. He has something of a druid's sensitivity. Ursula's power is of the same kind as Rhonwen's but stronger. It is a new magic. I would like to think it comes from the druids' death.'

Dan was silent. It all seemed wildly improbable. He had been forced to believe in Ursula's very real power when he saw her naked in the Great Hall. Believing it was difficult for him. It went against every concept he had of the way the world worked. Ursula's magic was so immediate, so undeniable, it upset him greatly and he preferred not to think about it.

They rode on, far enough behind the King's party as not to cause attention. Bryn for all his youth was an experienced tracker and Macsen was not attempting to disguise his trail. They rode all the hours of daylight. They spoke little. Dan was deep in thought. When it became fully dark they camped some distance from Macsen. The smoke from his fire was clearly visible. They camped without a fire, in a dry ditch. Once more Dan was grateful for his huge hound's warmth. It was still not a good way of spending the night.

'Do you want a song to soothe you, Bear Sark?' Taliesin whispered over the sleeping head of Bryn.

Dan grunted.

'I don't want a song. I want some real answers. I have been thinking. How can Ursula's power save the Combrogi? I don't see that because she changed her shape it follows that she can save anybody. I don't understand what you mean. You must have something in mind. What do you want Ursula to do with her power?'

There was a long pause as if Taliesin was weighing up Dan's likely reaction. Dan was suddenly aware that to the bard, he represented serious danger. The bard knew how easily a threat to Ursula could turn him bear sark. It had nearly happened when Macsen did not speak of her with enough respect. Dan did not want to kill the bard. The pause lengthened. At last Taliesin spoke. His voice was a whisper.

'Ursula has to find a bridge between worlds, raise "the Warrior's Veil" and either let us through or bring something else out. Something that will fight for us.'

'Something more than just Ursula and me?'

'You are not nothing, Bear Sark, as you well know, but you are not enough. A few thousand of you would do better.'

'And this is dangerous?'

'Rhonwen survived it. But yes, I think it probably is.'

'Thank you for being honest.'

'You deserve nothing less.'

Dan had not turned bear sark. That was good. The danger had passed. The bard yawned and soon the quietness of the night was disturbed by his even breathing.

They had not agreed it but Dan presumed he had first watch. He could not have slept anyway. He ran through in his mind all that the bard had told him about magic and the druids. The dark shadow of druid belief chilled his soul. He was bound by oaths he believed in to a people that not only took decapitated heads from their enemies but had practised human sacrifice. They wanted to use Ursula's power in a way he was sure was dangerous. Were the Celts really the good guys? He remembered Alavna and Bryn's beautiful sister. Good or bad he was on their side against the Ravens who had to be worse. If they were not, how could he live with himself?

~ Chapter Twenty-two ~

Betrayed!

U rsula could not sleep. The power of the land surged through her uncontrollably, as if just by existing she completed some electrical circuit. She wanted to ride all night. She knew Rhonwen was near. Ursula's head ached. She could dimly sense Rhonwen's continual pain and something else. It felt like fear.

Macsen insisted on resting the horses. Ursula could see his own exhaustion and near despair running marrow-deep inside him. Nervous energy and will-power drove him on. Common sense made him rest. He lay next to her by the fire. Sleeping, he looked younger. He was probably no more than twenty. Ursula knew he had little expectation of making twenty-one.

Huw was on first watch. Ursula did not trust him. She was rather surprised that Macsen did. She feigned sleep. She lay listening to the noises of the night, convinced that she could hear rustling and the anxious movements of the horses. She was not imagining it. Someone approached. Magic had made her hearing more acute. Her guts told her she was right. They churned. She reached for her sword. Huw was two or three metres away, doing what? Investigating? He was whispering to someone. She counted the number of sleeping forms. Gwyn, Prys and Macsen all slept. Who could he be talking to? Himself? Huw had not the imagination. Ursula was not good at moving quietly but crouched low and did her best. It was very dark away from the firelight but magic helped her there too. She could see once the memory of the firelight left her eyes. She did not want to wake the others if there was no reason. She strained her ears. They were speaking Latin. Most of the warriors had a smattering of the language. Kai and Macsen spoke it well. Because she had shared the Cup of Belonging with them, so did Ursula.

' … No more than two weeks' march.' It was not Huw's voice. This was harsh and guttural.

'We're tracking the sorceress. You have her?' That was Huw's voice. Ursula could only see a dark form and the glint of something metal catch the firelight.

Distance and a difficult accent muffled the man's voice.

' … Lud … sure of him. He is happy to live a civilised life for the price of a few taxes … two days' ride. What of Macsen?'

Huw's response to the unknown voice was chilling.

220

'You could take him now. He has only a couple of guards with him.'

Ursula felt sudden fear course through her. Macsen was asleep and undefended. Why had she not woken him? She got her sword ready and opened her mouth to shriek an alarm only to feel a burly arm compress her windpipe and the cold metal of a gladius nick the skin of her neck. For a short sword it was quite long enough to do what it needed to. She cursed herself inventively. She had been straining so hard to hear Huw she had failed to hear the arrival of the Raven scout. What if through her carelessness Macsen were to die?

She could feel the hot breath of the man on her neck. She had not dropped her sword. The man was small and wiry, that much she could tell from his arm. She doubted he could match her for strength. She could elbow him hard and wind him but the movement of her shoulder would get her throat cut. Whatever she did to him, he could slit her throat before she could disable him. Would he slit it anyway?

There was a scuffling, and a whinnying of horses. Several Ravens were approaching the camp. A dog howled. Braveheart? She thanked the God of this world. Instantly, Macsen was on his feet and so were Gwyn and Prys. They slept fully armed. However many men they had to face if they were armed and ready they might live. They stood a chance. Her earlier warning would not

221

have changed the odds. Each of them had their backs to the fire. Three against how many? She could not see. The firelight dazzled her. All beyond it was mere shadow and unknown threat.

Huw was suddenly in front of her. He was standing up. She was still crouching. He kicked her sharply in the ribs with his booted foot. His smile was full of razors. She could hear the pleasure in his voice as he spoke to her attacker.

'Don't kill him. I want to make this one beg.' The man with his sword against her throat released her with a chuckle. It was the last sound he ever made. Ursula moved quickly. The instant he removed the gladius from her neck she hit him hard in the solar plexus with her elbow. He did not expect the force of her blow and his sword hung uselessly at his side. He was winded and surprised. Before he could raise his sword, she had time to turn and raise hers. She was half standing now and had enough room to swing it in a powerful arc before it bit home at his unprotected neck. She had not given him enough time to recover. He slumped to the ground; his neck all but severed. Something welled from the massive wound and pooled around his head. It was too dark to see but it must have been blood. Hane's training worked. Ursula did not baulk at what she had done; she raised her sword again. Huw watched in frozen horror. He had missed his moment. Had Huw intervened when she had attacked his ally, Huw could have killed her. The thought was like the touch of an icy blade down her back. She could not have fought the two of them. Now he was at her mercy. He held his sword limply in his hand. He stared at her slack jawed and then ran. Ursula watched him run. She would not waste time in chasing him. Macsen might need her. Ursula got to her feet ready to run to Macsen's side. There was a throng of armed Ravens storming the small group of Combrogi. Macsen was hard-pressed and his bodyguards were too busy defending themselves to be able to move nearer to his side. Ursula began to run towards him, when a tall slender man sprinted from the cover of the undergrowth and stationed himself at Macsen's side. Dan! He was bear sark. She could tell even from that distance. He unsheathed Bright Killer, which trembled in the firelight like a living flame. In Dan's hands it became a blazing flame of death, flickering, swift as a tongue of fire. All touched by it died where they stood. The four warriors spread out to form a defensive ring around the fire. Ursula willed it to blaze more fiercely to protect their backs. They were outnumbered. That much was clear, but the enemy came more cautiously now. Dan's presence tilted the balance. Braveheart stood by his side and defended his left side. His jaws and unusual height served only to encourage the enemy more directly onto Dan's sword arm and the searing force of Bright Killer.

223

The enemy did not rush in so recklessly but weighed their moves and tried to calculate Macsen's weakness. The Raven scouts did not lack courage. They had been ordered to kill the tall prince and they did what they could. They died well but cheaply, no one got close enough to Macsen to draw his blood. Ursula did not think they needed her there. She did not want to prove the weak spot in the Combrogi wheel of bright knives.

She was distantly aware that her headache had returned. Perhaps it had been back for a while and she had just not noticed it. Rhonwen must be near. Had she heard the Raven talking with Huw say they had captured Rhonwen? The conversation had only been half heard but the headache was proof enough. A part of her was aware that she had killed a man but the wild energy of magic would not let her stop to consider it. She let the magic lead her. She ran from the battle, her mind focused on Rhonwen. Her long legs quickly put distance between her and the firelight fight. She could no longer hear the clash of swords and the howls of Braveheart. There was movement off to her left. Her sword was ready.

'Boar Skull!' It was Bryn and King Cadal's bard.

'I heard noises. The Bear Sark went to investigate. Is he all right? Braveheart's gone too. Dan made me promise to stay here and protect the bard.' Bryn's face was contorted with misery, equal parts anger at being left behind and fear for Dan's safety.

'We were tracked by Raven scouts. Huw was on watch. He spoke to them and did not give the warning. He's run off. I think the Ravens may have got Rhonwen.' Ursula's voice was surprisingly calm.

'What of The Bear Sark?' Bryn's voice was strangled with anxiety.

'Don't worry, Bryn. He's being a bear sark and killing everything that moves. I hope the others keep out of his way.' Ursula's voice was confident. Bryn's face relaxed, fractionally.

'Do you know where Rhonwen is?' The bard's voice was a whisper of concern.

'I think I can find her. I can sort of feel her if I concentrate. As I get nearer my headache gets worse.'

Odd though this statement was no one made any comment.

'We will come with you. You may need help.'

Ursula would have liked to say no. She still did not like the thought of Bryn being involved in violence, but he was Combrogi and for the Combrogi it seemed to be a fact of existence. She could not protect him from that. She nodded her head. Bryn expertly hobbled the horses and they set off on foot, for the sake of silence. Both Bryn and the bard moved more quietly than Ursula.

It was further than Ursula expected. They did not come across any Ravens, though the camp must be guarded. There was also no sign of Huw. That he was a

225

traitor came as little surprise to Ursula, but she could not see how he could have manoeuvred everyone into this vulnerable situation.

They came at last to the Raven camp in a clearing surrounded by trees. Rhonwen was screaming inside Ursula's head. Ursula staggered and nearly fell over with the shock of the intensity of it.

The bard's hand was on her shoulder.

'I can hear it too. Concentrate on where it's coming from. Don't think about what it means.'

She did not dare suggest that they leave Bryn behind. He was too vulnerable to attack.

'Ursula, I want you to try something new. Do you trust me?' It was hard for Ursula to think of anything but Rhonwen's anguish. She forced herself to look at the bard. With her magic enhanced vision she could see the earnestness in his eyes. Yes. She did trust him, as much as she trusted Kai. She nodded.

'That is wise. I expected no less. I want you to think very hard about not seeing me or Bryn. I'm not being foolish. Listen to me. The druids could make themselves and other things seem invisible. I'm sure you could make us invisible if you were to focus on not seeing us. When you have made us so that we cannot be seen we will look for Rhonwen. You will have to be the decoy.'

The screaming had stopped now. Ursula felt a tingle as somewhere Rhonwen used her power. Then the

226

screaming was replaced by a desperate sobbing. It seemed even that was perceptible only to Ursula and the bard. Bryn gave no sign of having heard anything. Still, the sobbing was marginally easier to ignore than the screaming. Ursula concentrated on doing as the bard had suggested. She was not entirely sure why. The bard's idea was seriously implausible.

It was easier than she had expected. She had never thought of herself as a particularly imaginative person but it was not difficult to imagine that the bard and Bryn were not there. Indeed it took little effort to convince herself that she had only envisioned that they were there in the first place.

To Ursula's heightened senses there was only a small ripple in the air like a heat haze where a few moments ago she had seemed to see Bryn and the bard. A heat haze in November in the dark was certainly unusual but less threatening to the Ravens than two visitors to the camp. Ursula had no confidence that the bard's plan would work.

There were few scouts guarding the camp. Almost all of the Ravens must have been involved in the raid on Macsen's camp. There was one bored sentry tending the fire and another two dragging something along the ground. It looked like a body, or an animal carcass. She could smell the charred flesh. A bundle of disordered rags and hair lay a little way from the fire. It had been bound by the hands to some kind of branch of wood. It was Rhonwen.

Ursula turned to where the bard would have been had he been visible which of course he was not.

'That's Rhonwen on the ground. I don't think she's going to be able to walk. You kill the guard and I'll fight the other two. Then you might be able to get her onto a horse.'

'Bards don't kill, Ursula. We are forbidden. It's why we always had safe passage, at least until the Ravens came.'

'Where I come from no one is allowed to kill, especially not fifteen year old girls,' she snapped at him angrily. She had crossed a boundary. She had become a warrior. She had felt death at her throat and defended herself. The bard's scruples seemed almost an indulgence. Then the old Ursula reasserted herself. What had she become that she regarded killing as necessary? What was she thinking of? The bard was right. She sighed.

'Never mind, I will do it. You and Bryn concentrate on getting Rhonwen out of here.'

Ursula concentrated on the wild power that sung through her. She was Boar Skull, a warrior giant, of inhuman strength. She imagined her hair limed as Macsen's had been. She envisioned it standing up like a punk halo or a petrified lion's mane. She removed almost all her clothes. The man she was going to make herself into was too broad for the leather breastplate she still wore. She pictured the elaborate blue tattoos winding along her own muscled arms and chest. Kai was not around to deny her the long warrior's moustache either. She took Bryn's spear and raised her sword skyward.

'I'm going to count to sixty and then charge. Get Rhonwen out of here and on a horse. I'll meet you back where I left Macsen. Go!' She didn't see the bard and Bryn run towards the limp looking figure, because they were not there to be seen. She breathed deeply, inflating her huge naked torso. It was not a great plan but at least this way she might get away without more killing.

At the count of sixty she began the wild ululation of the Celts and charged. The man dozing at the fire leaped to his feet and ran, yelling out to his compatriots. They were burying something and had left their shields elsewhere. They were caught unexpectedly. They ran too. Maybe they thought Ursula was in the vanguard of a major Celtic onslaught or maybe the sight of a wild-eyed Celtic giant charging towards them was in itself terrifying enough. Either way they ran. Ursula felt almost disappointed. The magic was a dangerous force. Using it she found she craved action, if only to expend some of its abundant energy. Power surged through her limbs. Boar Skull's bulk could scarcely contain it.

Rhonwen was gone as well as two of the tethered horses. Ursula's headache had eased. She could have mounted a third horse but chose instead to run after Bryn and the bard. It was the only way that she could think of to discharge her unstoppered aggression.

~ Chapter Twenty-three ~

Rhonwen

Somehow the Combrogi found one another again at the site of the fireside battle. A neat pile of severed heads and a cairn of stones marked their victory. Gwyn, Macsen, Prys and Dan were blood-stained but little of the blood seemed to be their own. Dan sat apart from the others, who wisely kept their distance until the berserker frenzy was over.

Rhonwen had lost the silver mask along with all her self-possession. She had covered her ravaged face with her cloak. She did not want to speak. Everyone including Macsen gave her the courtesy of privacy. Ursula's arrival was met with surprise. She still retained her wild Combrogi appearance, which necessitated some explaining as far as Prys and Gwyn were concerned. They had not believed Rhonwen's claim that she was other than a man at the oath-taking ceremony. They nodded sagely when Macsen explained she was a woman who had learned the capacity to shape shift. They clearly believed none of it.

Rhonwen's presence brought back both the headache and the awareness of Rhonwen's inner anguish that Ursula found impossible to deal with. The bard nodded at her encouragingly.

'No one saw us,' he said enthusiastically. He was sure she had succeeded in making them appear invisible.

'No one looked,' Ursula answered shortly. The run had tired her but done nothing to reduce the thrill of eager power that pulsed through her veins. It made her wild. 'Can anyone lend me a tunic?'

Dan, roused from the foothills of madness by Ursula's voice, found a spare tunic in Kai's saddlebag. Bryn, like a good squire, had retrieved the horses before joining him. The tunic looked woefully inadequate to cover Boar Skull's excessively broad chest.

'It's OK, Dan,' Ursula said in English. 'I need to speak to Rhonwen. I think I had better do that as me, as a woman, I mean.'

To Dan the massive Boar Skull was the Ursula he knew best, but he knew what she meant. He stood in front of her, to shield her from view, while she reduced herself to normal Ursula proportions and put on the tunic.

She touched him gently on the arm. 'Were you hurt?' He shook his head.

'Between us we killed all of them – ten or fifteen, I don't know. I had the sense to walk away while the others … you know took off the heads. I was nearly sane by the time they finished. It was gruesome. Do you know what the really terrible thing is? The more you kill the less you think about it. I think my soul must be stained with the evil of it.'

Ursula nodded. It was a more poetic way of expressing the feeling than she could have managed herself, but she knew exactly how he felt. Magic lent her an exuberance, a pleasure in her own strength that distorted her normal reactions. Somewhere, underneath the overlay of magic, her own soul seemed pretty stained. She had killed a man who had threatened her. She had done it without ceremony, almost by the way. She was a murderer. Did it make it any better that he would have killed her? She remembered the Ravens who had captured Rhonwen. She had wanted to tear them limb from limb with Boar Skull's mighty hands.

She didn't like such thoughts. She shook her head as if to rid herself of them. She had things to do. 'I do need to talk to Rhonwen. There is some kind of connection between us. Perhaps she'll talk to me.' Ursula could not help but feel sympathy for the tortured woman but, less altruistically, she needed to somehow stop Rhonwen's mental anguish from reverberating through her own bones. Rhonwen's pain made it hard to focus on anything

233

else. 'I suppose I'd better ask Macsen for his permission to talk to her. I wonder what they did with her mask?'

'I could go back with Bryn to find it. The camp isn't far away.'

Ursula looked doubtful. 'There may be more men there now. Did any escape from you?'

Dan shook his head. 'I think they all tried to make us a path to a hero's glory. They all tried their luck against us.'

That made sense to Ursula, in this world where all soldiers were mad. Maybe they all shared her fevered need for action, for some kind of consummation in conflict, once their blood was up. Any one of the Ravens could have run away from rather than towards the Combrogi. They might not have proved their courage but they would have lived. Instead they had chosen to die.

She had no sympathy to spare for dead Ravens. Rhonwen's pain made her own heart beat more erratically. She had to talk to her.

'Maybe you should find the mask,' she said hesitantly. 'Maybe the mask might help.'

Dan nodded and looked intently at his friend. 'You forgot to get rid of your moustache.'

Ursula put up her hand to her face in horror.

'Just kidding!'

Ursula laughed. She had not known she still could. As

far as could be told in near total darkness she was Ursula, just as she should be, without illusion.

Ursula, just as she should be, was enough to draw looks of stark disbelief and admiration from Prys and Gwyn. Had she changed that much then? When they had met her first she had worn no disguise but her excess weight and her long lost red anorak. They had not seen her as female then. She dismissed the thought. She could not worry about such trivia any more. There were too many things to do.

Dan introduced her, grinning broadly. All trace of the bear sark killer was gone.

'Here is Boar Skull as you have never seen her. You may call her Ursula.' Ursula couldn't help smiling at their confusion. It illuminated her face. Macsen was the first with a courtly compliment.

'Ursula, you are as beautiful as a woman as you are heroic as a warrior.' It was the first time anyone had called her beautiful. She smiled again and then wondered if he was making fun of her and scowled.

'With your permission Prince, I mean, King Macsen, may I speak to your sister?'

Macsen nodded. His smile disappeared. A pall of gloom descended on the small party. They'd hoped to find her in a better state. Gwyn and Prys could see the hope of marriage to Cadal fading. Dan whispered in Macsen's ear, and at Macsen's nod Dan gathered Bryn,

Braveheart and Taliesin and set off for the Ravens' camp to try to retrieve Rhonwen's lost mask.

Rhonwen was sitting a little way away, wrapped in her cloak. She made no sound, but the wailing in Ursula's head grew worse, bludgeoning her thoughts, making it hard to form a sentence. Her head ached as if it would split. Rhonwen's internal wailing was building to a crescendo. Ursula touched her gently on the shoulder.

'Are you all right?'

Rhonwen answered with a kind of gasp then croaked.

'They ambushed me on the road to King Lud's. They tied me and took me to the camp. They ripped off my mask and mocked me. Most left except for the few who guarded the horses. The men tried to ...' Rhonwen's voice broke. Ursula would have patted her shoulder but she had been burned there too.

'One of them tried to ... touch me, but I found my power then. I made fire come. It was real, wild, like before,' Rhonwen spoke as if to herself. 'This time I did not care if I got burned. I didn't want to live with the shame, with this ugliness and...' she started to sob. It was a blessed physical release of mental anguish. The wailing in Ursula's head died down. It made sympathy easier.

'It's all right, Rhonwen. If you tell me how, I may be able to heal you.'

It was not an idea that had even occurred to her before, but Ursula suddenly remembered Kai's disappearing wound long ago, after his first encounter with Dan as Bear Sark. There was no obvious abatement to the sobbing. She did not know if Rhonwen had heard her. Ursula felt awkward, at a loss. She may have changed her appearance but she still lacked the right words, the right tone to comfort.

'Dan, The Bear Sark, has gone back to find your silver mask.' She began tentatively, 'I could try to heal you, you know. I'm strong I …'

Rhonwen's words were unequivocal.

'I am a princess, do you think I could be healed by one such as you? You … you … ! I have no word for some-one who is both man and woman. Leave me. I will effect my own healing.'

Ursula was taken aback, but at least there was no ambiguity. Rhonwen really did, as she had always sus-pected, hate her. Ursula had done her duty. There was nothing else she could do.

She gathered her shredded dignity and walked slowly back towards Rhonwen's brother. She felt as if she would have rather stood in the Great Hall naked than meet the questioning eyes of Macsen and his men.

'They attacked her. She burned one of them. I think she wants to be alone.'

Ursula accepted the proffered horn of ale, grateful that it wasn't mead. She rejoined the circle conscious of the sudden distance that had sprung up between them.

Boar Skull was a comrade in arms but who, by Lugh, was Ursula? She was tempted to be Boar Skull again but did not have the strength. The electric pulse of magic had slowed. She was suddenly very tired. She could terrify a foe but she could offer no comfort to a suffering woman. She did not like the feeling of impotence. Someone covered her in a fine wool cloak and she slept.

She awoke to the confusion of rapid action, Prys shaking her and the sounds of jangling bridles.

Dan's voice was clear, if breathless, above the clamour.

'There must have been fifty, sixty, a whole century of them back there. I don't know where they came from. I think I saw Huw with them. I snatched the mask but I'm afraid they saw me and followed. We've got to go!'

Macsen pulled Ursula to her feet and threw her in the direction of her mount. Gwyn was dragging an unco-operative Rhonwen towards a horse. Ursula quickly checked. Bryn and Braveheart were OK. The bard had a cut above his eye. He was staunching it with his cloak. It did not look serious. In less than a minute they were mounted and riding like the gods.

It did not take long for them to hear their pursuers. Ursula thought back to the Raven camp as she had left it. Surely there had not been enough mounts for fifty men? The steady drum of hooves not far behind could have been fifty thousand. It was a very frightening sound. It was an earthquake-like vibration, rumbling as if the Goddess herself were coming after them.

Macsen was urging them south towards the Brigantes' land. Rhonwen spoke up for the first time, her beautiful voice still harsh with pain.

'Macsen, Lud fights with the Raven, the carrion birds. I heard it in their camp. Huw's working with him. It's certain. Ride the other way!'

Macsen reined his horse around with a muttered curse. Ursula knew that the last thing Macsen would want to do would be to bring an enemy back to his fortress, but they had little choice; to the east lay the marsh, to the west their enemy and to the south their enemy's allies, the Brigantes. They were all tired and the odds were against them. They turned north. They turned towards Craigwen. Under the thunder of hooves Ursula could hear the bubble of water as they approached a shallow stream. As they rode towards it she had the germ of an idea. She spurred her horse on to catch up with Macsen.

'Macsen,' she yelled above the noise, all reverence for his royal station forgotten. 'I'm going to try and create an illusion of us being swept away by the river. It might stop them.'

'Do what you can!' He was looking for a good place to stop and make a stand, his eyes sweeping the landscape in the grey dawn, searching for high ground, something to give them an advantage that could be gained in the minutes between them and their pursuers. The lie of the land was uncooperative. Maybe the earth herself was against them. Ursula could not ride and think at the same time. Galloping terrified her. She needed to concentrate if she were to help them.

'Dan!' Her voice sounded lost in the tumult of sound, but Dan was there in a moment.

'Can I ride with you? I need to do something!'

Dan did not hesitate. He rode alongside her and leaped from his own horse to hers. He did it effortlessly, without pause or thought. Perhaps it was the type of thing that you couldn't do if you thought about it. Somehow in the confusion she had ended up on Kai's horse. He was faster than she was used to and a trained Combrogi war-horse. Luck was on her side there for he scarcely faltered at the sudden additional weight. The Combrogi favoured such tricks and he was used to it. It took Ursula a moment longer than Dan or the horse to adjust to the new situation. She forced herself to be calm. She made herself feel the pulse of magic that thrilled up her spine. They galloped through the stony riverbed. The river here scarcely justified the name, but she could change that. The cold spray from the splashing hooves inspired her. She thought of the wetness of water, the icy chill of melted ice. She concentrated on creating an illusion of water, great torrents of water, a river full to overflowing. In her mind she saw it bubbling up all round them. When she saw the vanguard of the Raven century she focused on the picture of a river bursting its banks she had once seen on TV. She imagined the water flooding its banks. She willed the deluge to be.

'Ride!' she heard Prys behind her. 'The banks burst!'

They rode as if their lives depended on it, which they did. As she looked over her shoulder she saw the Ravens' lead horse rear at the sudden rush of white water in front of him. They would not ford that in a hurry. Instinctively everyone rode away from the illusion. Even Ursula could not argue with her instinct to ride like she had never ridden before to escape the treacherous water.

When they reached safe dry ground, they dismounted breathless and exhausted.

'You nearly killed us.' It was Gwyn. He sounded angry.

'What do you mean? It was an illusion that just saved your life,' Ursula answered hotly.

'By Lugh, that was no illusion. I'm soaked and freezing!'

It was true. Real water dripped from Gwyn's boots and horse. He shivered. The Combrogi eyed her with weary respect. She had made the river actually burst its banks.

'Not so much next time, eh?' said Dan and grinned.

'I'd rather an ally who didn't drown her friends,' said the bard shaking his wet cloak.

'You ungrateful dung-skulls,' said Dan dangerously. 'Thanks to Ursula we're alive, and we nearly weren't.'

Rhonwen's voice had recovered some of her silver poise.

'It takes subtlety the outlander has not yet learned to compose an illusion.'

Ursula bit back a response. Rhonwen could be as vindictive as she liked; anything was more bearable than that awful mental wailing.

~ Chapter Twenty-four ~

Veiled Hints

Macsen would not allow them to stop for long. Ursula had no idea how much of the river had burst its banks. It was only a matter of time before the Ravens found a safe place to cross and continued their pursuit.

Macsen was depressingly certain that they had come across the vanguard of the advancing legion. The cavalry and auxiliary infantry would not be far behind, and behind them the artillery and the main body of the legion. The whole might of Rome was only days away from Craigwen. Macsen's face was as grey as the dawn. Ursula told him about the betrayal of Huw and what she'd overheard. Her evidence backed up Rhonwen's. The Brigantes under King Lud were clearly a lost cause. They would have to fight with what they had. The only thing to do was to ride like the wind for Craigwen and get ready for the battle to come.

'There's no point in sitting out a siege, though we have three months' grain and clean well water. There's none to relieve us if the Brigantes have sided with the Ravens.' Macsen's voice was grim.

'I'd like to bet that Huw will be riding back to Lud by now, leaving the Ravens to finish us off. Huw knows the fortress too well for my liking. We'll have trouble if any of Huw's friends are traitors. It takes little courage to poison a well.' Gwyn's voice was equally gloomy. He'd never liked Huw, but he had shared a horn of ale with him only the previous night. If he saw him again he would kill him very slowly and keep his skull for a rat-trap in the fortress stables.

'Maybe we should go with Cadal, if he will let us cross with him to the Sacred Isle. We could regroup there and rebuild a force to retake Craigwen. I can offer my warriors only death if they stay to fight it out.'

Macsen's normally commanding voice was no more than a thoughtful whisper. Ursula thought he looked simultaneously very young and very haggard. He bore a huge responsibility – the survival of his people.

'How many men do they have?' Dan sounded very unsure of himself. He needed to understand the odds.

'They have around five thousand men plus the auxilia – another four thousand maybe.'

'How many Combrogi?' Dan did not really want to know the answer.

'If Kai has done his job and sent out the call, we will have between three and four thousand men, but less than half are warriors. The other half are farmers, servants of the tribes. They will die as well as any man if I ask them too, but they can't be relied upon to take many of the enemy with them.'

It was not many against the Ravens but it was more than Ursula could envisage within Craigwen's walls.

'But what about Cadal?' she asked. 'He's an ally isn't he?'

There was a pause. It was the bard who spoke.

'Cadal will have sailed for Ireland by now. He's a prudent man. He will have taken advantage of calm waters.' The bard paused to consider his words. 'Before we left he entrusted me with the task of finding the Princess Rhonwen and ensuring that she still intends to honour the marriage proposal. He'll need my word that Princess Rhonwen intends to keep hers before he will fulfil his. We are tied here in a tangle of oaths. Of course my witness to her marriage oath would be better surety still. Then he'll send men, but they will stay on the sea to protect the fortress' seaward side. The Ravens may bring ships – we don't know.'

Rhonwen's face was unreadable. Dan had given her the mask.

'You can have my marriage oath now, if it will help us.' Rhonwen had recovered much of her composure. She sounded her old smooth-tongued self, though her hand, when she gave it to the bard, trembled.

'Very well.'

The bard adjusted his cloak, combed his wild beard with his fingers and adopted a more formal stance. Macsen and the others formed a small tight circle around Rhonwen and the bard, as witnesses to her vows. It was the oddest wedding ceremony Ursula could imagine: a wet, travel-stained and bloody congregation, a silver masked bride and no bridegroom. But by the law of the tribes it was binding and Rhonwen had kept her word.

It was one small burden lifted from Macsen's back. He managed a smile and kissed his sister's silver cheek. 'Fertility and prosperity,' he whispered. Rhonwen said nothing. Ursula found it impossible to imagine what she was thinking but whatever it was it did not impinge upon Ursula. There was no silent wailing in Ursula's head, nothing more than the usual headache to remind her that Rhonwen and her antipathy were near. They mounted the scarcely rested horses and rode, fast, for Craigwen.

Afterwards Ursula could remember little of the journey itself. She could ride adequately now, provided she was not required to gallop or doing anything too difficult. She was tired after her magical exertions but the power in her had scarcely ebbed. It was increasingly clear to her that her magic was the only way out for Macsen and his men. There must be something she could do, if only she could think of it. Could she make the earth quake and somehow destroy the army before it reached them? Could she do that and could she bear so much death on her own conscience? She knew deep within herself that the answer lay in the Veil that haunted her dreams.

What Macsen really needed was more men. Where could she get an army to fight a Roman legion from? The answer was obvious but impossible. Even if she could raise the Veil, which was at best unproven, how could she make it work where she wanted it to? She gnawed at the problem all the long ride back. She would have asked Rhonwen, but the woman's hatred of her darkened the air between them. In the end she asked the bard.

'Do you mind if I ask you something?' The bard was himself deep in thought but he nodded. 'Do you know about the Veil?' She was breathless from the pace of the ride. His eyes were guarded, but he nodded again. 'Can you tell me how it works?'

'Not exactly, Lady, I know of no one living who could do that and I'm sceptical about the dead.'

Ursula paused. The bard knew something she was sure. He was, after all, a magician in his own way.

'Tell me what you know, please. I can't ask Rhonwen and I need to know.'

Dan had ridden up beside him and was listening with an almost painful intensity to every word.

'The Veil is just a name for one of the places where the walls between worlds is thin,' the bard began. 'The druids conjured what they thought of as bridges through blood sacrifice, prayer, fasting and very complicated rituals. I don't know if the new magic works the same way, but I was taught that the aim of the sacrifice is to pay the toll; the aim of the ritual is to focus the mind; the aim of the fast is to free the spirit and the aim of the prayer is to call on the well of power that holds the universe in place. These are sacred things Ursula, only a few years ago I would have been eviscerated for telling you this, and in truth I don't know much more. I suspect it is like all magic. I believe it is your will that guides it and the power that permits it. Your soul calls to the power even if you give it no name. That is all I know. I am sorry it is not more.'

Dan nodded, as if it all made perfect sense to him, as if the bard had just given him instructions to Basingstoke from the M25.

'And is this very dangerous?'

It was Rhonwen who answered. No one had even known she had been listening.

Her voice sounded distant, wistful. 'It is like riding a tempest balanced on a chariot's axle, like swimming through a whirlpool. Of course it's dangerous.' She was

248

all scorn. 'I do not think one who fears to be a woman will have the courage.'

Dan had a retort on the tip of his tongue but before he could say it she had ridden off, black hair streaming behind her like a dark flag.

'If it's dangerous I don't think you should do it.'

Dan was unequivocal. Taliesin looked uncomfortable. 'That is not for me to say. I know only that if you doubt and try it anyway you will die. There are many stories of druids who could not find their way home when they lost their … faith in the power and their will. You cannot be persuaded to do it, and if it is your destiny you cannot be persuaded against it.' Looking deeply miserable, the bard too rode off.

'Ursula, you mustn't.'

Ursula's expression was granite.

'If I do not, we will all die. You heard the odds.'

'Ursula, we could flee to Ireland.'

'Macsen doesn't believe that. What Combrogi King will let another King and his fifteen hundred warriors stay in his kingdom? Hell, even I know that couldn't work. Five of them can hardly be in the same room without a fight breaking out about something. The mind boggles at the trouble fifteen hundred or more would cause. That won't work, Dan. Macsen will choose to fight. You know he will. All of them will, not to would be eternal shame. They're warriors.

They're scarcely sane when it comes to battle and honour.'

Dan had to admit that the Irish option had struck him as a long shot.

'Well, what would you raise the Veil for?'

'To bring men to fight for Macsen, of course.'

'I don't see how you can even think about that. Where would you get them from? Anyway, even if you could do it, you'd be taking them from their homes, their lives like we were taken. What gives you that right?'

Ursula sighed. 'Don't have a go at me. I'm just trying to find a way to keep us alive and keep my promises at Alavna, to Macsen, to you. Do you think we can go home unless I learn how to raise the Veil? Did you hear Prys say that the men who were chasing us were from the legion that destroyed Alavna? They were probably some of the same men, the scouts of the Second legion.'

'I'm not meaning to have a go, Ursula, but the Veil business is …'

'Mad? Yes, it is. Being here is mad. You being a super-man berserker is mad. Me doing magic is mad. None of it makes sense.' Ursula's tone was angry, then she took a deep breath and calmed herself. 'I think I can raise the Veil. I've dreamed of nothing else since we came here. I think I could do it and I know where I would get the men from too.'

'What do you mean?'

'Remember history with Mrs Enright in year seven?'

'Yes, of course. I reminded you about it.'

'Yes, OK. Remember the stuff about the legions?'

'Vaguely.'

'Do you remember, she talked a bit about a Roman legion that disappeared. There was a book written about them. It was a story, I forget what it was called, we read some of it in class, but the thing was, there really was no record of what happened to them.'

'The ninth legion, Hispana.'

'That's right. I might have known you'd remember the name. Well, what if they disappeared because they came here? And they came here because I brought them!'

'You're mad. Anyway, that was nearly two thousand years ago. They're long dead.'

'If we were in our time they would be, but when are we now?'

Dan wrinkled his brow. 'I don't know. I don't even know which emperor's in power. Boudicca was sometime before AD 70 I think.'

Ursula snapped at him in impatience. 'It was a rhetorical question, I didn't mean you to try to work it out. What I mean is we've either gone back in time or crossed into another world, right? So I don't think it matters with raising the Veil when or where it is.'

'How did Rhonwen get us, then? What was she looking for?'

Ursula was hesitant for the first time. She dropped her voice. 'I've been thinking about that too. I think the Veil is almost tuned in to battles at the moment. I used to dream of walking through the yellow mist of the Veil into the sea or the desert or something and once I even dreamed I was stuck in the middle of a rock. That was horrible. But now I mainly dream of battles, all kinds of battles. One was in space. I don't think it's even happened yet. I mean, well you know what I mean. But we were at Hastings, right? I think Rhonwen was chasing a dream of the Norman army. They would have helped Macsen, even the Saxons would be useful here.'

'What, you mean she got the time wrong?'

'Yeah, not by so much either when you think of it.'

'More than 900 years!'

'Well, yes, whatever, but …'

'And you think you can do better than that?'

'Yes. I know what I'm looking for. Rhonwen was just looking for an army. I'm looking for the ninth legion in … when?'

'Around AD 110 I think. I don't know. I can't remember.'

'Near enough.'

Dan could tell by the look in Ursula's green eyes that this was not a fight he could win.

'But Ursula if we have gone back in time the ninth

legion might already be here.' There was a pause as Ursula weighed the thought.

'I don't think we have gone back in time, Dan. This is not our earth. It doesn't feel like it. I never felt magic pour through me on our earth. You weren't, you know berserk on our earth were you? I know that I'm supposed to find the ninth and bring it here. I just know I am.' Ursula's face was contorted into a mask of obstinacy. Dan thought she was quite as mad as he had ever been. He knew better than to argue with her.

'Promise me you won't try this alone.'

'You sound like one of those kids' programmes. "And remember children don't try this at home, be sure to get an adult to help you."' They both laughed, not because it was particularly funny but because they needed to break the tension somehow.

They were riding through the valley that ended in the steep cliffs of Craigwen. Both of them were surprised to find that it felt like coming home. It was much later that Dan realised that Ursula hadn't promised anything.

~ Chapter Twenty-five ~

A Good Plan

Macsen wasted no time in holding a Council of War with Kai and the other tribal leaders. As Taliesin had anticipated, Cadal had already left to take advantage of calm seas. Queen Usca, Macsen's formidable grandmother had gone too. The bard lost no time in sending messages to Cadal confirming Rhonwen's marriage oath. As Rhonwen showed no symptom of being a happy bride, Cadal may have feared that she might change her mind with disastrous consequences for the alliance. Gwyn and Prys turned the fortress upside down in search of evidence of further plotting against the King. Their methods were not always gentle and anyone who had not actually hated Huw was interrogated. It was a small enough number. They found nothing. They discovered no hint of treachery in the fortress. Every man avowed total loyalty to Macsen. They put a trusted guard on the food stores, well and armoury.

Dan and Ursula were invited to attend the War Council. Macsen urged Ursula to adopt the dress of a priestess and wear the flowing robes favoured by Rhonwen. He said it would help inspire the confidence of his allies. It took all the persuasive skills of Kai, Bryn, Dan and the bard, but in the end she accepted the deep violet blue cloak and the rich red dress that was offered her. Her hair had grown anyway in her months as a warrior, but she augmented it a little with shape shifter magic, so that it hung to her waist like a pale blonde curtain in the manner of Rhonwen's. Bryn was impressed.

'You look like a real woman.'

'I am a real woman, you stupid squire.' But her smile was warm. You could rely on a kind of honesty from the eight year old. It helped.

Nothing helped the Council of War. The men were grim and, in spite of her careful preparations, Macsen gave Ursula only the most cursory of glances and carried on talking. In front of him was a three-dimensional map made of clay.

'My plan would have been to have Lud's men hidden here, in the wood above the valley. We could have waited for the Ravens to get settled in the valley, start building their siege engines, set up their ballista for an assault on the walls, their usual tricks. Then, probably at night, we would swarm out of the castle and attack from three sides. If I'd had enough men I'd have put some chariots behind too, to deal with any retreat.'

'It would have made a fine song for Cadal's bard,' the Ordovices' chief, a beefy man with a red face and bristling ginger moustache, interjected. 'But what is your plan, now Lud has thrown his lot in with the carrion?'

Macsen hesitated and Rhonwen spoke.

'I see no reason for the plan to change. I will raise the Veil and bring in reinforcements.'

The men glanced at the silver masked woman with scarcely disguised amusement.

'And if the Princess' plan yields only ...' the Ordovices' chief glanced briefly at Ursula and Dan, 'more outlanders?'

Dan found his hand on his sword hilt before he could stop himself but Kai's restraining ham of a hand on his shoulder calmed him.

'We fight still.' Macsen's voice remained firm, commanding. 'We allow the siege to begin. We make life difficult. We corrupt their water and food; encourage pestilence; weaken the troops. We spread rumours of the power of our sorceresses. Show them a few tricks, weaken morale, make them afraid. Then we attack at night, kill as many as we can and ...'

'Die,' finished the Ordovices' chief. There was silence. The men of the tribes looked at each other and at the clay model in front of them. The pause went on for a long time.

'It is a good plan.' There were nods of assent.

'I'll drink to that.'

Macsen allowed himself a terse smile. Dan breathed again. Ursula was right. The Combrogi had more honour than sense, but Dan had a lump in his throat. He felt proud to be accepted by such brave, obdurate people.

The tribal leaders and everyone else proceeded to drink gargantuan quantities of ale, consume a small herd of cattle and sing of past victories through most of the night. If they had only a few days left of life they were not going to waste them in sleep. Macsen's plan did not require that they husband their stored food and it was a shame to waste it or leave it for the enemy. In between times they honed their blades to bone-slicing sharpness, oiled their leather breastplates and overhauled their shields. Many limed their hair and generally readied themselves. Caradoc informed them that the enemy troops were massing. They would be at their gates within the day. The Combrogi had decorated the battlements with the spiked heads of the Ravens they had killed in the fireside battle. The head of the man Ursula had killed was among them. She could not look at it.

Ursula knew what she had to do. She rose at dawn after a nightmare sleep filled with Veil visions. She would have liked to make herself into Boar Skull. It was a more comforting form than her own. The months of relentless exercise had changed her true body into something she scarcely recognised, something lean but definitely feminine. Her new fitness made her move differently, but the balance of her limbs seemed all wrong somehow. She had learned to fight as Boar Skull. She had had no time to get used to Ursula. But she had an instinctive feeling that she should approach her task without illusion of any kind, mental or physical. She bathed and oiled herself as she had before the warrior's ceremony. She put on a plain wool tunic and mousy brown coloured leggings, male clothes that most closely resembled the things she'd worn at home. She made her hair the length it should have been, an awkward length between short and long. It was in her eyes so she tied it back from her face with a strip of cloth. She took her sword, her cloak and a stoppered drinking horn of water.

She had eaten nothing since the bard had spoken of fasting. She would have liked to say goodbye to Dan or at least leave him a note, in case she didn't come back, but the Celts didn't write and there were no writing materials anywhere in the fortress. She hoped he'd understand. She did not take a horse.

The men were on war alert so to leave the castle she had to try the trick she'd used on Bryn and the bard. She was not sure it had worked then, but she had no option but to try it again. She willed herself to be unseen and she was. She did not know if she had made herself invisible, not to be seen was good enough.

Dan had himself woken with the dawn. He had slept fitfully. He was certain that Ursula would waste no time in trying to raise the Veil. He dare not miss her. He asked Bryn to keep watch. Bryn followed her as far as the bathhouse. Bryn was much better at silent tracking than Dan. Bryn saw her disappear. He reported back to Dan.

'She's done the disappearing trick, but you can see her if you make yourself concentrate. Look for the place where the air ripples like a pool.'

Thanking Bryn, Dan followed her. Luckily Prys was on watch at the main gate. He let Dan through, but Dan knew that Macsen and Kai would be alerted within minutes. It was not something he had the time to worry about. Dan had to protect Ursula.

Dan stayed well back. He moved with all the care he could muster. He did not want to alert her suspicions. Ursula's senses were sharp. He hoped that she would be focused on what she had to do. He hoped that she would not expect anyone to follow. Bryn was right. If you looked hard enough the air shimmered in places. He assumed Ursula was somewhere in the vicinity of the shimmering air.

There was a place high above the valley, which had haunted Ursula's dreams. It was close to a tree that had a sort of witch's face. It was not hard to find. The valley's sides were not as steep as the rocks on which Craigwen was built but she was breathless by the time she reached the top and her headache had returned.

She drank some of the water and knelt beside the witch tree. Mum had taken her to church sometimes. She would have to pray to the only God she knew. She did not know Rhonwen's Goddess but if she herself could manage to be male and female she expected no less of her God.

She ran through the bard's checklist in her mind: fasting, prayer, blood sacrifice, ritual. Dan had told her about the druid Prince, Lovernios. His death would have to stand for the sacrifice. Enough blood would be shed in the next few days to make considering shedding more, now, an obscenity. The ritual was a problem because she knew of none except the oath-taking she had witnessed and participated in. She unsheathed her sword with the spare grace of the warrior she had become and stuck it into the ground.

'I am Ursula Alavna ab Helen and by name I swore to avenge Alavna. Let this be my revenge.' Her voice sounded feeble and uncertain. She felt stupid. Surely this could not be the kind of ritual the bard had meant? It occurred to her that perhaps all her preparations for this moment, the bathing, the anointing herself with oil, the selection of her clothes, had themselves a ritual significance. She hoped so. She could think of nothing else to do.

She had done the fasting. She didn't know if it had

freed her spirit. It certainly left her feeling hungry and rather light-headed. Now it was the time for prayer.

She did not know what to say. She had been taught that killing was wrong. There was no way out of this that did not involve killing. Could she ask the power that holds the universe in place to bring men through the Veil to kill and to die? The wall between worlds was very thin here. She could see the legion in her mind's eye waiting for her. She could smell the sweat of the men, hear the jingling of their mail, the thump and the squelch of their marching feet as they toiled through mud. She knelt in her church's attitude of prayer.

'I don't know if I have the right to ask this. I don't even know what name to give to you. I know that the ninth legion waits for me. They are there. The Combrogi need them. Perhaps it is not up to me. If it is your will may the Veil come into being.' Head bowed, Ursula waited for her answer.

Dan could see her clearly now, no more than twenty metres away. There was a pale yellow glow in front of her. Ursula did not notice because her eyes were tightly shut.

The yellow mist seemed to whirl and shift. It was a maelstrom more than a mist. It was coming closer to Ursula whirling round as if about to consume her.

'Urs ...' he began but a man's strong hand was over his mouth.

'So you would run away, would you? You treacherous runt! I knew we should not trust you, outlander. Are you going to run to the Ravens? You can throw yourself on their mercy because I'll show you none.'

It was Gwyn. There was no time to explain. Dan had to get to Ursula.

He tried to pull himself free of the warrior's clamp-like grip.

'You'll have to fight me, alone, without your little witch friend.' For a moment Dan had no idea what he meant. Then he remembered Gwyn's wounded pride at being bested in training what seemed like years ago. Dan groaned inwardly. He did not need this now.

Gwyn released him but only so that Gwyn could pull out his sword. Bright Killer seemed to leap of its own volition into Dan's hand. Gwyn attacked furiously with a viciousness Dan could not match. He was too worried about Ursula to give himself up to madness. He dare not enter his quiet place of certainty. He didn't dare surrender to it. Instead he held on to his limb-slowing sanity and did the best that he could. Gwyn was pressing his advantage. Dan kept moving out of his way but Gwyn was Macsen's champion and Dan knew he could not beat him, sane. Gwyn raised his arm for what Dan knew would be a fatal blow and Ursula screamed. Gwyn hesitated. Dan recovered. With all his strength he swung Bright Killer so that it clashed with Gwyn's own sword.

With a vibrating ring, Gwyn's sword was thrust out of his hand.

'Ursula!' Dan panted and ran to save her.

She was standing now. She had her back to him. Why had she screamed? The yellow mist swirled in front of her like the maw of Rhonwen's dragon. It was ten metres high and growing. Ursula raised her arms as if in blessing. Suddenly a tall figure ran towards her screeching something Dan could not hear. It was Rhonwen. She pushed Ursula aside and raised her own arms and the mist advanced. With a cry that could be ecstasy or anguish, Dan couldn't tell, the mist enveloped Rhonwen, curling around her like a coiled snake made of yellow cloud and she disappeared.

'Ursula! No!' It looked like Ursula was about to follow but the mist unaccountably stabilised. It seemed less like a living creature, more like a meteorological feature. Something about it had definitely changed because Ursula staggered backwards as if suddenly released from the grip of some powerful physical force. Dan's relief at her apparent safety was short-lived. The mist was parted by a gladius and the bulky form of a soldier emerged from the yellow tainted gloom. The soldier would not have been able to see much. Dan guessed that he must have been operating on instinct for his short sword was held ready to strike. He was moving inexorably towards a dazed-looking Ursula. She was unarmed and seemed unaware of her danger. She was seconds away from a soldier's blade. Dan ran towards her but Gwyn got there first. He could not guess what Gwyn must have thought. Perhaps Gwyn believed that Dan and Ursula were both in league with the Ravens. This soldier wore Raven clothing and must therefore be an enemy, consequently, Gwyn prepared for the attack. With a war cry as blood-curdlingly terrifying as Dan had ever heard, Gwyn charged forward to tear out the enemy's heart. By the time he got there the first soldier was flanked by ten more. Gwyn learned Hane's lesson the hard way. Hand to hand against an enemy fighting in close formation he stood no chance. Dan saw Gwyn Alavna ab Mog die but he died a warrior's death.

Dan threw himself in front of Ursula who was trembling uncontrollably.

'It's OK, Ursula, I'll protect you!'

'Against a legion!'

As more men marched through the Veil, he could see that she was right. She had raised the Veil and the ninth legion was marching through it. He gripped Bright Killer firmly. What did they do now?

~ Chapter Twenty-six ~

Strength and Weakness

Ursula seemed calm. Dan thought that she might have been in shock. Her eyes looked strange.

'Strength or weakness?'

'What do you mean?'

'Will they respect strength or weakness?'

Dan looked at the blood-spattered corpse of Macsen's champion.

'They just killed strength.'

Ursula nodded, her eyes never leaving the face of the man she had picked out as leader.

'When I move forward, I want you to run and get Macsen and Kai and the bard. Hurry, I can't hold the Veil stable for long.'

Ursula spoke through gritted teeth. He glanced at her. She was very pale and although it was too early for the sun to have warmed the cold hilltop, beads of sweat glistened on her face. Dan wanted to argue. He couldn't

265

leave Ursula to face an army alone, but if the situation turned nasty he couldn't kill a legion on his own. Reluctantly he nodded. He didn't expect they'd let him get away anyway.

The first row of the column had not advanced so that Dan could see only about thirty soldiers plus the odd arm and leg of others still in the mist. He had no doubt that the rest of the legion would march through if the Legate ordered it.

Ursula moved forward and very deliberately knelt at the Legate's feet. True to his word, Dan ran. Ursula must have done her 'not-there-thing' again because no one seemed to notice that he'd left. How could he persuade Macsen that the arrival of a second Roman legion outside his fortress was a good thing? From the high ground, Dan could see in the far distance a cloud of dust to indicate the progress of the vanguard of the second legion. His guts churned with fear and he ran for the fortress. There was so little time.

Ursula bowed her head for a moment in a gesture of prayer. The Romans watched her coldly but at least they made no move to kill her.

'Thank God, you have come. You are an answer to my prayers. Welcome Legate of the Ninth! Never was a sight more welcome.'

Instinct told her that this man had to be the Legate. She had called him through the Veil first in her mind.

She was trembling as much from uncontrollable nerves as from the strain of maintaining the Veil. She looked at him and did not have to fake the appeal in her eyes. God! May this work!

The man was clearly a veteran soldier, short but broad shouldered and powerful looking. His eyes were a very piercing blue and his dark hair was touched with grey. He did not look Roman, if anything he looked like an older version of Caradoc. Was it possible that he too was of the Silurian tribe? Ursula tried to remember everything she knew about the Roman military. It was not a great deal. She did recall that conquered nations served in the Roman army but could a non-Roman reach such high rank? Did it matter? The man was probably going to kill her. She found that she did not care over much whether her executioner was of Celtic stock or not. She hardly dared breathe. He stared at her in a very deliberate and appraising way. He stretched the silence between them until her wracked nerves all but snapped. She kept herself very still. When the Legate finally spoke he seemed remarkably calm for one who had walked through the Veil and killed a man. Ursula would not look at Gwyn's butchered body.

'Woman, this is a strange welcome, first we are attacked and now you offer prayers of thanksgiving. What is this place?'

'This is Craigwen, sir. We are just beyond the gates of

the fortress doomed to be besieged by a rogue legion. The warrior you fought thought you our enemy. It is my earnest prayer that you are not.'

There was a pause.

'I know nothing of a rogue legion. I know of no Craigwen. What is going on here? Tell me truthfully, woman, I am not an over patient man.'

Ursula did not, truthfully, know where to start.

'The yellow mist that surrounds your men,' she began, hesitantly, 'it marks a quicker road. It has brought you far from where you started. I pray that it has brought you to help us.' Ursula took a deep breath. She was not dead yet. She continued more confidently. 'I am of the tribes, but the Romans here, we call them Ravens, are massacring our people. Even our women and children are being slaughtered in the name of their dark emperor.' She had never actually heard anyone talk much of the emperor dark or otherwise. Macsen had no leisure for the wider politics of the Empire. But the Ravens fought on someone's orders. Anyone who ordered the likes of the Alavna massacre could not be good. She was improvising furiously. She had worried so much about raising the Veil and bringing the legion through, she had not thought about what she would say to them. 'I have some power over the yellow mist and this quicker road. I raised it to bring you. I have dreamed of you and your legion. I saw that you were not a man to kill innocents. I prayed that a noble and a honest man might lead his army to our aid against the Ravens who wish to annihilate the only British tribes left. '

'Are you of the druids?'

'Not exactly.'

'I have never heard of this mist. And who is this dark emperor?' The Legate's tone remained hard. He did not believe a word of it.

'Sir, I do not know his name, but his men march under his banner, the sign of the raven and a man named Suetonius does his work.'

The man scowled. 'The only Suetonius I know is dead, but he was a fine soldier, though hard enough on the tribes.' The suspicion in his eyes had not softened. Ursula felt her heart sink. She could not have achieved so much to throw it away at the last. She wished for Dan's gift of inspiring trust.

'I cannot tell you more except that I have seen with my own eyes what has been done to us by men wearing the dress of Rome. You are here in answer to my prayers – how can you not help us!'

Ursula was getting desperate. She felt hope and her control of the Veil slipping from her.

'Why do you sweat? Are you afraid? Is this some trap you have lured us to?'

Ursula shook her head. 'The road I made through the yellow mist is hard to sustain. I am afraid that if it falters some of your men will die and you and they will be separated.'

'You threaten me?'

She shook her head. 'Look back, you can see some still stuck in the mist.' A quick glance confirmed the truth of this.

'Advance forward ten paces!' the Legate commanded.

Ursula backed out of their way and more of the column emerged through the mist to blink confusedly in the watery daylight. The ones who had been stuck in the mist looked predictably spooked. Behind them, she was sure, many others remained.

'What is happening here?'

The Legate's gladius was centimetres from her throat. With an effort of will Ursula kept her voice steady.

'I don't know how deep the mist is. I cannot change its nature. Unless you all march through it some of your men will be stuck in it.' She fought down her panic. What else could she say? This was all going horribly wrong. She could feel tears of frustration prickling behind her eyes. There had to be a way to convince them to help. For the first time she realised what she had done. She had conjured a Roman legion and intended to ask them to fight on the side of their enemies against their own people. Why had she not thought this through? What if the legion would not fight for them? What would Macsen think if she brought a whole army of potential enemies through the mist? Surely they had enough enemies already.

'I don't think you should all march through until you have spoken to King Macsen.' She said quickly. Her voice trembled. She was angry with herself for showing such weakness. She was bathed in sweat as she struggled to maintain the Veil.

'And who is King Macsen? I hope he makes more sense than you woman, I grow impatient.' The Legate sheathed his gladius.

Ursula felt little sense of relief. There was another very long silence, in which she faced some sixty, armed Roman legionaries alone and with not a clue what to do next. She knelt down and closed her eyes, partly so that she didn't have to look at the ranks of shiny armour, plumed helmets and cold eyes, partly so she could focus on maintaining the Veil. She prayed too, in a way; a panic-stricken repetition of, 'Oh God, what have I done?'

After what seemed like a very long time Dan arrived with Macsen, Kai and Caradoc. They looked angry and wary. Dan was pale and he had a cut under one eye. It looked like someone had punched him. He was not mad. Ursula was so confused she did not know if that was a good thing or not. Ursula thought Kai and Caradoc looked magnificent in full battle dress. There was a kind of purposeful shuffling among the legionaries as if they too recognised power when they saw it and respected it.

Would she have done better to meet them as Boar Skull?

Macsen's face grew tighter with fury as he saw the troops and the slain body of his champion, Gwyn. He kept a tight rein on his emotions. He nodded to the Legate and showed that his hands were empty of weapons.

'I see my sorceress has excelled herself. I wish I could offer you welcome, but as we speak one of your legions gathers at my gates. I cannot claim any pleasure at seeing another.'

Ursula fought the urge to throw herself into the Veil and be swallowed up by it. The thought of finding herself with the remainder of the legion dissuaded her. Strangely the Legate seemed more comfortable with Macsen's aggression than with her own words of welcome. She threw a look of anxious appeal at Dan. His face was stony. Even Dan thought what she had done was wrong. She would not cry. She would face this like the warrior she had proved herself to be and not cringe with apology. Even if she had been wrong they had lost nothing. The Combrogi could not win; she had tried to give them a chance. If the gamble had failed, well, they could only die once just the same.

She was so deep in thought that she did not at first notice sixty-five pairs of eyes staring at her. When she did it was to Dan she turned, 'What?' she said in English.

'Ursula, you've turned into Boar Skull.' It was true. It

was no wonder the Romans gaped at her in surprise. The clothes she was wearing threatened to cut off the circulation. She ripped off her tunic and leggings to reveal the massive physique of her alter ego.

'That is indeed a sorcerer,' said the Legate, his composure ruffled for the first time.

Macsen snorted. 'Boar Skull is a shape shifter and more beside but I did not ask that she call you to fight for us. Wherever you came from you are Roman and that makes you our enemy.'

The Legate appeared to weigh this up. 'She … er … he told us the Romans here have tried to annihilate the tribes. Is this true?'

Macsen nodded tersely. There was some muttering in the ranks, silenced by a glare from the Legate. 'Who is emperor here?' the Legate asked.

'Master and god, Caesar Domitianus Augustus.' Macsen's answer gave the Legate pause.

'That man is dead, I have that on very good authority.' The Legate flushed a deep red, and Ursula got the strong impression that he had some personal knowledge of his death. 'If a man by that cursed name now claims to be emperor here I do not serve him. I serve Caesar Nerva Traianus Germanicus. Why have I not heard of this false emperor before?'

Dan chose this moment to enter the conversation.

'I understand, sir, that you have been stationed at

York. It is not hard to keep news from such a distant base. While you have remained there knowing nothing of what is going on, the second legion has been able to continue with its reign of terror over the tribes.'

'How many of the tribes survive?'

'We number three thousand men.' Macsen's reply was firm. He was too desperate to dissemble.

'And how many live in the towns?'

'No free men.'

The Legate's face darkened. He gave Caradoc a hard look. The intricate tattoos on Caradoc's forearms marked him clearly as of the Silurian tribe. The Legate must have recognised them and spoke to him in Silurian.

'How many of the Silurians still live?'

'I am the only warrior here of that tribe. I do not know how many others still live. I have not heard.'

The Legate's jaw tightened.

'My grandmother was Silurian of a noble line. Many of my men especially the auxilia are of British tribes. We are unusual in having so many of the conquered fighting for their conquerers in their own country. It is not an easy situation.' The Legate stared thoughtfully at Ursula in her Boar Skull guise. 'I do not like the sound of this emperor. I lived briefly in Rome under the real Caesar Domitianus Augustus under his last reign of terror. I cannot say that my family prospered under his cruelty. Whoever has chosen to revive his name deserves only his fate.'

'And what was that?' asked Macsen levelly.

'He was assassinated, though most of his killers were later killed themselves by the army. He had wit enough to keep the army well paid and loyal.' The Legate's tone was bitter. 'This false emperor has not chosen a propitious name, though it is one that would appeal to some of the army. What you say is difficult to believe, what proof can you offer me?'

Macsen took from his belt a pouch of Roman gold. He handed the pouch over. Each coin was stamped with the head of Caesar Domitianus Augustus, on the reverse side there was a Raven. The legate examined each coin carefully.

'No legion known to me fights under the banner of a carrion bird.'

He handed back the coin.

Macsen spoke carefully, weighing each word.

'I know no honourable Roman would accept gold to fight, but if you could help us rid the land of the scourge of these followers of a false emperor, all the wealth we had would be insufficient to express our thanks.'

The Legate's eyes narrowed. 'If, in truth, this legion you speak of fights to support a false emperor, no honourable Roman could do else but join with you to destroy them. No loyal Roman could turn a blind eye to rebellion. It may be that I am not your enemy, but I need more proof than this.' The Legate paused. 'I am concerned for my men. Will you let your sorcerer bring them through this ...' He waved his hand in the direction of the yellow mist.

Macsen looked at Kai. Ursula was startled to hear a reflection of her own thoughts from his lips.

'We can only die once,' Kai said with a grim grin.

'How many men do you have?' said Macsen slowly.

'Six thousand.'

Something like hope began to light Macsen's eyes.

'Ursula, Boar Skull, can you hold the Veil firm for so many?'

Dan had given Ursula still in Boar Skull mode his cloak to hide her necessary but rather ostentatious nakedness.

All eyes were on her again. She nodded. 'Do you have supply trains?'

'Of course.'

Ursula sensed Macsen's relief. If the Legate proved to be an ally they had nowhere near enough supplies to feed his army.

'I'll try to bring them through too.'

It took a long time. The sun was high by the time the last man was through. Macsen and the Legate had not ceased talking for nearly the whole time.

The Legate had not lied. Many of the men spoke to one another in the languages of the tribes. There was more than one blue tattooed arm encased in the chain mail of the ninth. Under the orders of the Legate, the army organised itself swiftly and in good order. As the first eight man section emerged through the Veil they set up a camp among the trees. Each new section joined them until the century was complete. The six centuries, which formed each cohort, arranged their camps in adjacent groups. It was a miracle of military organisation. Soon the entire hilltop was full of men. Men were provisioned, campfires lit. The hill above the valley was covered in thick wood. There was plenty of wood for fires and plenty of cover. It would be hard to see the legion even from Craigwen itself. From the valley beneath it would be impossible. Was it possible that Ursula's half-baked plan could work? That Roman would fight Roman? She felt very cold and drained. For some reason her head ached as if Rhonwen were near. She had a chilling thought. She had forgotten to tell Macsen about Rhonwen's disappearance into the Veil. She swayed and Macsen was there to catch her. Her last conscious thought before she passed out was one of horror. In the effort to sustain the Veil, Boar Skull's comforting bulk had dissolved into Ursula's true form again. She was herself again and vulnerable.

~ Chapter Twenty-seven ~

Not All There

U rsula woke in the darkness of Macsen's chamber. Bryn and Braveheart slept together in an untidy heap on the floor. She was still naked but for the cloak she was wrapped in and she was still Ursula. A pile of clothes lay on the bed, warrior's clothes. She thought herself into Boar Skull's bulk and nothing happened. The magic that coursed through her veins had gone. She felt bereft without it. She dressed herself nonetheless in Boar Skull's garments, merely tightening the belt several notches and tiptoed past Braveheart. He opened one eye and drifted back to sleep.

She thought she heard someone call her name. The courtyard was thronged with people, most of them strangers. There was no one there that she recognised. Still the feeling persisted. Men were stamping their feet against the cold, swigging mead from drinking horns, playing dice or sharpening their swords. Whatever they seemed to be doing, Ursula knew they merely waited. Expectation and fear flavoured the air like spice. The Combrogi's day of judgement was at hand.

She listened to the talk. The Ravens had arrived and set up their camp. They filled the whole base of the valley. Macsen was not going to give them much time to get comfortable. They expected a siege. Macsen was going to give them a battle. Come dawn the Ravens would taste death prepared the Celtic way. No one mentioned allies. Did they not know or had she dreamed the whole encounter with the ninth legion? She went in search of Dan or Kai. No one took any notice of her. She had the strangest feeling that she wasn't really there at all.

It had not been a dream. The Legate sat within the Great Hall. His Roman dress was covered in a long hooded cloak and he had removed his distinctive head-dress. He and Macsen pored over the clay map. Perhaps seeing the encamped Ravens fighting under alien banners had given him the proof he needed. Macsen had spoken truthfully in one sense; the Ravens did follow an emperor other than the Legate's own. Whether this was because the Legate was from a different time or a different world or because the second legion really was a rebel group, serving a false emperor, she could not say. She could not quite get her mind round all the possibilities. Her grasp of history was not good enough. Perhaps Dan would know. All that mattered to Ursula was that the Legate seemed prepared to fight on their side.

The two leaders were alone but for the guards which surrounded them; equal numbers of Combrogi and centurions. They had been busy while she was sleeping that much was clear. It seemed that the ninth legion had hidden itself in the trees on either side of the valley, according to Macsen's former plan. The two men discussed only the details of their formation: where to place cavalry, where the auxilia and where the main body of the legion. She did not know how long she had slept. It must have been for a long time because it seemed that Cadal had returned from Ireland and was moored out to sea in readiness for a sea war should it prove necessary. She wondered if anyone had told him about Rhonwen. Rhonwen! Now that she came to think of it she was sure that it had been Rhonwen's voice she thought she'd heard calling her name. Had she returned from wherever the Veil had taken her? Ursula would have liked to tell Macsen what had happened to Rhonwen, but he did not seem to know she was there. Both he and the Legate took no notice of her at all and even the guards failed to challenge her. Where was Dan?

She found him at last in the old barracks arguing with Kai.

'I am grateful for the helmet, but I can't use a breastplate or a shield in battle, Kai. Look, I've never fought in one before, really. I'm not ungrateful. Don't think that. But they hamper my movements too much. I appreciate what you're telling me but I can't fight defensively when I'm mad anyway.'

Ursula stood next to Dan, but he ignored her. It came to her suddenly that she was stuck in her 'not-there-thing' without the magic to get out of it.

'Dan!' Her voice sounded shrill and desperate to her own ears. It did not sound at all in his.

'How's Ursula?' Kai said by way of changing the subject. 'Any change?'

'No. She breathes but that is all. It's been three days. How long can you go without eating?' Dan's expression clouded. Kai touched his arm comfortingly. Dan pulled himself together. 'Is Macsen still waiting for her recovery?'

Kai shrugged. 'Rufinus, the Legate, is pushing him to attack at dawn. That's the word among the men too. I don't think they can keep the ninth legion secret for much longer.' Kai glanced round and lowered his voice so that even Ursula had to strain to hear him. 'There have been rumours that Macsen's sold them out, that he and Lud of the Brigantes will fight between them to see who is to be the more powerful Raven puppet. Not all the men believe it but enough are worried. I don't think Macsen can wait any longer and still have the warriors behind him.'

'I don't see why he's been waiting for Ursula to come round. I mean he's never shown any interest before.'

'You mean he's not been the same since he saw her naked!' Kai laughed robustly. 'Oh, he cares enough for Ursula all right, she's a lovely-looking woman, but it's not that. Macsen needs to present our men with a real live sorceress or sorcerer so that she can vouch for the ninth being from another world. There is a risk that our men will fight the ninth, not the Ravens, if he doesn't explain and that they won't fight at all if he does.'

Both men were silent for a moment. Ursula knew that she blushed.

'She picked a risky strategy all right,' said Kai.

'But she's given us a chance where we had none,' answered Dan hotly.

'It's "OK", Bear Sark. You don't have to defend your Ursula against me. Let's go and find the man himself. Even he must have tired of battle tactics by now. He's as bad as Hane. The way I see it, you charge, kill the enemy and go home. What's so complicated about that?' Dan laughed and the two men headed for the Great Hall.

Ursula sat down heavily. Macsen needed her and she had been unconscious for three days. Kai thought she was lovely. Dan thought she'd done the right thing. No one could see her. She had no magic and she hadn't eaten for three days. She was too weary to hold so many disjointed thoughts in any kind of pattern in her head.

Worse still she thought she could hear Rhonwen calling to her mind. It was a distant echo of a call as if Rhonwen was a long way away, but it was a call none the less. Ursula could have done without it. Maybe she should eat something.

A feast had been prepared. Food was carried into the Great Hall. The aroma of roast pork reminded Ursula that she was indeed hungry. She grabbed a haunch but nobody seemed to even notice that. With the succulent juices of the meat running down her throat and chin she felt strength and magic return. The magic was trickling rather than pouring through her, but at least it had not deserted her. She found a quiet corner of the crowded Hall and steadily worked her way through three days' worth of food.

Few of the men seemed to be eating with their usual enthusiasm. Many refused the drinking horn and sipped goblets of water. She heard more than one whisper of battle nerves and the need for clear heads and many more whisper of battle nerves and the need to be blind drunk. There seemed to be two distinct schools of thought. She saw the men of Alavna eating together. There was someone missing. She realised with a sudden unexpected pang that it was Gwyn. They were eating but sparingly and sharing the comradeship of thoughtful silence. As her magic returned she could perceive the strange multicoloured aura of fear and excitement that fogged the room like another kind of mist. Just to breathe it was intoxicating. She felt the first flutter of nerves.

Three thousand men could not congregate in that room, large as it was. The doors were opened wide to include the others who ate and sat outside in the courtyard. The Legate, Rufinus and the other war leaders shared Macsen's couch, or knelt by its side.

Macsen gave the warrior's hand signal for silence. For once it came almost instantly and all eyes were on him. Ursula stepped carefully over the seated warriors to stand by his couch. No one saw her.

'We are here together, the noblest of what is left of Britain. We all know why we are here because today is the beginning of freedom for Britain. For all of you have united together and have no taste for servitude. We are here to defeat the Ravens. They plunder, they butcher, they ravish, and call it by the lying name of "empire". They make a desert and call it "peace".' There was a roar and a stamping of spears and shields. Macsen raised his hand again for silence.

'Here on the last free soil of Britain we can have victory. We can defeat the carrion crow that casts its black shadow over this land. They have raped our women, murdered our children, destroyed our sanctuaries and yet we still have power they lack. Remember the druid Prince who died at Lindow. The magic of the land that

284

his death unleashed is with us now and can deliver victory into our willing arms.' There was more foot stamping and roaring though fewer people knew what he was talking about.

'Ursula Alavna ab Helen known as Boar Skull, a proven warrior of our people, has called an army through the Warrior's Veil to fight to rid us of the unkindness of Ravens. An army from another world is with us and together we can free this land.'

At Macsen's signal Rufinus stood to his feet. He was wearing the armour of Rome but around his wrists he wore the newly-painted warrior tattoo of the Combrogi. The spear thumping ceased abruptly. The men were quiet. It was now or never. Ursula felt again the electric pulse of magic through the conductor of her spine. She was suddenly there in front of the assembled men, like an apparition. There was a massed gasp; then, while all eyes were on her she transformed herself into Boar Skull at his most massive, complete with moustache and tattoos.

She had failed before. She could not afford to fail again. Macsen had nearly lost them, for all his rhetoric. The very air had cooled to near hostility. Rufinus was too much a Raven to be acceptable to the warriors of the Combrogi. This time maybe she could make a difference.

'I am Ursula Alavna ab Helen, I got my name for an oath I made at Alavna. I saw there what Ravens had done. I swore an oath to avenge it. To many of you I am known as the warrior, Boar Skull. I trained here and proved myself a warrior of the Combrogi. I swore an oath to my King. I am a sorcerer. With my magic I raised the Warrior's Veil. I did it to keep my vow at Alavna. I did it to keep my oath to my King.

'The men I brought through are not Ravens, but Eagles. They come from another world but they can fight like Ravens, they can kill Ravens and they will do it for us. For where they come from they have tribes like ours, speak languages like ours and feel like us that the Ravens are wrong. It is up to you, whether you fight with King Macsen or let this moment go. This is your last chance to make Britain free. But whatever you choose, I am Ursula Alavna ab Helen, the sorceress, and Boar Skull, warrior of the Combrogi and I stand with Macsen and the Eagles for freedom.' It was the longest speech Ursula had ever made in her life and the most eloquent. It was met by a stunned silence. Then the warriors of Alavna started to cheer, then Hane's men joined in until the whole hall erupted. Rufinus sat down. He did not wish to put a foot wrong and jeopardise what was gained. Macsen raised his hand for silence.

'Here is our power, in our magic, in our strong hearts, in our allies and in our swords. We will not bend our knees to the Ravens. On then into battle and as you go think both of your proud ancestors and your free

286

descendants!' The roaring and shield banging turned into the frenzied war cries of the Combrogi. Hane signalled and those he'd trained attempted to group themselves in battle order. Macsen's plan was for them to follow the first onslaught of Combrogi warriors and finish off what they had started. The Ravens were not expecting attack from the besieged fortress. With luck, many would be sleeping. Combrogi warriors mad with the frenzy of blood-lust might keep them from remembering their discipline for a while and when they got it back they would be prey for Eagles. Ursula got in position next to Dan, her heart still thumping from her speech. They all greeted her with pride and affection, with much manly shoulder patting and arm grabbing. It felt very good. Then Macsen was there.

'My thanks. You cut that very fine. I thought you would never wake.'

'I was very weary after raising the Veil.'

'I know it was so with Rhonwen, though she ...'

'You know what happened to her?' Macsen nodded.

'I'm sure she's not dead. I think I've heard her calling me. She just went through the Veil. She could get back.' Ursula's words tumbled over one another in her effort to reassure Macsen.

'I cannot talk of this now. I need you to stand on the battlements and act as priestess. The men expect it and it will help our cause. It would be good if you could wear Rhonwen's robes and …'

Macsen's iron will kept his voice calm and expressionless but Ursula could sense his anger and sorrow. He did not seem like either King or war leader at that moment. For some reason she found herself agreeing.

Dan intervened.

'My King, I would not wish Ursula to be undefended – I …'

'Bear Sark, I myself will stand by her side on the battlements to spur the men on. But only after I have led them in the first charge. If I do not return from it then it will be Kai who will stand duty at her right hand. Do not fear for your Boar Skull, my friend, she is precious to us. I need you in the field. A bear sark such as yourself brings pleasure to the gods.'

It was not the answer that Dan wanted but Ursula nodded firmly.

'It's OK, Dan. This is the day for keeping our oaths. When the Combrogi are free, then so are we.'

She switched dizzyingly back to Ursula and hugged him, kissing him on the cheek. 'Keep safe, Dan,' she whispered. 'If we can survive this I know that I can get us home.'

With the dampness of Ursula's kiss still on his cheek Dan took his place between Kai and Prys and readied himself for battle.

~ Chapter Twenty-eight ~

The Battle of Craigwen

Ursula could see more than she wanted to. Her vantage point on the fortress walls gave her an unhindered view of the vast Raven army. The Raven army also had an unhindered view of her. There were no crenellations to hide behind, only a low wall, lower than waist height that afforded minimal protection. She felt very exposed. She felt very uncomfortable. She'd never had much of a head for heights.

She could see the whole second legion stretched out before her. Each century camped together in neat rows of ten men tents. Cookfires flickered brightly in the paling darkness that was this dawn. She could see the half-constructed siege engines that would allow the Ravens to breach Craigwen's stone walls. The ballista were already arrayed at the foot of the slope. The Combrogi were ready at the fortress gates. Macsen had silenced them for the time being. They wanted to give the Ravens as little notice of their intentions as possible. There was only the ominous quiet that precedes a storm. Taliesin, King Cadal's bard, stood unarmed, next to Ursula on the dizzying heights. He was ready to immortalise the battle in song, the Combrogi's own war reporter. Ursula found that she shivered in the finery of her borrowed cloak. Rhonwen's thickest gold torque fitted too tightly round her own less fragile throat and the crown of mistletoe and holly that Macsen had given her prickled her scalp uncomfortably. She no longer heard the distant call of Rhonwen in her mind, but her influence was all too powerfully present in the scent of her robe and the sorrow in Macsen's eyes.

'Why don't the Combrogi go?' Ursula nerves were stretched too taut. The magic flowed through her so violently she was surprised that her silhouette was not outlined in neon against the still dark sky.

'Macsen will be winding them up a notch more before they open the gates. It's a pity there are no chariots, you can compose good stuff about chariots.'

Ursula glanced at the bard to see if he was joking, but then there was a boom as loud as thunder. The great gates opened and Macsen led the Celts in a wild screaming charge down the treacherous slope to the plain.

The first Raven soldiers the Combrogi came to were dead before they could find their weapons. The Combrogi slashed through tents with their great hacking meat cleavers of swords. They massacred their occupants. The Combrogi's savage cries became whoops of triumph at a slaughter more like farming than battle. It did not last. Within minutes the legionaries had mustered into some kind of battle order and the real fighting began. The legionaries formed themselves into ordered ranks while the auxilia, wild men themselves, engaged in close combat with the Combrogi. Their shorter swords were better suited to fighting at close quarters and the sheer weight of their numbers hampered the Combrogi attack. The Combrogi needed room to swing their long swords. Men began to fall.

Many of the Combrogi carried slings. Those that avoided the onslaught of the auxilia managed to use them to good effect at a longer distance. They threw their spears too into the ranks of the legions but though almost every missile found a target it was because the targets were too numerous. There was a lot of shouting of orders, a lot of screaming, but the initial Combrogi advantage was being lost. There were too many enemies. Ursula looked for Macsen in the mêlée. All men were equally blood-spattered and his distinctive scarlet cloak did not distinguish him. She had not seen Dan at all.

'Now would be a good time for a bit of magic,' the bard prompted.

'What do I do?'

'Can you do dragons? Birds of prey go down well.

Lightning would be good. Something to give the men heart and terrify the Ravens witless. Scream a bit! Invoke curses. Use your imagination!'

The bard appeared to have taken refuge in flippancy. He was sweating profusely. Ursula sensed that the sensitive bard was struggling to deal with the carnage below. Ursula understood what he meant. He was right. The men needed to be given heart. What would Rhonwen have done? Ursula was not by nature a dramatic person but she felt the electricity of the magic run through her. She willed it to emerge from her fingertips. She didn't know of any curses but they had done *Macbeth* at school the previous year.

'When shall we three meet again. In thunder, lightning, or in rain?' she shrieked, in English. The magic amplified her voice so that it echoed round the battlements. Forked lightning sizzled from the end of her fingers. It illuminated the sky. A stray bolt unexpectedly ignited the wooden siege engines which burned like a beacon in the darkness. She had not intended the destruction but it heartened the Combrogi whose cheering almost drowned out the sound of thunder. How could they fail with the gods and Ursula on their side? A hail of arrows and slingshot showered in her direction, but the fortress was on so steep an incline that all of it fell short.

Hane's men charged to assist the struggling warriors.

Dan was among them. In the leaping firelight of the blazing siege engines Ursula saw the cold otherness in his face. He was bear sark again. He held a short dagger in his left hand, Bright Killer in his right. With his left hand he cleared enough space in front of him to enable him to swing Bright Killer in his right. A large gap appeared around him as he advanced. Braveheart snarled at his side. His fellow warriors gave him wide berth; the veteran enemy foot soldiers knew him for what he was. Only the young or the very unlucky tried to beat him in close combat. One of the unlucky was Huw. There was no mistaking their former comrade. He was with a small knot of Lud's men who had been inspecting the troops when the Combrogi charged. Ursula did not think Dan recognised him, but Huw recognised Dan. To Ursula's heightened perceptions it seemed that she could almost smell his fear from the battlements. She turned her head so she would not see Huw die.

By now the Raven general had worked out what was happening. He organised men into wide ranks to fill the valley floor. They marched forward one hundred and fifty men at a time, each man's shield ready to defend his neighbour. As they advanced they stabbed with their short swords. Their advance had the mechanical precision of a machine and there was nowhere for the Combrogi to go. They retreated and were herded backwards towards the fortress gates. The ground was littered with bodies and many were Combrogi. What was Macsen doing? Had Rufinus let him down?

Macsen was suddenly at her side, blood-stained and sweating.

'We need some kind of signal. I thought Rufinus would have charged by now. What's keeping him?' The sun was fully up by now, under the blood-stains his face was ashen and his jaw set.

'Ursula?'

What was he looking at her for? Surely he and Rufinus had arranged some signal?

'I was going to torch the siege engines when we needed him, but he will have seen the lightning do that.'

'He must be able to see what's going on?' Ursula fought to keep the impatience from her voice. Surely after all they had done they could not lose the battle for the want of a signal?

'Not necessarily – they're keeping well back so as not to be seen. He must be waiting for some other signal.'

'What do you want me to do?' Ursula's voice trembled. She was suddenly very scared.

Macsen looked at her in anguish.

Below her she could see that even Dan had been driven back by the disciplined advance. They needed the Eagles.

It happened so effortlessly that even afterwards Ursula was unable to describe how she did it. She jumped down from the exposure of the battlements, ripped off Rhonwen's cloak, golden torque and woollen robe. Macsen and Taliesin stared at her wide-eyed. They feared that the risk to Dan had unhinged her. Then suddenly, there was a ripple in the morning air and Ursula was gone. In her place there stood a six foot Golden Eagle, crowned with mistletoe. It hopped with little grace onto the battlements and spread its immense wings and took to the air. It flew over the steep wooded sides of the valley calling. One by one the Raven soldiers looked up to see the giant bird and then all hell broke loose. The eagle was all the signal Rufinus needed.

Combrogi chariots and Eagle cavalry charged down the valley's slopes into the tightly packed ranks of the Raven infantry. It was the Ravens who now had nowhere to go. They were trapped by their own tight order. Their own cavalry was too far back to assist in any way. The second legion was doomed.

Macsen's Combrogi chariots gained momentum as they hurtled down the incline. They attacked from both slopes simultaneously. The impact when they finally reached the Raven ranks was serious. The second legion was well disciplined. The centurions had their men raise their shields in a double shield wall, but none could hold against the force of charging horses. Their nerve broke. Once the Eagles' heavy cavalry followed through, there were gaps in the lines and a panic that the infantry could exploit. They followed hard behind. They did not charge like the Celts but marched from both sides in disciplined order. If any hope had remained in Raven hearts it must have died then. The Eagles marched at a steady pace with inexorable rhythm. The Combrogi backed against the fortress took advantage of the confusion wrought by the chariots. They hurled missiles and spears and curses into the legion's ranks. The Ravens fell over each other in an effort to get away from the heavy hooves of the war-horses, to escape the cavalry swords and spears of their riders. The silver tide of the Eagles' infantry surged forward through the struggling ranks of Ravens. They dealt death the Roman way with the quick sharp thrust of the gladius. The Eagles worked their way through the chaos. Eagle warp cut through Raven weft. Small groups of Ravens managed to take up defensive positions, crouching under their shields, but the Ravens had never expected to fight others as disciplined as themselves. The sight of the gleaming ranks of Roman Eagles ravaged their morale. There was carnage. Some centuries tried a controlled retreat but the chariots and heavy cavalry, having destroyed the order of the ranks, contented themselves with cutting off the retreat and hunting down survivors like game for the table.

The cries of the injured and dying were terrible. It was a scene of horrific ugliness. Dan clung to his madness for sanity was too painful. There no longer was a second legion.

Ursula flew high above the battlefield to escape the stench of death. Birds are not intelligent creatures and Ursula had truly become a bird. She soared high above the carnage, the victory and the tragedy on golden wings. As night fell, a vague memory of something else, a nest maybe, or an egg halted her flight. Something was calling to her. She dived down through the chilly air to land on the battlements. That sparked some memory. Something was waiting for her there. She heard a name being called, 'Ursula'. What did it mean? The name rang in the great bird's thoughts as if, from far away, someone was calling to her.

Dan had watched as the giant bird descended to land on the high stone battlements of the fortress. His own madness was gone. His arms ached with the death he'd dealt. Men were still looting and disposing of the Raven dead on the red-stained plain. He was pleased for the Combrogi. He'd kept his vows. He'd survived. Not even that meant much if Ursula was gone. He looked aghast at the beautiful giant eagle. No spark of intelligence glinted in the shining eyes. Dan's voice cracked with desperate emotion.

'Taliesin, play! You got to her before. It's got to work.'

Macsen, Kai and Rufinus joined him on the battlements.

'We saw her land.' Kai's face was grave as he touched Dan's shoulder with his left hand, his right had been badly injured. He should not have been there.

'It may not work, Dan, it is what sometimes happens with shape shifters they …'

'Play, Taliesin!' Dan could not bear Kai's kindness.

Taliesin played. Dan moved cautiously forward, the giant bird's talons were on the same scale as the rest of her.

'Ursula?' He could not prevent the word coming out as a kind of a sob.

'Ursula.' The giant bird swayed as if she had lost her balance, there was a shimmering and then Ursula was there. Dan leaped forward to catch her as she fell.

'Get her to the bathhouse! We have to get her warm.'

All that long night Dan kept vigil. Macsen, Kai and Rufinus took turns to leave the victory feast and stay with him. The bard's duties kept him away but Kai told Dan how the song of Ursula the Golden Eagle who led the Eagles into battle was the highlight of the saga. They brought Dan mead and the champion's portion. He was given the finest cuts of pork and beef the fortress had to offer. His name was lauded in the highest terms as one of the heroes of Craigwen: The Bear Sark with his bright killing sword who reaped a harvest of Raven heads unmatched by any man alive.

Dan tried to smile but he felt terrible. He found it

impossible to join in the joy at what had been a terrible slaughter. Caradoc had joined Gwyn in the ranks of the dead, Prys was seriously injured, and Kai might well lose his arm but was too drunk to feel the pain. There were around eight hundred Combrogi dead and not a Raven breathed. It was a victory, but when his madness had gone, his ecstasy at killing went with it.

Ursula still breathed and her skin felt warm to the touch. They had wrapped her in layers of cloth. Rufinus brought her a silk shift from a far country and then they had wrapped her in layers of wool and fur. She had not yet spoken. Dan was secretly terrified that she had lost her mind.

It was dawn of the second day after the battle when she finally opened her eyes. Their emerald colour was now so deep it was nearly black, the colour of the deepest waters.

'Dan? Are you OK? Was there a battle? Did we win?'

'Ursula! Yes we won. You've been sleeping, how do you feel?'

'Weird. My arms are aching like I've been carrying a ton of shopping around for days and my shoulders are stiff.'

Dan's grin threatened to split his face in two.

'What's so funny?'

'Don't you remember?'

'Oh, no, did I do something embarrassing?'

'Only if you consider turning into a Golden Eagle and turning the battle into a rout embarrassing.'

'I thought that was a dream.'

'Nope, you really did it – hence the sore arms.'

Ursula groaned. 'I could murder a cup of tea.'

Dan was suddenly serious. 'You said that you knew how to get us out of here now. Do you want to go home and get one?'

Ursula sat up.

'Can you find me some clothes? Not one of those awful shift dresses – trews and a tunic. If we've won and Macsen gives us leave, we will have fulfilled our oaths.'

~ Chapter Twenty-nine ~

Farewells

It was the Eagles who now camped on the blood-stained valley in front of the fortress. Rufinus had promised to ask Ursula to reopen the Veil for those of his command who wished to return, back to where they had come from. He himself would stay. As Ursula had suspected he had been involved in the death of Caesar Domitianus Augustus in his own time. Finding another emperor by the same name in Macsen's world had made the Legate determined to stay and oppose that enemy too. To him, no one by the name of Caesar Domitianus Augustus could be other than an enemy. As a blood Celt, Rufinus also wanted to aid King Macsen in rebuilding the Combrogi kingdoms. Dan did not know whether the Legate thought he was in another time or another world or just another part of Britain from his point of origin. He did not even seem to be very interested in the question. Rufinus was wholly engrossed in planning military strategy with Macsen. Lud was furiously trying to re-establish himself as an ally. The total removal of all the Ravens from Britain was now looking like a real possibility.

After talking it over endlessly with Ursula, Dan was pretty sure Rufinus had left their own world at a point about thirty years into Macsen's future. Only Dan seemed to care.

Rufinus and those of his men who had agreed to stay had also agreed to drink the Cup of Belonging, if Kai could still perform the rite. There was plenty of land for the taking in abandoned tribal territory. There was a future for those who wanted it in this land and it was a Combrogi future. Dan salved his conscience with the thought that those who wished to stay were content with their lot.

In the end, no more than a few hundred soldiers of the ninth legion wished to return to their own place and those followed Dan and Ursula to the witch shaped tree.

It was a strange gathering. The soldiers were in awe of Ursula, the sorceress who could fly like a bird. They spoke in hushed whispers and there was fear in the air. Ursula was afraid too. Rhonwen's presence still haunted her. There was still the echo of an echo of her call. Had she somehow got stuck within the mist itself? Would she re-emerge when Ursula raised the Veil again? It was with a determined effort of will that she put these fears to one side and calmed her mind. She had made her preparation. She had fasted and bathed as before. She took a deep breath, stuck her sword in the ground and prayed for the return of the Veil and safe passage for the waiting legionaries.

The yellow mist billowed out from an unknown source as before. With obvious trepidation the men marched through it in close formation. The Combrogi made a kind of honour guard for them, their allies in the Combrogi's darkest hour. Bryn and Braveheart were there and the veterans of Alavna, as well as Hane's men, Taliesin, Rufinus and the King. As the rump of the ninth entered the mist the Combrogi all raised their swords in silent salute until the last of the Romans were swallowed by the mist. No one spoke. Ursula released the Veil.

Macsen stared after them for a moment, a haunted look on his face. If Ursula had been afraid that Rhonwen might reappear then Macsen had hoped that she would. The disappointment was written on his face. Rhonwen mattered to Macsen. In the end she had not mattered too much to Cadal. Though he had been unhappy to lose his magical bride, he had been content to settle for a beautiful young cousin instead. The alliance was safe without Rhonwen and the women and children were returning on the next tide. There was a real hope that a whole new era was about to begin. It was to be a Combrogi renaissance, but Macsen had paid dearly for it.

He didn't care what he paid to reward Dan and Ursula who had served his cause so valiantly. He had wanted to burden them with many gifts. He had offered them gold and silver and fine woven cloth. Reluctantly Ursula had accepted a brooch in the shape of an eagle. It was bearing a sword entwined with mistletoe. He'd had it made especially from Raven gold. Dan had been prepared to give up Bright Killer and wanted to give it to Bryn. Bryn refused to take it because it was moulded now to fit Dan's own hand. Dan had very mixed feelings about the sword. For him it was a potent symbol of his madness. His fondness for it was the sign that he was unfit for the civilisation he had left. Ursula knew his fear. It was not so far distant from her own. Anyway, Dan had taken the sword and in a part of himself been glad to possess it. He also accepted a particularly beautiful Celtic leather sheath tooled with gold.

Dan looked at the Combrogi who remained by the witch shaped tree. It was hard to say goodbye. It was hard to know that they would never see these men again; Kai who had been a kind of father to them both, Taliesin and the men of Alavna. Dan would have liked to take Braveheart back with him. He loved the dog and knew that his feeling was reciprocated. Because he loved him he knew that he could not condemn him to the restricted life he would lead in Dan's small suburban house. He gave him to Bryn in so far as Braveheart was his to give and Braveheart seemed to understand. Dan could not bear to be parted from Bryn either. His guilt at leaving him was not as great as that he had felt on leaving Lizzie, but it was bad enough. Bryn had wanted to go with him through the Veil until Dan shocked him with tales of school. It amused Dan that after all the horrors he had seen, Bryn could be so horrified by the concept of sitting in a room and learning to read and write. As for most of the Combrogi, writing was anathema, a curse of the Ravens. Bryn would do well enough. Kai had promised to care for him and train him in the warrior's ways. Kai would give the boy more affection, Dan knew, than Dan's own father had managed to give to Dan.

Ursula found she was crying when she kissed Kai and the others goodbye. She was part of their tribe now. She was one of them. It was a liberating feeling to know she belonged somewhere. It was very difficult to give that up. Saying goodbye to Macsen was difficult in a different way. He was a complex man. She could not forget what Kai had said about his liking her. He kissed her hand and looked at her very intently.

'Ursula, you do not have to go. You could be Queen here of all the Combrogi if you wished it.'

'Thank you, King Macsen. I am flattered to be so well regarded but in my country I would not be expected to marry for a good while yet. Perhaps later if we were to meet again it would be different ...'

He grinned, suddenly a younger-seeming, more care-free man. His burdens would be of a different kind now his people were victorious.

'Why, Ursula, I do believe you are learning diplomacy. What has happened to Boar Skull of few words and most of them ill-tempered?'

She grinned back. 'Goodbye Macsen. I wanted to let you know about Rhonwen. I know she lives still. I have heard her calling to me. She saved me, you know, when I was an eagle. It was her voice calling to me that brought me back to the fortress.' As she said it she knew that it was true and also that she had refused to admit it to herself before. 'She is alive somewhere and still connected to this world. I'm sure she will find her way back.'

Macsen nodded, sombre again.

'Thank you for telling me, Ursula. I have thought I sensed her too, in the battle. Let us hope she finds her way back to us.'

He kissed her then just once, swiftly, on the lips. 'You come back to us too, Ursula. I have not released you from your oaths.'

'Good luck, Macsen,' she whispered, and tried to hide her scarlet face from Dan.

Dan embraced Kai and Macsen, Bryn and the bard in warrior fashion. He patted Braveheart and stood alongside Ursula.

'You're sure that this won't take us to second century Roman Britain?'

Ursula nodded.

'As sure as I can be.'

Nothing was sure. Craigwen had taught her that. First they had looked like they could not win against the Ravens and then it had looked like they could not lose, but they *had* very nearly lost, in spite of Rufinus. No, nothing but death was sure. That rather dismal thought gave her courage. If death was the only certainty, in life there was everything to play for. She had no intention of ever standing back and watching from the sidelines again. She moved a little way from her friends to focus her strength on her last act of magic. It was hard to give up such power, such energy, such exhilaration. She knelt down on the damp earth and felt the now familiar magic of the land flow through her. It was time to go. She stuck her sword into the earth, bowed her head in prayer and raised the Veil for the last time.

Dan joined her. She could tell by the look on his face that he too felt the building of that inner tension they knew so well as fear. They were not afraid of the Veil. They were not afraid of landing in the wrong place. Dan trusted Ursula and Ursula trusted herself. Their worst fear lay unspoken between them. Had they been so brutalised by their warrior life that they might be unfit to live in their own world? The deaths they'd caused weighed heavily on both their minds. They felt shy too. They had been so important to each other here. It was hard to imagine being back at school and just being two people in the same year group. Dan was the first to break the silence.

'Well, this time I'm not losing you in the mist.'

With a final wave to Bryn, Dan grabbed Ursula's hand. It was cool and strong and comforting. Ursula smiled, grateful for his gesture. Thus linked, Boar Skull and The Bear Sark stepped from Craigwen's bloody soil into the mists of the Warrior's Veil.

The events described in this book occur in a parallel world, but one which has a lot in common with First Century Britain. In 1984 the body of 'Lovernios', a man from this period, was found preserved in a bog and investigations of the body suggest that he may have been ritually sacrificed. I have used the theories of Ann Ross and Don Robins from their book *The Life and Death of a Druid Prince* (Rider Books, 1989), as a starting point for the fictional Lovernios of my story. My version of druidic belief is, however, true only of the parallel world and is not intended to represent the beliefs of British druids of the period. I'm not sure that anyone really knows what they were. First Century Britain was also a time of genuine conflict between the indigenous peoples of the British Isles and the Roman invaders. In AD 98 Tacitus wrote a biography of his father-in-law, Julius Agricola, who concluded the conquest of Britain. It is a key source of information about the period. Macsen's speech to his army at the Battle of Craigwen borrows a little from Tacitus' account of Calgacus' speech at the *Battle of the Graupian Mountain*, translated by Anthony R. Birley (Oxford University Press, 1999). The world, the battle and the outcome are very different in his story, but I suspect that the feelings of the men about to meet their enemy would have been the same. Even though the events of this story occurred in another world, this one has had its share of Alavnas throughout its history and continues to have them with horrible regularity.

N. M. Browne

The line from William Shakespeare's *Macbeth* featured on page 292 is taken from the opening scene, Act I.

If you have enjoyed this book why not try . . .

holes

louis sachar

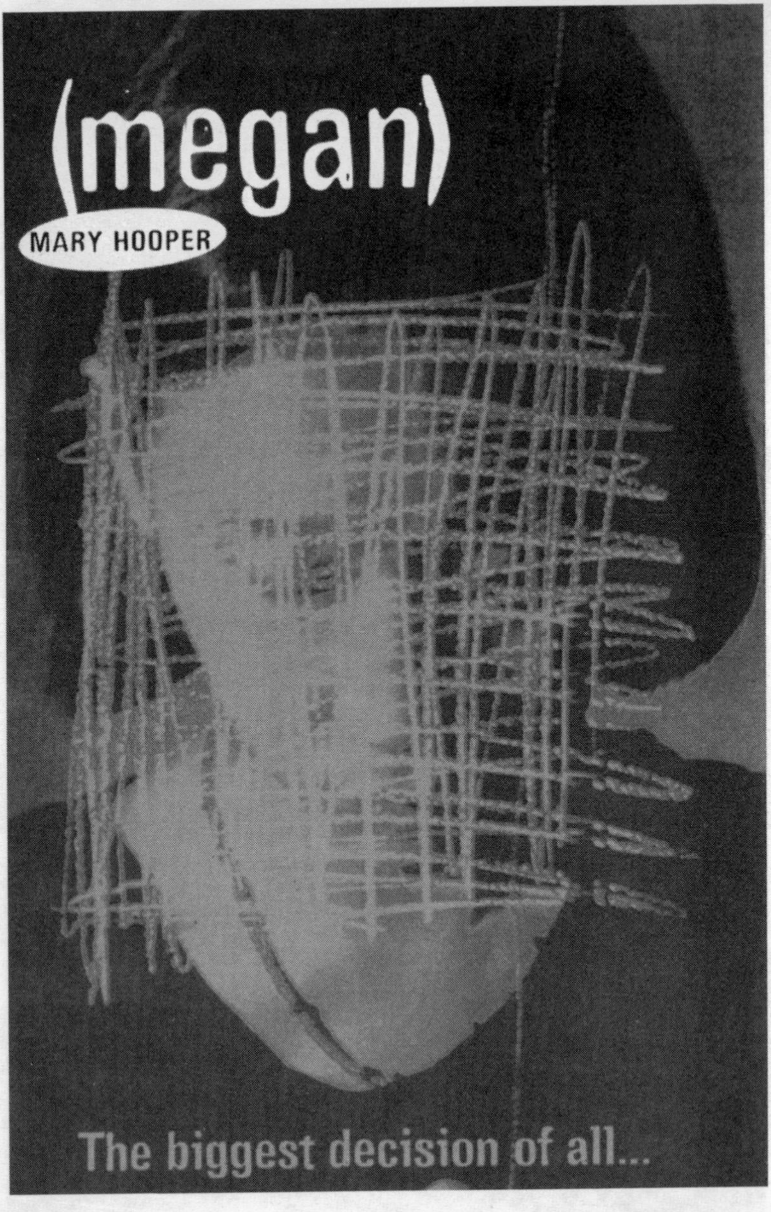
(megan)
MARY HOOPER
The biggest decision of all...

(megan)²

MARY HOOPER

...and then there were two...

face

benjamin zephaniah

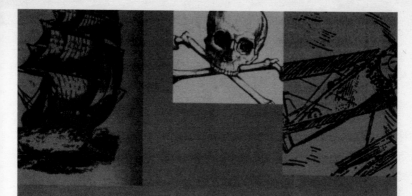

Jack Black AND THE
SHIP of THIEVES

BY *Carol Hughes*